To Anne
All best wishes
Nick Cowen
Dec 2019

THIS WAY NOT THAT WAY

NICK COWEN

Privately printed for
Nick Cowen
trustharrison@kingsoflounge.com
(all enquiries to the author at this email address)

by The Hobnob Press
8 Lock Warehouse, Severn Road
Gloucester GL1 2GA

Design and typesetting by John Chandler. The text is set in 12 point Doves Type leaded 3 points. Doves Type is a digital facsimile, created by Robert Green, of the celebrated face made by Edward Prince in 1899 for the Doves Press, based on Jenson's 15th-century Venetian type.

ISBN 978-1-906978-75-4

ℂ DEDICATION

To those with whom I have indulged in a mutual passion for paths and maps, under the guise of employment, and to all the dedicated volunteers who have been so generous with their time.

ℂ DISCLAIMER

I

SIMON BOLIVAR

"NOW LOOK HERE," I said to Harrison, "I am not going to be intimidated by you and I'll tell you exactly what the situation is. I am the employed representative of the local authority who manages the public rights of way and undertakes their statutory obligations and you...are not. You are a volunteer and an uninvited volunteer come to that."

"Who does all the work," said Harrison, poking me in the chest. I could not decide whether this was intended to be a statement or a question and I certainly did not appreciate being poked in the chest.

"You can cut that out for a start," I said, "what about the law in all of this? I am the one with the delegated powers whilst you operate on a ways and means basis through some sort of local tribal law, enforced by a bunch of happy go lucky vigilantes."

"They ain't 'appy," said Harrison giving me a cold stare.

This was a different Harrison, an uncompromising and somewhat threatening Harrison. Gone was the apparent indifference with those long enigmatic silences and blank expressions.

On reflection I did not come out of last night's dream particularly well either but as it was my dream I could gloss over my rather pompous behaviour. At the very least I was able to demonstrate a bit of backbone for a change which I found pleasing. Dreams will vaporise, often before breakfast but I was still contemplating this new version of Harrison as I sat down to answer some e-mails with my second cup of tea at work.

After a while the chap from the other end of the building popped his head around the door.

"Good morning Victor. Just in case you were wondering, Simon Bolivar called by first thing this morning to pick up his boots."

I had already sensed that something was missing from the office. It was like that old party game where you have many objects on a tray that you have to memorise and then the tray returns after one object has been removed.

"That's the object from the tray," I said, "the boots."

"They weren't on a tray," said the chap from the other end of the building.

"No, of course they weren't," I said impatiently, "and his name is Harrison not Simon Bolivar and the boots belong to the council."

When he had gone I checked up on the internet to find out exactly who Simon Bolivar was.

The phone had been ringing quite a lot this morning so I thought I ought to answer it when it rang again. I listened to a complaint from a lady about a man who had sworn at the group of walkers that she was leading as they had passed through his property. Once I had established the location, I informed the customer that I was not entirely surprised by this news but I would investigate further. Another caller rang to say that everything was down. I replied that I was sorry to hear that and suggested that he might have the wrong number.

"Oh no," replied the man, "don't you be going anywhere, it's you I want to speak to all right, you're the waywarden, isn't that so?"

"Well, I don't call myself a waywarden exactly.." I said.

"Do you not? Anyways, it's all down."

"What is down exactly?"

"The signs is down and the fences is down. So is the trees and there's a line down as well."

"Is there anything left standing?"

"Neglect is the thing, neglect is the boy, pure and simple. You'll be wantin' me to sort it all out, isn't that the game now, on the volunteerin'?"

"I'm sorry but I don't have your name or even which part of the county we.."

"Oh no you don't, you won't be gettin' me out there in a smart yellow safety jacket persecutin' the speeding motorists. Just use your eyes, you'll see it's all down when you come."

I did not record any details from this call except the words "down-just use your eyes". I hoped that I would recognise the place if ever I passed through it.

I was just squeezing in a third cup of tea before I went out on my rounds when I bumped into the chap from the other end of the building in the tea room.

"Simon Bolivar," I said, "isn't he one of the very few people to get a country named after him, Bolivia in 1825 I believe?"

"I've no idea," he said, "I noticed his face on one of our tea towels at home. My wife is a sucker for communists, Tolpuddle martyrs, revolutionaries, you know the type? I'm no freedom fighter me, I just do the washing up."

Even though Harrison had picked up his boots I knew better than to think that he would suddenly materialise, but something was in the air. Perhaps I had even sensed it before the boots disappeared and that might account for last night's strange dream. A couple of days prior to the dream I had watched a female dog owner struggling woefully to control her dog. The dog had strayed well away from the footpath and was happily blundering about in the long grass unwittingly terrorising the wildlife with the owner shouting "Ronaldo" over and over again at the top of her voice. The thought must have entered my head that had Harrison been present, he would have sorted it out. In no time at all the errant dog would be gazing up at him, no sweets, no treats. I now imagined the conclusion of this little scenario with the breathless owner finally able to catch up with her dog. The dog owner would say something to Harrison like; "How did you do that? He never listens to me, naughty Ronaldo. Oh there, look at his face, doesn't he look just like Ronaldo?"

This question would have drawn the blankest of blank expressions from Harrison and he would probably just walk away at this point leaving the owner to wrestle with her dog.

The telephone rang to stir me from my reverie. I was pleased to establish that it was Nancy, my counterpart who looks after all the public rights of way in the east of the county.

"Victor, we're in trouble," said Nancy.

"Surely my dear you're not in the family way?" I said, "it was nothing more than a peck on the cheek."

"This isn't the time for silly voices, please be serious."

Nancy went on to explain that her local MP has said that he is going to challenge his own local authority to kerb all spending and, in his words, "Cut it to the bone". He was also really pushing for the sale of any council owned land for housing.

"This is coming our way Victor, how are we going to be able to provide any kind of service? The bastard's angling for a place in the cabinet, he's already a power crazed megalomaniac so god knows what he'll be like further up the greasy pole," said Nancy.

"I see," I said, "and when did you get to be so interested in what our politicians are up to? You just used to shrug if I ever mentioned politics or politicians."

"Have you met him? He's a right...."

"Say it Nancy."

"No, I'm not going to say it, I really must stop swearing so much."

"Oh, go on, please, if nothing else you'll make an old man happy."

"There's that silly voice again Victor, what's got into you, why all the silly voices?"

"All? I've only managed to perfect one so far. Oh, I don't know, I think I'm quietly going mad."

"You're spending too much time on your own, have you done anything about it like I said? Have you looked?"

"Oh, I've looked all right, plenty of looking."

"It's time you found someone and there are loads of dating sites now."

"Hmmm. Anyway, changing the subject, Harrison picked his boots up this morning before I arrived at work."

"That's great," said Nancy, "you badly need Harrison's help again."

"Hang on a minute, I am coping," I said.

"Coping by going quietly mad? I know you wanted to retire Victor but let's not go down without a fight ok? I've really got to go and no more of those silly voices. I wish I had a Harrison, I'm not sure how he does it but he sorts stuff out."

Nancy calls it "stuff" as well and she got that term from me ten years ago when she first joined the authority. Stuff is the unfinished business out there on the public rights of way network. Take your pick there is plenty of stuff to chose from; missing signs, craterous potholes on byways, stiles akimbo, gates jammed shut, encroaching vegetation, silted up ditches, paths obstructed and other paths illegally diverted. I look forward to the day when I can go for a walk and not worry about stuff. That day very nearly came before Christmas but at the last minute I had declined the very reasonable voluntary redundancy package that was on offer. At the time I thought that Harrison needed the direction in his life that volunteering on public rights of way could provide. I was concerned about Harrison's wellbeing, unnecessarily as it turned out.

It had been a strange morning. Firstly contemplating a rather unsettling dreamt version of Harrison and now wondering why Nancy was behaving differently of late. She has definitely been less tolerant of my nonsense and neither could I account for her sudden interest in what politicians were up to. Did Nancy really think that I was struggling to cope?

"I can manage perfectly well on my own without Harrison," I said out loud to myself and then glanced up towards the open office door to make sure that nobody was lingering and listening.

I left the office and set out on my rounds in the van with a list of stuff to look at and an unannounced visit to make at the end of the day.

I cleared a small ivy clad tree from a footpath with a bow saw before putting up a few directional waymark arrows on an old oak gate post a bit further along the path. I replaced a stile step which was only a ten minute job as the two uprights for the stile step still had a few years of life left in them. I dug out a couple of silted up ditches that I visit every couple of months throughout the year.

My final visit of the day took me to a converted farmyard where a walking group had been sworn at by the owner. I had visited this site many times over the years and spoken to various owners who were unhappy about the well used public footpath that crossed the yard diagonally beside the farmhouse. As I had explained, over and again, there was no possibility of diverting the footpath as there was nowhere to divert it to and each new owner was well aware of its existence before they purchased the place. The latest owner was Mr Peter Knowles who was undertaking substantial developments to the property and he and his wife had thought that they had seen the last of me when I announced that I was going to retire just before Christmas.

At the time Peter Knowles hoped that my replacement would be "more reasonable".

"Oh Christ, not you again Wayland, we thought we'd got shot of you, once and for all?" said Peter Knowles when he caught sight of me in the yard, "thank god my wife's not here. It's because of you and your bloody footpath that she left and refused to live here. I'm still trying to persuade her to move back in again and I'm getting the cold shoulder over it all. What do you want anyway, at least you haven't got that street urchin with you?"

I informed Peter Knowles that I had received a complaint from a member of the public that they had been sworn at when using the public right of way across his property.

"No, definitely not," he said, "oh hang on, wait a minute, there was one group who shuffled through here a few days ago. A right sour-faced bunch they were, I think I might have called out after them something like; "cheer up you miserable buggers, at least try and look as though you are enjoying yourselves." Well, honestly, it was a pretty poor advert for the supposed pleasures of the great outdoors. Are you going to clap me in irons Wayland?"

I looked around the yard and there were still contractors working in the outbuildings. I noticed from the vans that they were not local businesses and I wondered whether he had now managed to fall out with the local firms and had to look further afield. Mr and Mrs Knowles had certainly fallen out with their neighbours almost immediately and this was one reason why the public footpath could not be diverted as any new route would have to cross the neighbour's property and they were having none of it. The public footpath across the yard was clear enough and not obstructed, the main impediment to the public using the path was Mr Knowles himself.

"Vic isn't it?" said Peter Knowles, "now you're here and to save a wasted journey, come inside and have a cup of tea. I know how you council fellows like your tea. I'm sure that it must be possible for us to have a reasonable discussion about moving this bloody footpath, don't you think?"

I found myself back in the kitchen sitting at the breakfast bar whilst Peter Knowles searched for tea bags. There was no sign of King and Kong, the two large slinking wolf-like Alsatian dogs that Peter Knowles had produced on an earlier visit. These beasts were supposed to have provided the ultimate deterrent to the public using the footpath but Harrison had made a mockery of that plan by getting them to chase sticks in the yard.

As I waited for my tea I was thinking about how I was going to proceed with the swearing complaint against Peter Knowles. I had witnessed groups of walkers myself that could barely raise a grunt of acknowledgement when they encountered you out on the public rights of way network. Most groups are pretty cheery on the whole but with the odd sour faced exception.

"Do you think that it is a membership requirement to look as miserable as sin?" said Peter Knowles as he placed a mug of tea before me on the breakfast bar, "you know, before you're allowed to join the sour faced walking club?"

"Um, there are plenty of cheerful walking groups out there as well," I said.

"Crikey, you do know what I'm talking about don't you? Finally a bit of common ground after all, biscuit?"

"Thank you," I said.

"Now then, about this path? You wouldn't want it through your garden would you?"

"Are you offering it to me?"

"Ha, ha, I wish it was that easy. I must say Vic, you're a lot more relaxed without that street urchin in tow. You're well shot of him, take it from me."

I was not sure about being more relaxed without Harrison around. I think that I was just getting worn down with it all. Not exactly ceasing to care but perhaps ceasing to raise the energy levels at the appropriate moments to demonstrate that you care.

I told myself that I did care. I tried to imagine Harrison sitting alongside me, what would I be doing differently if he were here?

"Another biscuit Vic?"

Enough was enough. I needed to inform Peter Knowles that his behaviour was obstructive and that swearing at a passing group of walkers amounted to intimidation. It did not matter whether they were sour-faced or dressed as clowns, they were walking the legal line of the public footpath and it was my job to do something about it. I could not imagine a policeman in uniform drinking tea with someone who had committed an offence. Policemen act as policemen, soldiers act as soldiers and public rights of way officers should act as public rights of way officers.

"Christ, it's my wife," said Peter Knowles suddenly, snatching the half drunk mug of tea out of my hand and hiding it in a cupboard, "for god's sake don't let her see you or the balloon will go up again, quick Wayland, out this way. I hope she didn't notice your van up the road, anyway I'll just lie about it and say I haven't seen you."

As Mrs Knowles entered through the front door I was being bundled out of a rear entrance.

"Coooee," said Mrs Knowles, "Peter, I'm back."

"Ssshh," hissed Peter Knowles as he closed the door behind me.

I tried in vain to walk silently on the crunching gravel and upon reaching the narrow lane I walked briskly to the van, fumbling for my keys on the way. Once in the van I sat behind the wheel, staring blankly ahead. What was I doing? I had failed to discharge my duty.

I ate a soft apple and thought about it.

I decided that I would write formally to Peter Knowles

outlining the details of the incident and the nature of the offence. This would then provide an official record on file should a similar incident happen again. It was after all just an unfortunate interruption that had prevented me from spelling it out in the kitchen at the breakfast bar.

I disposed of the apple core and wiped my fingers on the back of my trouser legs, behind the knees. It was nearly the end of the week after all.

I must have closed my eyes for a moment and I was startled by an abrupt tapping on the driver's window.

"Did I make you jump?" said an elderly man brusquely as I wound down the window, "does the public footpath go through the farm yard?"

I paused for long enough for the man to continue talking.

"I'm leading a walk through here in a week's time and to be frank the signage is pretty poor in this area. It's much better in the neighbouring county where I come from."

The man dug a finger into his right ear and frowned.

"Do you know a Mr Harrison?" said the man, "I was told that he's the one to get hold of if you want to get anything done around here. Apparently there's no point in talking to anyone else as they are all completely useless," the man's eyes narrowed and he sucked in his cheeks as he viewed the route of the footpath entering the gateway to the farm house, "I take it that you're not Mr Harrison?"

"No, I'm not," I said, shaking my head slowly.

"I'm going to ask at the farmhouse," said the man as he walked away.

My finger and thumb were poised to turn the key in the ignition but instead I heaved myself out of the van and called out after the elderly man.

"Wait, I'm not .. Harrison.. but I may be able to help."

2

DEMENTED ELECTRIC WASP

HARRISON HAD APPEARED at work before me and was waiting at the bottom of the yard, standing before my accumulated muddle of footbridge timbers, old metal kissing gates awaiting restoration, heaps of stone and the general disorganised residue of twenty eight years of public rights of way maintenance. He turned around to face me as I approached.

"Tit," said Harrison.

"I beg your pardon?" I said.

"Big tit."

"Big tit? Who?"

"Sshh," he said quietly.

"Why sshh?" I said, lowering my voice, "what's going on, is it a bird?"

Harrison nodded slowly with his head slightly cocked to one side.

I listened for the bird.

"For a supposed countryman," I whispered after a pause, "I am shockingly bad at bird song identification, better when you can see the little blighters. Anyway, I'm pretty certain that there is no such bird as a big tit. A great tit possibly?"

Harrison nodded gently in acknowledgement and continued listening.

A sudden squabble of sparrows, that even I could recognise, drowned out the rapid bicycle pump sound of the great tit, if indeed it was a great tit. The sparrows then moved on, en masse.

"I can hear a different bird," I said, pointing towards another area of neglected vegetation in the council yard, "I think it might be a .."

"Robin," said Harrison.

"That's what I thought," I said, "we could just do this all day I suppose, or shall we go out in the van?"

As we drove away from the yard Harrison did not enquire where we were going or what we were going to be doing for the rest of the day, he had just turned up after nearly four months of no contact and now here he was. At least he was wearing his Doctor Marten safety boots.

"Anyway," I said, breaking the silence, "why the sudden interest in birds? It seems a world away from leaping about on the top of buildings. I suppose birds do that but they can actually fly. Dolores sent me the video of you doing your freedom running, or whatever it's called."

"I ain't doin' that no more," said Harrison.

"No? Well I would call that a sensible move. Quit while you're ahead. Have you been away? I haven't seen you about since the end of last year. What did you get up to over the winter?"

As it had been a while since I had spent any time in Harrison's company I had forgotten that asking direct questions was inevitably a fruitless exercise. I glanced across at him and he took the trouble to shrug in response.

"What are you like at pub quizzes?" I said, trying to inject some enthusiasm into the conversation.

"Why is that?" he said.

"There's one next week at my local and I am trying to get a team together. My old team has dumped me because I keep talking them out of the right answers."

"Nah, no fanks."

"How's Dolores?"

"Busy."

"Is she thinking of coming out in the van with the lads, like last year?"

"I guess."

"Righteo," I said, "you can put on a cd if you want to, they're in the glove compartment."

Harrison leant forward and rifled through the cd cases until he opened one and slotted a disc into the player on the dashboard.

"Great," I said, as the music started, "Bob Wills and the Texas Playboys, do you like this one?"

Harrison turned his head to frown at me and then looked away.

After the first two tracks Harrison leant forward and turned the cd player off.

"Is you goin' to sing along wiv the whole fing?" he said.

"Oh, I suppose I was singing wasn't I? I'm normally on my own and then it doesn't matter."

At that moment my mobile phone rang and I tugged it out of my fleece pocket.

"Do you mind?" I said, handing it to Harrison, "can you say "this is Victor Wayland's phone, he is currently driving but may I take a message?""

Harrison took the mobile phone and answered it.

"Yeah," he said.

I turned to look at Harrison and silently mouthed my instructions again.

Harrison ignored me and continued listening and looking straight ahead. I found it hard to concentrate on my driving and began slowing down. I wanted to ensure that he answered my phone as instructed.

"Yeah," said Harrison after a long pause, "ok, cool."

He then handed me back the mobile phone.

"Who was it?" I said, "you didn't say what I wanted you to say, it's important, you can't just say "yeah"."

"It weren't for you," said Harrison.

"What do you mean it wasn't for me? It's my phone."

"It was nuffin'," he said, turning away to look out of the passenger window.

I was beginning to wonder why I thought I needed Harrison's help at all. The idea of Harrison seemed to be better than the actual thing.

Almost immediately my mobile phone pinged to indicate that I had received a text message. I contemplated returning the phone to Harrison to let me know what it said but I had never satisfactorily established whether he could actually read or write. I pulled over into the next available lay-by.

"Forgot to say, will be in the yard first thing fri. D," I said, reading out the message, "is that from Dolores, was it her that just rang? That's good news then, she must have the van back on the road."

Harrison nodded and yawned at the same time.

"I guess," he said, once the yawn had passed.

Before I drove on I quickly checked to see if I could save Dolores' number for future reference as I no longer had any contact details for her but it came up as number withheld.

We continued in silence for a couple more miles before I turned off the road. In the daylight hours there was always a steady trickle of vehicles that were prepared to chance this unmade track to gain access to a wide expanse of open grassland on the crown of Snowy Hill. On this bright and clear morning there were already a number of visitors in the parking area with dog walkers either setting out or returning back to their cars.

There was one larger vehicle at the far end of the car park that had a long shiny metal trailer attached behind it with lots of small compartments along the sides. The driver was sitting in a folding chair beside it, reading a newspaper.

"I'm not certain but I think that trailer's full of racing pigeons," I said, getting out of the van, "fancy being a pigeon fancier, what with your new found interest in birds? Anyway, that's not why we're here."

A curious message had been left on my office answer phone at the end of last week. It was from an equestrian who reported that a "demented electric wasp" was flying around Snowy Hill and frightening the horses. I had a fair idea what this could be and I hoped that it might be evident today so that I could gauge the extent of the problem. Apparently on Friday an organised long distance ride was passing over Snowy Hill and the concerned equestrian was imploring me to do something about this "demented electric wasp" before then.

The views from this elevation were spectacular with the far horizon crisp and clear. It was fresh enough for there to be no haziness yet I could feel the sun's warmth on my skin, which after a long, dull and dreary winter was very heartening.

Leaving the car park we passed the truck and the shiny metal trailer which was indeed full of racing pigeons.

"Are you letting them go this morning?" I said.

The man flicked down his newspaper.

"Yeah, as soon as that bloody thing stops flying about, it'll send 'em in all directions" he said.

Apparently he had driven two hundred miles south to reach this spot and once the racing pigeons had been released, they would be home well before him. He went back to reading his newspaper and drinking straight from a thermos flask.

We ventured out onto the open grass area, or I thought we had until I realised that Harrison was still standing beside the trailer, peering at the pigeons.

At this point the bridleway was unfenced and the route on the ground was a bit vague. Further along, as the bridleway left the ridge, it was contained between fences but up here horse riders could enjoy the open turf and would often canter along this section, if there weren't too many dog walkers and loose dogs about.

From nowhere I heard a sudden buzzing sound and an object sped a few yards above my head. Here was the "demented electric wasp" that had been terrorising the horses and, as I had anticipated, it was a small drone. I looked around for the operator who was standing on the brow of the hill one hundred yards away. In a matter of seconds the whirring machine was out of sight on the other side of the ridge and it was altogether in a different league from the remote controlled model aeroplanes that have been around for years. These types of drones, from what little I know about them, have four small rotary helicopter type blades that provide the speed and manoeuvrability. I imagined that it was a military technological development that had now, in this form, filtered down to the domestic market. In my book this kind of hobby should have ended with toy balsa wood gliders.

I walked up to the crest of the ridge where the operator had a three hundred and sixty degree view of his drone playground.

"Good morning," I said, as I got my breath back from the steep climb.

"Mornin'," said the man, who was perhaps in his late twenties.

"Great view from up here."

"Perfect."

"Um..I'm the public rights of way officer for the west of the county."

"That's nice."

The drone was now flying in a rapid figure of eight.

I could see two horse riders approaching along the bridleway and they were now entering the open grassland of Snowy Hill. One sweep across of the drone in their direction had stopped them in their tracks and both riders began calling and waving frantically.

"Excuse me," I said, "but would you mind pausing for a moment to let those horse riders pass and also, the chap in the car park can release his racing pigeons."

"I haven't been here long," said the man, "it's a new machine and I've got to get some practice in."

"So, is that a no?"

"Yes, it's a no."

I could hear the two horse riders calling out again.

Further down the hill Harrison had walked some way up the slope and had stopped to watch the flight of the drone as it occupied the clear blue sky.

"How about a bit of consideration for other people?" I said, "those horse riders down there can't continue their ride and the racing pigeon man has driven two hundred miles to come here to release his pigeons, but he can't because of you."

"I was here first," said the man.

The thing buzzed just over our heads and it really was quite intimidating.

Another machine appeared out of nowhere and the two objects paused to hover side by side.

"Christ, they're breeding," I said.

The drone operator waved across to the car park and a man waved back, approaching with a control panel in his hand.

"You'd better get used to it mate," said the man, "it's the

future."

"I hope you're satisfied," I said, "The horse riders have now given up and turned back. How long are you here for?"

"Actually, I've taken the week off to do this."

"So, will you be here on Friday?"

"I dunno, yes, maybe on Friday, now can you just...push off mate, you're getting on my nerves."

I walked back down the slope to where Harrison was standing on the open grassland watching the aerial display.

"They're a bloody menace," I said, within earshot of the second drone operator as he passed us on his way up to the crest of the hill.

Harrison did not comment.

"Come on, we've got other things to be getting on with," I said.

The racing pigeon man was now leaning against his vehicle, smoking a cigarette. I informed him that they were not prepared to stop the activity.

"Right," said the racing pigeon man, "I might 'ave to go up the 'ill and 'ave a little word then."

He looked like the sort of chap where "'aving a little word" might be a euphemism.

I left him to find his own solution for today and we headed back towards the van. On the way I bumped into Chris, an old colleague, long since retired and we had a quick chat beside his car as he was putting on his walking boots. He had a pair of binoculars around his neck and I recalled from earlier conversations that he was now a keen bird watcher. I informed him that he would be lucky to see any bird life up here with two drones whizzing about. He told us that he was going to check out some short eared owls that had been resident over the winter in a field of long grass, further along the ridge. He described the location and I think I knew where he meant.

"They should be around for another couple of weeks before

they return to Scandinavia for the breeding season. Fascinating birds with long wings, there was about six of them last time I went over there. Better to go later in the day when they're hunting but I might be lucky. They don't seem too bothered about people, which is good. How's the job going Victor, is this your new assistant?"

I introduced Harrison to Chris.

"Nice bins man," said Harrison.

"These?" said Chris, lifting up his binoculars, "a bit of an indulgence actually, not cheap. Well, you work all your life and there has to be some pleasures to look forward to in your dotage. Keep up the good work Victor, bye Harrison."

We drove out of the car park to go and clear a fallen tree that was blocking a bridleway, a couple of miles away.

"Every time I meet an ex colleague who has retired," I said to Harrison as we bumped along the track towards the road, "they always say "keep up the good work". I'm looking forward to saying "keep up the good work" when I eventually leave, if there's anyone left to say it to. Talking of keeping up the good work, what on earth am I going to do about those wretched drones if they are back again on Friday? As far as I know the horse ride is coming through in the early afternoon."

Harrison did not seem to share my concern but I thought I would press on and try to keep some sort of conversation going, as I so rarely had any company when out and about at work.

"What do you make of these drones? That's the first time I have seen one in the flesh, so to speak. I don't know if you watch the news?" I glanced across at Harrison just to emphasize that I had asked him a question and he obligingly shook his head slightly, "anyway, you now get these ghostly floating rooftop perspectives of devastated war torn cities that look like some sort of dreadful video game that you see advertised on telly. Drones to kill and then drones to film it all afterwards, I just think there's something very sinister about drones."

"My mate Fido 'as got one," said Harrison after a pause, when I thought I was talking to myself, "'e uses it to bring 'im biscuits in 'is workshop."

"Excellent, I like that," I said, laughing for the first time today.

I thought about Harrison having a mate called Fido. This was a new piece of information to add to what little I knew about his world. I conducted a quick mental roll call of Harrison's associates that I was aware of. There was Dolores, of course, not his girlfriend, as she was quick to point out one day, much to my embarrassment. Dolores was doing some sort of part time film making course and undertook the running maintenance on the old Trust Harrison van that was fuelled by used chip fat from a Chinese takeaway; Harrison's brother Marlon, very similar facially but stockier and a couple of years older. Marlon was a cool customer and he talked normally, unlike Harrison's mishmash language but they did share the same innate reticence. Marlon lived in an old coach with a number eight for a destination on the front. The coach had now moved from the byway where I had first encountered it and I had no idea where it was now. Marlon's mate had lived next door in an old GPO van and I had never established his name. Potentially there were five of them, if Fido and Marlon's mate were not one and the same.

I had not included the lads who came out in the Trust Harrison van into this calculation; Nigel, Knocker, Ollie and Council Peter. I already knew them through the old Gilbert Trust days as long term helpers. Once the Gilbert Trust charity had decided that they could no longer afford to provide a gang to do footpath work then somehow the lads had reappeared in the old van, with Dolores now driving. The word "Gilbert" had been painted over on the side of the van and "Harrison" had been added, so that it now read "Trust Harrison". Since Harrison's still rather unexplained visit to Cuba last year, the

Trust Harrison gang had been issued with green Fidel caps, with the red star on the front and Cuban flags had been attached to the roof-rack of the van. Some of the lads also wore military style fatigues to add to the impression that there was now a splinter group of Latin American revolutionaries at large in the English countryside.

I had also begun to sense that there was a deeper mystery connected with Harrison and his associates. Inexplicable things had happened and the number eight had been a reoccurring feature. Perhaps I was just reading too much into it all.

"I like the sound of Fido," I said, but when I glanced across at Harrison he appeared to be asleep.

Before I went to start on the bridleway clearance, I took the opportunity to deliver some waymarks to a parish councillor and gave him a bit of guidance as to where to put them up so that they made sense. I then spent a good twenty minutes digging out the mouth of a ditch on a tarmac footpath, just off the road, that had become silted up. Rainwater was collecting in a big puddle and the local school children had been clambering along the bank and steadying themselves by holding onto a wire fence to avoid getting wet. Harrison did not stir, despite my clanging about unearthing a spade from the back of the van.

We were able to drive right up the bridleway to the reported blockage where a large elder bush had collapsed underneath a mass of ivy. I changed into my chainsaw gear and dug out a hard hat with ear protectors and a pair of thick hedging gloves for Harrison who stretched and yawned, once he had emerged from the van. I did a quick safety check for any overhead wires or cables that might have got tangled up in the vegetation and then launched into the obstruction with the chainsaw. Harrison knew the form and began pulling away the cut sections and stuffing them in any available space that he could find amongst the bushes to the side of the path. Once I had partially cleared the route he pushed his way around to the far side of the fallen bush, dragging a large piece behind him to find some more space to dispose of the bush further up the path. The cuttings mounted up around me and I hauled and pushed the accumulating vegetation to the sides as I went but Harrison had not reappeared. I made the last few cuts to separate the elder and ivy into manageable sections and then switched off the saw, putting it to one side after removing my safety helmet.

"Hello?" I called out to Harrison, wondering why he had stopped assisting me.

I pushed my way through the clumps of dark green ivy and found Harrison crouched on the ground with something in his hand. Beside him were the remains of a small nest and a scattered clutch of minute broken egg shells.

"What's happened?" I said, Harrison seemed to be trying to reassemble one of the broken eggs, "do you think it came out of the bush when it went over? It must be something like a wren's nest as the eggs are so small. I guess a magpie or some other opportunist has made a very small meal out of it, ripping open the nest to get at the eggs. Oh well, these things happen, I'm afraid. It's just nature at work and there's nothing you or I can do about it. Let's get this stuff cleared then."

I returned to pulling the elder and ivy from the path but Harrison remained on his haunches and began arranging the component parts of the destroyed nest on the ground. He then took out a penknife that I had not seen before and seemed to be whittling a very fine point to a twig and stripping small sections of bark into lengths. I periodically stopped to watch his progress as he began to reconstruct the small ball of dried grass, leaves, moss, wool, delicate feathers and strands of horse hair. By the time I had cleared the track and changed out of my chainsaw gear, Harrison had completed stitching the nest back together with his twig needle and fine threads of shredded bark. He used his little finger to redefine the small entrance hole into the side of the nest near the top and then stood up to observe his handiwork.

He now looked around before finding a suitable relocation for the little nest and then ensured that it was firmly supported and sufficiently concealed from the beady eye of any larger predatory threat.

"I've got to eat something before we move on," I said, "did you bring anything?"

Harrison shook his head.

"Can I offer you a ham and mustard sandwich?"

"No fanks," said Harrison.

As I ate he wandered off up the bridleway and returned ten minutes later, slumping down into the passenger seat.

"All clear ahead?" I said.

"Yep."

"That's good."

We drove away in silence and sorted out a few odds and ends throughout the afternoon but mainly stuff that I could have undertaken on my own.

At three o clock I dropped Harrison off in town on my way back to the office, where I had some pressing e-mails to deal with.

"Ok, thanks for coming out today. I imagine that I'll see you on Friday with Dolores and the lads?"

"Yeah, I guess," said Harrison, as he got out of the van, still cupping the tiny reconstructed egg in the palm of his hand. He raised his other hand in a subtle gesture of farewell as he slammed the van door.

I watched for a moment as he walked away along the pavement with his characteristic short, urgent, paces. I had no idea what would happen now that Harrison had reappeared. From previous experiences, with Harrison around, it had felt as though nothing was beyond the bounds of possibility. On today's performance it really had amounted to nothing and even that seemed like an effort.

3
TIME

YESTERDAY THE CLOCK in my office had stopped at a quarter to four. This morning I tried changing the batteries but it still did not make the hands go around. It was a cheap clock and now it would end up in a landfill site, frozen forever at a quarter to four, a time capsule demonstrating to future generations, or aliens, the false economy of purchasing a cheap clock.

"Your clock has stopped at a quarter to four," said the chap from the other end of the building, as he wandered into my office.

"I know," I said, "it stopped working yesterday and it's not the batteries."

"I wondered why you were still here at a quarter to five last night. Hang on, I might have just the thing for you," he said, disappearing back out of the door and reappearing a minute later.

"There you go," he said, placing a large hour glass on my desk, "the team brought me this when they thought that I was taking voluntary redundancy before Christmas. I don't think you contributed towards it, no, I remember, you gave me that old stick didn't you? Anyway, I find it very distracting and could watch it for hours, wasting time rather than measuring it."

"Thank you," I said, "but it doesn't really replace a clock does it?"

"Yes it does, you've only got to turn it over seven times and then you can go home."

I turned it over and we both stared at it for a moment.

"The sands of time, slipping away," he said, "I've forgotten why I came in to see you now, anyway, time is money, must press on."

I carried on answering some e mails but kept half an eye on the trickling sand. When equilibrium had been reached, Nancy rang and I told her that Harrison had reappeared yesterday.

"So, he's back on the scene?"

"Yes, in all his reticent glory. He wasn't much help to be frank, or company come to that, but, as you say, he's back on the scene. I turned down my redundancy package because of him, not that he'd care about that."

"Now you're just being grumpy Victor, time will tell. Talking of time, that's why I rang, to see whether you're going on that course tomorrow morning?"

"Time seems to be a reoccurring theme today, anyway, isn't it some sort of life management course, why on earth would I want to do that?"

"It's good, I went on the last one. We don't get any training courses offered now, what with the cuts, but I really think you would find it useful, and yes, it's not just relevant to your working life but, you know, to your home life as well."

I let out an audible sigh.

"Come on Victor, I hate to say it but considering your age, time and time management is important. Just go to the course and if you don't want Harrison then send him over here."

I had to go out in the van to deal with some stuff but waited for the final grain of sand to fall before turning the hourglass over.

I pulled in at a crossroads where a bridleway sign had somehow been turned around on its post to point down a busy road. A cyclist on a touring bike was just about to join the busy road and I thought that I should advise him that there were better, safer options on minor roads that he may not be aware of, if he was a stranger to the area. The cyclist was German, a bit younger than me and like all Germans he seemed to be able to command a reasonable conversation in English. I established where he was going and there were indeed safer options.

"Don't go that way," I said, "it's a death camp, I mean a death trap."

The German cyclist smiled.

"Ja, don't mention *ze* war, I know your Baseel Forty, very good."

"I'm sorry," I said, my face reddening immediately, "it was a slip of the tongue."

"You have a split...in your tongue? Let me see. I am a doctor, back in Hamburg."

"No, I haven't, it's just an English expression, a slip of the tongue, a mistake, a very unfortunate mistake."

"A slip of the tongue? Ja, I see, you want your tongue to go das way and your brain makes it go dis way. You did not want to mention the war, the last thing you wanted to do was mention the war and so you say "death camp". The brain is very funny, ja?"

I was now sorely regretting my intervention in trying to help the cyclist.

"Yes, I'm sorry, but anyway, let's start again. You don't want to go that way as you'll probably get flattened by a juggernaut."

I had a sudden further panic that juggernaut was perhaps a German word for unstoppable world domination.

"Jug? I do not know dis word?"

"Oh, good, a big truck then, a container lorry?"

"Ok, ok, it is a bad road."

"Yes, it is a very bad road, for a cyclist."

I pointed out on a map a much safer alternative for his onward journey.

"Ah so, danke, you are very kind. Have a good life."

With that the cyclist scooted away on one pedal before cocking his leg over the cross bar and setting off up the minor road.

I was left wondering how I had managed to confect such an unfortunate muddle but the German cyclist seemed cheerful and forgiving enough. After the embarrassment of the situation had receded, I was left considering his parting wish that I should "have a good life". Was this just a casual offering like "have a good day"? I am 62 and certainly most of my working life is now behind me. What is there left before me? Had I had a good life? Will the remainder of my life be good? As the day wore on I was getting increasingly depressed by this unexpected reflection. Rather than be upset by my ridiculous faux pas, the German cyclist had continued happily on his way but by his parting pleasantry I had been left re-evaluating and doubting the worth of my life.

I tried to put these things to the back of my mind and listened to a radio programme about the art of defensive driving. I had always prided myself on my unblemished driving record and completely concurred with the voice on the radio who said that you should try to anticipate another driver's potential for stupidity. Having mentally congratulated myself I then thought that I ought to touch a piece of wood as some sort of flaky insurance policy. My hazel stick should be somewhere close to hand and I reached across to the passenger seat and felt for it under my coat. I then thought that as it was a bit muddy on the end I might have pushed it through the grill into the back. I glanced across and could just see the tip of the handle poking out. Despite stretching and feeling with the flat of my hand I still could not locate it. I glanced across again and at that moment the large van in front must have braked suddenly in the stop start traffic as we passed through the town.

It was a fairly standard driving into the back of the person in front at slow speed sort of accident. The sort of everyday occurrence that you drive by and tut at, wondering how they could be so careless. Nobody was hurt but it was a bloody nuisance all round.

We both found somewhere to pull over and then got out to inspect the damage.

"And what's more, I'm not even superstitious," I said to the van driver, concluding my statement of guilt. He had remained silent throughout my confession and it was probably the shock of actually having a collision after all these years that made me sing like a canary. We exchanged details and he pointed out that my radiator was now leaking.

This unfortunate affair seemed to take up the remainder of the afternoon. I managed to coax the van along to our vehicle maintenance depot which fortuitously was quite nearby and I was hoping for a replacement vehicle to tide me over until my van could be fixed.

"This is all we've got," said the mechanic, directing me to a van that had been adapted to house a roadside speeding camera, "it should only be for a couple of days."

As there was no other option I took the keys and headed back to the depot. There were no police decals on the vehicle but it was unmistakably a speeding camera van with small, square smoked glass windows in the back doors and another one on the side. In my office the hourglass had long since emptied itself but judging by the exodus from the staff car park it was now time to go home.

Having slept on the matter, I thought that I would take Nancy's advice and attend this morning's half day time management course. I held no great expectations but I did not think that it could do me any harm either.

"That's the spirit Victor," said the chap from the other end of the building, giving me a wink, as we mustered to find a seat in the small hall.

"Have you got something wrong with your eye?" I said, "anyway, I'm surprised to see you here, you used to moan about having to go on pointless courses in the good old days when there were plenty of pointless courses to go on."

"Well, I think we're all here for the same reason, aren't we?"

"Really?" I said, "I don't know much about it and I've no idea who is actually running the course."

"Gina...Bellarosa," he said, with relish and then nodded towards the audience, "look at this sorry lot, sat there with their tongues hanging out."

The small hall was now rapidly filling up with middle-aged men.

"Do you know anything about her?" I said, "other than her name?"

"Well, no, but you'll have to agree, as names go in our grey and dreary world, now we're at the fag end of local government, it is pretty exotic."

"So, you're expecting somebody like...Gina Lollobrigida, to turn up on a Wednesday morning and talk to you about time management?"

"Hmm, Gina Lollobrigida, now she was a cracker. Ok, yes, it's fair to say we're all expecting something in the Gina Lollobrigida league, that's reasonable."

"I see. I just came along because I hoped it might be helpful and interesting."

"All will be revealed shortly," he said, rubbing his hands together in anticipation, "incidentally Victor, why are you driving that speeding camera van around?"

"I had a little shunt in my van."

"Your fault?"

"Yes, it was stupid really."

"A stupid little shunt?"

Before we had time to conclude our conversation, such as it was, the lady running the course walked down to the front and introduced herself.

"Good morning, my name is Gina Bellarosa and welcome to making the best of your time, here in your place of work, but also, more importantly, in your life as a whole."

I could sense the chap from the other end of the building moving about in his seat and he then leant across to whisper in my ear.

"Most disappointing Victor," he said, under his breath, "I was convinced that she'd have thick black hair, tumbling down to..."

"Shh," I said,

"Her hair's what I would call...mousey..."

"Shh," I hissed again.

There were general, restless shuffling sounds coming from the audience of middle-aged men.

"It is interesting," said Gina Bellarosa, "that these seminars do seem to attract the male employees of a certain age, if that's not being rude. Perhaps it is the time of life, and more specifically a lack of time left, that focuses the mind. Perhaps women are more naturally attuned to juggling their day to fit in with their various commitments? Certainly, these short courses do attract a particular demographic and that's fine."

Gina Bellarosa then embarked upon the essential housekeeping announcements regarding fire exits, toilets and coffee breaks, before concentrating on how we were all wasting our precious time.

It took me a while to adjust to the fact that I now had to sit and listen to somebody talking. At first the words meant nothing and I told myself that this was because I was simply not used to it, in this environment. It was all a matter of concentration, I had to banish extraneous thoughts and just focus on the words.

Gina Bellarosa was slim and healthy looking and probably of average height. It was difficult to judge her age, older than Nancy and certainly younger than me with an expressive face and good cheek bones. She had a self assured manner, a confidence to deliver her phrases slowly and then wait for them to sink in. It was the sinking in that I was struggling with, my fault, not hers. I had to tell myself again just to focus on the words.

"A cynical person may say, "well things take as long as they take and you cannot recalibrate a local authority". I suppose that may be like trying to penny pinch seconds from the eons of geological time."

I rather liked this analogy and heard my lone voice chortling amidst the silent torpor of my fellow colleagues.

Having finally received some sort of response, I was now Gina Bellarosa's go to face in the audience. I tried to offer visual, facial encouragement as the morning progressed. A smile here, a raised eyebrow there, in fact all the signs of somebody being interested and attentive.

"And after the coffee break," she said, concluding the first half of the seminar, "we're going to address the subject of procrastination."

On our return I noticed that a number of attendees had slipped away, including the chap from the other end of the building.

This had not gone unnoticed.

"We always lose a few mid morning," said Gina Bellarosa, "but never mind, never mind. Perhaps they have become so inspired that they can't wait to seize the day. Now, what is procrastination?"

As I was being singled out and looked at, I felt obliged to say something.

"Putting things off until tomorrow," I said and then immediately regretted stating the obvious, wishing that I had been more imaginative or humorous in my response.

"Procrastination is the death of a good idea," said Gina Bellarosa, ignoring my suggestion, "by the time that you have thought about your good idea, slept on it, even told somebody else about it, it might feel like this idea is still alive and fizzing but all the while, time is passing. Tick, tock, tick, tock. Time will dilute your good idea, devalue it, suffocate it and ultimately be the death of it. We are often our own worst enemy, I'm sure you've heard that expression before? So, what is stopping us? It's us, we are. You might think that you've got all the time in the world to carry out your good idea. Well, I've got news for you mate, you haven't. Nobody has."

Despite being looked at encouragingly for the remainder of the half day course, I resisted any further interjections, even though her occasional prompts to the audience were being met with a deathly silence.

The winding up at the end caught me by surprise and I wondered whether I might have nodded off for a bit. Gina Bellarosa clicked her finger and thumb together in a loud snap, causing me to make an involuntary jerk and sit up straight.

"There goes another second," she said, "so, do you remember the saying, "look after the pennies and the pounds will take care of themselves"? Well how about, look after the seconds and the minutes will take care of themselves? Thanks for listening, whatever it is, please make sure that you do it now...oh yes and don't forget to enjoy yourselves, it's later than you think."

The audience clapped dutifully, followed by a lot of stretching and yawning.

Despite being left high and dry with my bland suggestion about the definition of procrastination, I felt drawn to walk down to the front and thank Gina Bellarosa for the seminar.

"Thanks," she said, "I hope you found it interesting, inspiring even?"

"Yes, very. Time is precious and we needed reminding of that. I don't suppose that you would like to...," I said, surprising myself and also being unsure where this question was heading, "to join my pub quiz team?"

"Now you're talking," said Gina Bellarosa, "I love pub quizzes but unfortunately my partner's not that keen, when is it?"

"It's this coming Monday, but I've only got one place left...as it happens," I said.

"Sorry, got a union meeting on Monday, maybe another time? Thanks for asking though. Now, I've got a train to catch, time waits for no man," said Gina Bellarosa.

"Or woman," I said.

"Especially not for women."

"Would you like a lift to the station?"

"No thanks, I should be ok if I walk briskly, I've worked it out down to the second."

"I'd expect nothing less," I said.

"I'm sorry, I don't know your name?" said Gina Bellarosa, offering her hand.

"Victor. Victor Wayland," I said, "I'm the public rights of way officer for the west of the county."

"Are you now? Ok, that's interesting," she said as we shook hands, "Victor Wayland, victory, a way across the land. Great name, very evocative. Arrivederci."

"Thank you," I said, I almost asked after her Italian origins but time was against me and so I said "goodbye" instead.

After eating my lunch, I set off in the speeding camera van to check some stuff that I had been meaning to look at for ages. No time like the present I told myself.

After a few miles I was feeling very heavy lidded and opened the driver's window for some fresh air. Even with the window open

I was still struggling. Perhaps it was sitting still all morning or even Harrison's very soporific company from yesterday that was rubbing off on me. The signs that you see on motorways "Tiredness can kill, take a break" kept flashing through my mind. I had already had one accident this week and I definitely did not want another. I had to close my eyes. I would seize the moment and do the sensible thing as to procrastinate for even another minute could be fatal. Midway on a long straight section of road I pulled into a small lay-by, turned off the engine and wound the window back up.

The driver's seat in the van was very uncomfortable and I peered into the back to see if that was any more accommodating. There were a heap of three large padded fluorescent yellow safety jackets in one corner. I struggled through the narrow gap between the front seats and picked up and shook the jackets. The floor in the back of the van was plywood and by spreading out the jackets I could make a comfortable place to lie down, just for a moment.

I woke up to the sound of something heavy walking around upstairs. I opened my eyes to be confronted by the fluorescent yellow from the nest of coats that I had formed to lay down upon, which only added to my confusion. Eventually I worked out where I was and that it must be a pigeon or a crow plodding around on the roof of the speeding camera van. How long had I been asleep? What was the time? I had left my mobile phone on charge in the office and this van had no clock on the dashboard. I rubbed my eyes and thought that as it was probably too late to continue with the inspections that I had planned for this afternoon, I would now return to the office.

The yard was all locked up and I drove home to find Leadbelly howling on the doorstep. I always fed him when I got home from work but judging by his indignation and dismay, I sensed that something must be badly awry. On entering the house, I was stunned to find out that it was now in fact seven thirty and I hastily opened a tin for his supper. Feeling bewildered and somewhat disorientated, I flopped down into my armchair without putting any lights on. After a couple of minutes Leadbelly leapt up onto my lap, breathing cat food odours and clawing at my groin, punishing me for my neglect in feeding him so late. He then jumped off and sat beside the armchair, staring up at me from the shadows. In the half light his eyes were black holes with the pupils fully dilated. I stared back, mesmerised by these portals into deep space where time and even light years were meaningless. I blinked, losing this thread, falling back to earth, back into my armchair, unfocused.

"Forgiven me?" I said, just as the cat flap rattled and I realised that I was talking to myself.

4
JIM PRINGLE

IT WAS THE day of the long distance sponsored horse ride and sitting at my desk on Friday morning, I was still no clearer as to how I could prevent it being disrupted by drones flying about on Snowy Hill. I had left a message with the local police but I had not heard back as yet.

I had just made another cup of tea to help me think when the phone rang. It was the PA to the new director and apparently Jolyon Bellringer wanted to speak to me in person.

"Victor, it's Jolyon here, glad I've manage to catch you, I'm sure that you're tremendously busy. We haven't had a chance to meet up yet but I hope to remedy that soon. I'm very keen to establish who is doing what out there, I don't want to be just a name, locked up in their ivory tower, do you know what I mean?"

My mind flashed back to Lucian Poole, the previous director and his ill fated attempt to meet and inspire the work force.

"Ok, hello," I said, "it's kind of you to take the trouble to get in touch..er..what do you.. how can I help?"

"Well, obviously you have already helped enormously and I'm tremendously grateful that you were able to act so swiftly. One of my goals is to ensure that we break out of that old silo thinking and be more flexible, you know, we've all got to be more adaptable? Your actions on Wednesday epitomised that approach perfectly and it was the least I could do, you know, to ring you up and thank you in person. So..er..well done."

I undertook a quick mental scramble though the events of Wednesday which comprised of trying to stay awake in a seminar and then falling asleep in a lay-by all afternoon.

"Um.." I said.

"Come on Victor, you're obviously one of those modest and self effacing chaps. Credit where credit is due I say. Anyway Mr X's people have been on to comms to say he's doing fine and once he heard that our traffic speeding van had been parked down the road from his gateway, the very next day after the accident, well, in his own words he was "touched". We drew a blank at first and no-one seemed to know who had arranged it until finally we established that it had been you, acting on your own initiative."

"I see," I said.

"And once he found out that it was actually our public rights of way officer who had taken the time out of his busy schedule to do it and for some hours well into the evening I understand, then he was even more touched. Mr X has a number of public rights of way on his land and, when he's back on his feet, he wants you to pop over there and give him some advice. As you know he's only just bought the estate and despite being driven into at sixty miles an hour when coming out of his drive, he says that he has been made to feel very welcome. Did you catch any speeding motorists by the way?"

"Er, no, well you know how it is, just the sight of one of those vehicles is a deterrent in itself."

"Exactly and it has turned out to be a brilliant PR exercise and we've made a very high profile friend, thanks to you Victor."

"Well, it was nothing really," I said, pushing back my chair on its castors to enable me to stretch out and put my feet up on the desk, "obviously, I'm very pleased to have been able to offer my services."

I took a sip of my tea and explained that I had felt a certain empathy having just experienced a road traffic accident myself, earlier in the week and it had made me realise how traumatic the whole business was. I pointed out that it had been my first collision in twenty eight years of driving a council vehicle and that I had been very proud of my unblemished record.

"Hello?" I said, but the director had gone and I realised that I had been talking to myself.

I quickly checked on the internet to find out who Mr X was and established that, amongst other things, he was a judge on a prime time television talent show. There was also a picture of Mr X's pearl white 4x4 after it had been struck by a speeding vehicle.

I finished my tea and heard the familiar sound of an old diesel van rattling over the speed hump at the entrance to the yard.

As the Trust Harrison van parked up, I savoured the smell of fish and chips in the air as I walked down to the bottom of the yard to say hello.

"Still running on old chip fat then?" I said, as Dolores opened the driver's door.

"Hey, we're back on the road," she said, "yes, still being supplied by the Chinese takeaway in town. Where's your van Mr Wayland, we didn't think that you were here when we drove in?"

I explained about the minor accident and pointed to the traffic speeding van.

"That's the only replacement vehicle that they had available in the workshop," I said, "hopefully I'm getting my old van back on Monday. Anyway, it's great to see you all again, it seems like..ages."

I walked around to the open sliding door to peer in the back.

"Hello lads," I said, but nobody spoke. Ollie was eating a large bag of crisps, Council Peter was scratching his leg with the stainless steel hook that served as a left hand, Knocker was extricating something from the depths of his long grey beard whilst Nigel made strange whistling noises through his nose as he slept in his seat.

"I really appreciate you all coming out," I said.

Harrison finally emerged from the front passenger seat to yawn and stretch expansively.

"It's a bit like that," I said, stifling a yawn of my own, "it's as though everyone's been hibernating over the winter."

"He's not been hibernating," said Dolores, nodding towards Harrison.

"Oh?" I said.

"No, he's been a stuntman on a film set in Italy for the last couple of months, he's only just got back in the last few days. Says he's tired, little lamb."

I looked across at Harrison.

"I asked you the other day what you'd been up to and you didn't tell me about that?"

"I don't do that stuff no more, I told you that," said Harrison.

"That's true, you did tell me that much. Is there any reason that you've given it up, apart from it being absolute insanity?"

"How about this for a dodgy excuse," said Dolores, "he doesn't want to eat pasta any more, or pizza. He's decided that he doesn't want to eat wheat. I don't know why I'm talking for him, just to hurry things along I suppose, to get to the point, to save time, life is too short, hey isn't it buddy boy?"

Dolores suddenly leapt on Harrison and held him tightly in a head lock. Harrison put up no resistance at all and eventually emerged with red squeeze marks on his face.

"And she's doin' wrestlin'," said Harrison.

"Are you?" I said, "where? Not that I'm going to come and watch or anything. I'm not sure that I believe anything anybody says to me anymore, I'm just glad that you've all come back. Oh yes, have you heard of someone called Mr X? Apparently he's famous?"

Harrison looked blank and Dolores shook her head.

"It's just that he's moved into the area and somehow I have managed to get into his good books, it's not worth explaining how to be honest, but the new director seems to think this is terrific news. So, you've never heard of him?"

"I have," said Ollie, calling out from the van through a mouthful of crisps.

Ollie emerged from the side of the van and started alternately kicking his short legs forward to resemble a lumbering Tiller girl whilst singing a song through a spray of crisps.

"I'm the one for you, you're the one for me, we'll always be together like chalk and cheese. I'm the one for you, you're the one for me, let's turn around together and touch our knees."

At the conclusion of this short demonstration Ollie staggered back towards the van to sit down and took a gulp from a large bottle of diet cola.

"Ok," I said.

"It's what he does," said Ollie breathlessly, "when he comes on."

"Well done man," said Harrison.

"Yes, thank you," I said, "that's great but I am a little confused about the bit "we'll always be together like chalk and cheese" as that is the whole point of chalk and cheese, they are opposites..."

Just at that moment my mobile phone rang and I indicated to Harrison and Dolores that I had better answer it as I hoped that it might be the local police getting back to me regarding the troublesome drones on Snowy Hill. It was not the local police but a disgruntled member of the public who was not happy about a forthcoming event in his village. I gathered that he was referring to the annual sports car hill climb that had been held for years and was very popular with the motor enthusiasts in the vicinity. The complainant, it seems, had just moved to the village from the outskirts of London.

"I didn't move to the countryside to listen to high performance cars racing up hills and whilst we're about it there's loads of sheep here making a right bloody racket. I came here for a bit of peace and quiet, a fat chance of that I can tell you."

In an effort to make this a brief conversation I informed the caller that it was lambing time, hence the bucolic racket and the track used for the hill climb was not a public right of way.

"But I walk that way with my dog every morning," said the caller.

"Yes, but it is a private track and technically you are trespassing against the owner, there is no right to walk wherever you.."

"I'll walk where I bloody well like and I'm not having you telling me where I can walk and where I can't."

"But I'm the public rights of way officer, I do know..."

"You can sod off mate and this bloody countryside's not all it's cracked up to be."

As the caller hung up on me I watched the Trust Harrison van disappear out of the yard and I had not even got as far as asking Dolores and Harrison what task they were going to be doing today. It was after all their first day back after many months so I imagine that they would just familiarise themselves with things and ease their way back into it all. They were unpaid volunteers after all.

Rather than fret in the office I thought that I might as well head out to Snowy Hill and see if the drones were flying today. If they were flying then I would have to try and reason with the operators and hope that they might demonstrate a bit of understanding when the sponsored horse ride came through.

Before I left the yard I put on a cd that I had searched for yesterday evening at home and eventually found at the back of a cupboard. I had felt a bit exposed by Harrison's sudden interest in identifying birdsong and I thought that I ought to brush up a bit. I had bought the cd in a charity shop some years ago and had only listened to it once. It was called "identifying birdsong the easy way" with Jim Pringle. Jim Pringle had evidently been out at various locations at various times of the day, recording various birds. There should be an accompanying booklet with the cd but it was missing when I bought the disc. From what I could remember there was a good burst of one particular bird and then Jim's soft and reassuring voice would enter the scene and confirm which bird we had been listening to. Either there was something wrong with the cd itself or it was the cd player in the traffic speeding van as each time Jim's whispered tones began then the cd would skip to the next birdsong recording, leaving me none the wiser. As I was driving down the road I turned up the cd player to make sure that it was not just Jim whispering inaudibly and this increased volume created an avian cacophony inside the cab.

"And there we have just been listening to a pair of.."

"That was some passing.."

"The "chissick" sounds are from a.."

I was getting more and more infuriated as the cd skipped and missed the essential identifications whilst being deafened by the intermittent birdsong.

"That deep cooing that you can hear is from a.."

"And that's an alarm call from a.."

"For christsakes Jim, talk to me," I cried out in frustration.

"Those shrill notes are from a.."

"We're now by an old barn, near some open fields.."

"Jim, I don't care where the bloody hell you are with your blasted tape recorder, I just need to know what I am listening to, it's not too much to ask surely?"

"Those single sharp shrieks are the.."

"Right that's it," I said, ejecting the cd and flinging it down into the passenger floor well, "I thought that it might be informative and relaxing but no, thank you very bloody much Jim Pringle."

I wound the window down and took some deep breaths. After a good lung full of cloying and nauseating oil seed rape pollen from the bright yellow field that now revealed itself on the other side of the hedge, I hastily wound the window back up again.

I have never relished conflict and it does not come naturally to me although it is an essential factor of my job to assert the highway law on behalf of the authority. Some folk like the anticipation of a show down but it gnaws away at me and I cannot stop thinking about it even to the point of not being able to get to sleep the night before. It is better when the situation is more black and white in legal terms and you can simply quote the law verbatim but when there is no clarity and it is down to persuasion and relying on someone's cooperation then uncertainty enters the equation.

I arrived at Snowy Hill with a sense of dread and sure enough I could see a drone occupying the clear blue sky above the crest of the ridge.

I parked in the car park and there were a couple of dog walkers undertaking a circuit of the hill but no sign of any horses at this stage and with the engine turned off I could hear the incessant buzz of the machine. I waited for a while to make a couple of phone calls in the hope that the drone operator might push off but there seemed to be no indication of that happening. I began the slow walk up to the summit where the operator was stationed. When I was about half way up the hill another vehicle entered the car park and I caught a whiff of fried food in the gentle breeze. I stopped and turned around to see the Trust Harrison van park up next to the traffic speeding van and I gave them a wave. The sun was glaring from the windscreen so I could not detect whether anyone had responded. I completed my ascent and approached the drone operator.

"Oh, it's you again," said the man.

"Yes, it's me again. Look, I'll get to the point, there's a long distance horse ride coming by at any time and you are going to disrupt it if you keep flying this thing up here. The horses will get completely spooked by your machine."

"You can't stop me."

"Why can't you understand the issue? I am just asking for a bit of cooperation here."

"Do I have to spell it out for you?"

"Spell what out?"

"P.I.S.S. O.F.F. Get the message?"

The operator then controlled the drone to buzz just above my head, dipping it up and down so that I could feel the draught from the whirring blades.

"If I had my stick I'd bloody well swat the thing out of the sky," I said, "get the thing away from me, get off."

I waved my arms at the drone as the operator laughed.

"Run along," he said, "off you go, back down the hill,"

As I flapped my hand at it, I lost my footing and began to slide down the steep slope until I ended up on my backside. My ankle felt strange as if it had flexed it over too far and I gingerly stood up again to see whether I had sprained it. The drone operator had now turned his back on me and the machine was sailing away out of sight behind the hill. I looked down the slope and Harrison was wandering up from the car park. I continued slowly downwards in short diagonals and met Harrison half way up the hill.

"Is you ok boss?"

"No, I am not ok, that thing is an offensive weapon and I think I've twisted my ankle. He's just an ignorant...bloody idiot. What have you got there? They look like ancient binoculars are you going bird spotting?"

Harrison held up the large binoculars that were hanging from his neck by a thick strap.

"My mate Fido leant them to me. I fort I'd come and check out them owls."

"I'm really cross, I feel like going back up there and punching his lights out, I might get the sack but at least it would solve the immediate problem," I said.

"Nah," said Harrison, lifting his binoculars skywards, "it's cool boss."

"I wish I had your confidence, that ride will be coming through anytime now."

I turned back to look up the hill as the drone buzzed back into view.

"The thing's stopped still," I said.

"Yeah, it ain't doin' what he wants it to do," said Harrison.

The drone operator held up the controls towards the drone which was hovering ten metres or so away from him but the machine remained in stasis.

"He looks like he's getting quite agitated with it," I said.

Harrison lowered his binoculars.

"It's moving now," I said, "he's bringing it down to the ground."

We stood and watched as the operator picked it up to inspect it and then sent the drone back up into the air.

"It's working again," I said.

Harrison raised his binoculars to have another look. The drone had obviously developed a problem and now froze no more than five feet from the ground.

"With a bit of luck the bloody thing's broken," I said.

The operator plucked the machine from the air and held it in his hand before turning the motor off. The man crouched down for a while and then tried it again. Harrison inspected the action through his binoculars with the drone refusing to respond to the demands of the operator.

"I think he's packing up and leaving," I said and glancing across to the side of the hill I could see some activity in the distance along the bridleway, "I think this might be the long distant horse ride coming through, crikey that was a close run thing. Can I have a look with your binoculars?"

"Nah," said Harrison, making no effort to look himself, "Fido said that they is only set up for me to use and don't fiddle wiv them."

"Here's that berk coming back down the hill with his toy. Such a shame it's broken," I called across.

The man stuck two fingers up in response and gave me an unpleasant scowl. Instinctively I set off across the slope to intercept his descent but my ankle gave me a jolt of pain and I winced audibly.

Harrison reached out and gripped my arm just below the elbow and maintained a firm hold to prevent me from moving until the drone operator had passed on down the hill.

"I was just going to...I don't know what I was going to do."

I slumped down on the grassy slope and watched as the long-distance horse ride approached. There were seven riders in the group and I could hear them chatting happily as they passed beneath our position before drifting away onto a connecting bridleway. Having packed up his gear the drone operator now drove out of the car park, bumping slowly along the byway towards the main road.

"I was going to get his registration number and report him to the police," I said, "he must have been committing some sort of offence."

Harrison had remained standing with the enormous old binoculars dangling from his neck.

"He ain't going to be coming up here no more," he said.

"How can you be so sure?"

"Trust me," said Harrison, "now where's them short owls boss?"

5
QUIZ

THINGS WERE GREENING up nicely in the countryside now that we are halfway through April. What with Harrison's recent concerted interest in birds I really ought to make more of an effort myself in describing the onset of spring and to settle for "greening up nicely" probably errs on the lazy side. In a month or so's time there will be more of a generic chlorophyll lushness everywhere that could reasonably be termed green but at this stage of springtime with all this unfurling, sprouting, flowering and budding there are a multitude of fresh pale grey greens that seem to defy my limited literary palette. Now that I am forcing myself to look more closely a lot of them are not even green at all and some of the browner tones seem to neatly echo autumn's decay so it is all rather confusing really. I think what I am trying to say is that I feel heartened and encouraged by the onset of spring.

"Have you noticed the whitening of the hedgerows Victor?" said the chap from the other end of the building as he strode purposefully into my office on the Monday morning, "you know, the what's it called?"

"Blossom?" I said.

"Yes, that's it. Very white this year and lots of it."

"If you have a closer look at the blackthorn blossom I think you'll find that it is probably more creamy than white."

"Trust you to be pedantic about it and I was being genuine in my praise of the natural world, I shan't bother next time. By the way, and more to the point, you haven't paid your tea money for three weeks."

The local policeman had rung this morning to say that his shifts had been altered and that he apologised for not being around on Thursday and Friday of last week. I described the potential conflict between irresponsible drone flying and equestrians and he muttered something about it all being a lot simpler years ago when boys had catapults hanging out of their back pockets. I thanked him for taking the trouble to ring back but the problem seemed to have resolved itself. There was also something reassuring about Harrison's statement that the drone operator would not be returning to Snowy Hill.

My ankle had recovered pretty well over the weekend with a combination of frozen peas and inactivity and I could now walk on it fairly normally.

I continued with answering some e mails and after a while the telephone rang again.

"Nancy, it's great to hear your voice," I said, "I'm always very pleased when you ring and it isn't someone moaning about being attacked by a belligerent goose on a footpath or reporting a fallen twig that's blocking a bridleway. Isn't it a lovely time of year? There's some fantastic blossom out there."

"You're full of the joys of spring Victor, now you come to mention it the hedgerows are very white this year."

"Yes, aren't they just," I said, "I'm glad you've rung, there's been a lot going on."

I told Nancy about the events on Snowy Hill on Friday and how disaster had been narrowly averted.

"Harrison appeared with some enormous archaic binoculars to go bird spotting and somehow the wretched drone stopped working."

"That's good then," said Nancy, "so the Trust Harrison show is back on the road?".

"Yes, I guess the van's all legal but I don't really like to ask."

I went on to tell Nancy about me driving into the back of someone and being given a traffic speeding van as a replacement vehicle for a few days. I skipped the bit about falling asleep in a layby and garbled something about the new director ringing me up and that I've got to go and meet Mr X when he gets back on his feet.

"Mr who?"

"Mr X, I hoped that you'd be mighty impressed but you've obviously never heard of him either. He's some sort of television celebrity who has just bought an estate with some rights of way across it in my area that I have got to go and look at. I'm not really sure what he wants to be honest."

"Well it all makes my life sound rather dull by comparison, actually, that's why I rang, do you still want someone for your pub quiz team? It is tonight isn't it?"

"It certainly is but I don't recall mentioning it to you, I didn't think that you liked pub quizzes, but you're more than welcome of course."

"Can Joe come as well?" said Nancy, "he's just passed his test and can drive me."

"Great, a team of three it is then, excellent, we'll show 'em."

A bit later on the workshop rang to inform me that my van had been repaired and I wasted no time exchanging vehicles as I was relieved to get shot of the rather conspicuous traffic speeding van. They told me that they could not replace a missing hub-cap that I had not actually noticed was missing.

"It's just one of those things," said the fitter, shaking his head solemnly, "in the old days I could have just ordered you a new one... but not now."

I thanked him all the same.

By one o clock the clouds had evaporated to leave the sun unchallenged in a clear blue sky with the blackthorn blossom now positively radiating from the hedgerows. Somehow things seemed a lot better after the anxieties of last week and I had the quiz and Nancy's company to look forward to later on. It is days like these that reminded me that I really did have the best job in the world. I felt a spring in my step and with my ankle now feeling a lot stronger I sorted out a few rights of way inspections that would keep me busy for the rest of the day and headed out.

I was pleased to be able to play cds in my van without them skipping and I even gave the "identify birdsong the easy way" another go after retrieving it from the passenger floor well of the replacement vehicle and dusting it off.

First on the list was a report of a fallen tree obstructing a footpath that ran along the fringe of a large wood. The place was alive with birdsong and after a few hundred paces I realised that it was my own voice that I could hear, mimicking the narrator Jim Pringle from the birdsong cd.

"And there we can hear the mocking laugh of the green woodpecker."

I walked a bit further along the path.

"That's the loud machine gunning chak chak chak of the magpie, up to no good I expect."

I stopped and listened to a sound from deep within the wood.

"It's a woodpecker pecking away like mad but I've no idea which one it is.. and now some bloody bird has just crapped on my shoulder. I suppose that is what you would call an occupational hazard Jim?" I said, searching for a screwed up paper tissue from my trouser pocket to clean it off.

I found the small fallen tree which I managed to clear with my clasp saw and I then pushed the separated sections to one side of the path. There were no other problems en route and I enjoyed the rest of my walk.

The next port of call was a report of a broken stile. After parking up on a broad verge I walked the six hundred yards or so to where the footpath left the farm track and sure enough I found a broken stile. It was beyond repair and needed replacing completely. After taking a photograph and setting off back towards the van I met the landowner driving towards me. From past experience he was always a cantankerous old devil and I braced myself to trot out the relevant bit of legislation to ram home the point that it was very much his legal responsibility to sort out.

"There's an old face from the past," said the farmer, winding down the window of his 4x4 and turning off the engine.

"Good afternoon," I said, thinking that perhaps we could try a civil conversation to start with, "how are you?"

"I'm alive, I had a triple heart bypass last year. I think everyone hoped that they'd seen the last of me but, sorry to disappoint, I'm still 'ere. What are you up to then?"

I informed him that we had received a report of a broken stile and I was just about to trot out the relevant section of the 1980 Highways Act.

"Yep, that one up ahead, we'll be sorting it out next week. There's a couple of others that need looking at as well and we'll do them all at the same time, if that's ok? If you can let me have some of them round plastic markers we'll put they up as well."

"Ok..," I said, faltering, having had the wind taken out of my sails by this unexpected reasonableness, "er.. have you got any other problems on the paths?"

"No, not really, people goes where they wants to go and we gets on with what we've got to do."

"What about dogs?" I said, probing a bit deeper, expecting to hit a nerve.

"Well, we loves dogs ourselves, it's nice to see 'em enjoying themselves, no we've got no complaints really. I'd better get on or the wife'll think that I've dropped dead again," said the farmer starting the engine before trundling on his way.

I looked around me for a moment. Had I stumbled into some parallel universe, into a world where everything was too good to be true?

"What do you reckon Jim?" I said, rather hoping that I did not get a response from Jim Pringle who now seemed to have wormed his way into my brain as a running commentary.

Everything else, for the remainder of the day, fell into place and I drifted home on empty roads.

I arrived at my local pub far to early and had already sunk a couple of pints before the quizzers started arriving. I bagged a decent table and could not help myself from checking the clock every five minutes. The usual suspects began to trickle in, the quiz bandits from the district who you never see in the place at any other time. My old team were down one player and a delegation was sent over to ask whether I would like to join them for the evening.

"I've got my own team thanks," I said, glancing up at the clock, "and god help you all if the questions have been set by a rights of way nutjob as we've got that particular avenue well covered."

Nancy and Joe arrived just before the quiz got underway and I got them both a drink.

"Sorry we're late Victor," said Nancy.

"You're not late," I said, "you're bang on time, we're sat over there. By the way, well done for passing your driving test Joe, you'll be driving your mother everywhere from now on."

"Yes, it's pay back time," said Nancy.

"I like driving," said Joe, "do you remember when you took me out in your van on the droves when I could hardly see over the steering wheel?"

"Shh," I said, "that was not strictly legal so best not let the entire pub know, if you don't mind,"

"Great fun though," said Joe, "I thought, this is the job that I want to do when I grow up,"

"There's a bit more to it than that unfortunately," I said.

"Yeah, all the hassle, mum always says it would be a great job without the public."

"I did not say that," said Nancy, "well I didn't mean it, even if I did say it."

"And then she started swearing all the time," said Joe.

"Great," said Nancy, "thanks Joe."

"We're simply driven to it Joe, it's probably my bad influence. Here we go, I think we're off."

The quiz did seem particularly hard or as I suggested to Nancy and Joe, they weren't asking the right sort of questions. Even a cricketing question, to which I would normally reel off the answer with no difficulty, was particularly obscure. I bought some more drinks in the interval having exchanged our sheet for the first half with the next table and Joe said he would do the marking when they read out the answers.

"I mean, take that last question, unless you were really into horseracing," I said, placing the drinks on the table, "who would know at which meeting the leading horse was nobbled by a spectator firing a sonic beam at it through his binoculars? It's just guesswork."

"Thanks," said Joe, sipping his orange juice and lemonade.

"Thanks Victor," said Nancy.

"Cheers," I said, chinking glasses with the team.

"I'd better not have any more or I'll be useless at work

tomorrow," said Nancy.

"Hand me the pen," said Joe, "they're reading out the answers to the first half."

"Well," I said, after the marking had been completed, "here's hoping for a better second half, so it was Royal Ascot, what did we say?"

"I said Ascot," said Nancy, "it's the only racecourse I know but you said it was Aintree."

"Sorry," I said, "up to my old tricks again, talking people out of the rights answers. Right let's knuckle down, shh."

Neither Nancy or Joe wanted another drink at the end but I slipped up to the bar before the rush and sat back down to commiserate with the Trespassers, our team name for the night.

Once the scores were in, we ended up somewhere in the middle but I was heartened that we came one place ahead of my old team.

"How much was it to enter?" said Nancy.

Despite her protestations, I refused to accept any money.

"It could have been worse, fellow Trespassers, but thanks for coming. A bird shat on me today when I was out walking a path, I thought that it might bring us a bit of luck but there you go, no such luck."

Nancy and Joe glanced at each other.

"I've just seen a kid that I was at school with," said Joe, "I don't know what he's doing all the way over here, excuse me."

"Such a polite boy," I said to Nancy, "you brung him up well, despite everything."

"He's alright," said Nancy, "er..so you went to that time management seminar then?"

"Yes, I did, on your advice, excuse me, I think I must be a little bit pissed, I detected a little slur then."

"What did you think?"

"Ah, Gina Rosabella, yes it was good. There were a lot of bored and listless middle-aged men in the audience who expected Gina Lollobrigida, the Italian screen goddess, to turn up on a Wednesday morning and talk to them about time management, poor woman. Actually, I rather liked her and I even asked her whether she wanted to come out to this quiz tonight. Anyway, she had a partner who didn't like pub quizzes, so..."

"Yes, she's my partner and I don't really like pub quizzes, well I'm not very good at them, as we have discovered."

"What did you say? I'm..I'm..stunned," I said.

"No, I really am crap at pub quizzes."

"No, not...not fucking pub quizzes..I mean..."

"I know what you mean," said Nancy, "so, there you go."

"You and...Gina Rosabella?"

"Yes, great name isn't it? She's made a living enticing bored and listless middle-aged men to go to seminars that they would normally avoid."

"How..?...How long?"

"About nine months now, properly. We met on that kayaking holiday, when you were on strike that day, do you remember? I just had to tell you, I couldn't let it drag on any longer."

"Is that why you came to the quiz? Came out at the quiz?"

"Well, yes it was really, I couldn't tell you at work, could I?"

"What about Joe? I mean, what does he think?"

"He's seen me being happy, he didn't like it at all at first but he gets on well with Gina now."

Nancy leant across and squeezed my hand just as one of my old quiz team mates passed by.

"Ok then Victor? Good evening..?"

"This is Nancy," I said, "she does what I do..at work..this is Wayne. Bye Wayne."

"I'm going, I'm going, good to meet you Nancy."

Nancy smiled at Wayne as he moved on towards the bar.

"Great," I said, "now they'll think...I don't care what they think. I don't know what I think. I've got to go home."

As I stood up to leave Joe reappeared.

"Joe," I said, extending a hand, "thank you very much for coming and for bringing your mum."

"Ok?" said Joe, looking at Nancy who nodded gently.

Joe took my hand and shook it.

"I've got five words to say to you Mr Wayland."

"For god's sake Joe, call me Victor," I said.

"Ok. . .Victor. Self..contained..underwater..breathing..apparatus."

I let out a long sigh and hung my head in shame.

"I know, I'm very sorry, you were right. As this is probably the only ever pub quiz outing for the Trespassers team, I sincerely hope that you will both forgive me. Please drive home safely."

"Are you sure you don't want a lift Victor?" said Nancy.

"No thanks, I need the walk, it's not far. Goodnight."

I stepped out into the night feeling numb. It was less than two miles back to my village and once I got beyond the streetlights I heard an owl hooting in the darkness.

"Come on then Jim," I said, "do your stuff."

The owl hooted again.

"Have you ever experienced hopeless optimism Jim?"

The owl gave one final hoot.

"It's just that I didn't realise how hopeless my hopeless optimism was."

"Well, you know what they say, when one door shuts, another door closes?"

"That's not funny Jim, or appropriate under the circumstances, in the future please just stick to identifying birds, if you wouldn't mind."

The remainder of the walk home was conducted in silence.

6
PAPERCLIP

THE PHONE IN my office rang and I watched it until it stopped ringing. The recording of my rather muffled voice, apologising for not being available, started to play but the caller then rang off without leaving a message. I immediately picked up the phone to check the caller's number. It was a number that I did not recognise and so I rang back.

"Oh, hi, it's Victor Wayland here, I believe you just rang, sorry but I couldn't get to the phone I was just..."

"Thanks for ringing back, you're the rights of way chap aren't you?"

"I am indeed, how can I help?"

The male caller went on to explain that he had not long joined the parish council in his village and had been out walking some of their paths. There was one public footpath up a steep incline that he thought more people would use if there were some steps created and perhaps a handrail. I have always been cautious about creating any structures that will require ongoing maintenance, particularly in the current financial climate. At some point, perhaps five years down the line either the wooden supporting pegs will rot or the boards will fail and what folk assume is a reasonable flight of steps is in fact an accident waiting to happen. They will need inspecting and a liability has been created whereas a steep path is just that, a steep path and you accept it as such. I began visualising future claims when one of the steps gives way and somebody breaks an ankle.

"Do you know what I mean?" said the caller, in my resulting pause after he had explained the scenario and the potential solution, "it seems pretty straight forward to me."

"Yes, well," I said, "actually it's a bit of a slippery slope."

"Exactly," he said, "and that's why we need some steps."

"No, I mean from a maintenance point of view," I said, applying some caution to his suggestion, "they'll need regular inspections and maintenance, which we can't afford and in the long run it could make matters worse, that's what I mean by a slippery slope."

"But it's already a slippery slope, how can it get any slipperier?"

"Sorry," I said, "it's my fault for confusing the issue by mentioning slippery slopes."

"No, I raised the matter at the last council meeting, it's been a slippery slope for a long time, especially in the winter."

On days like these you wonder how you ever make any progress at all. I wound up the call by promising to have a look at it when I was next out that way. This is what it has come to, I told myself, a reluctance to do anything positive in case it caused a risk or a liability in the future. It was this kind of engrained negative mindset that has been getting me down and it reaffirmed why I had wanted to take voluntary redundancy before Christmas.

My computer pinged and a colleague from the mapping team at county hall had just sent me an e-mail to remind me to send up some paperwork as part of the process when there had been a legal path alteration. There were three footpaths in my area that had been recently diverted and having inspected the new routes it was part of my job to confirm that I was happy with the created alternatives. This was a necessary administrative process of record keeping and the three signed and dated sheets had been sitting on my desk for a couple of weeks now.

She replied that I should scan them but as I had already printed out a copy of each I responded that she may as well have the originals and I would keep a paper copy. She replied that they weren't permitted to file paper any longer and it had to be stored electronically. I replied that this was nonsense, although I was aware of the supposed paperless world that we were now all supposed to inhabit. If you insist, I concluded, begrudgingly. I felt incensed that we should kowtow to the hot desking tribe and their witch hunt for those that still smuggled paper to one another. I had a sneaking suspicion that my colleague kept a secret bulging filing cabinet somewhere, perhaps in a disused boiler room, a broom cupboard or even in her mother's shed and was being understandably cagey about it. If I sent the completed forms up to her, I felt certain that she would squirrel them away somewhere until such time that paper would again come into its own and save the world.

I walked the length of the building with my signed certificates to the photocopier.

"Where's the photocopier?" I said, looking at the square of unworn carpet where the photocopier used to be.

"Gone," said the chap from the other end of the building, looking up from his computer for a moment, "taken away, removed, the photocopier has left the building."

"But..that's crazy, how are we supposed to do any work? I was going to use the scanner."

"Ah yes, they didn't really think that one through, ne'er mind, we can only do what we can do."

I stomped back to my desk and hammered out another message on my keyboard stating that I could not scan the wretched things and would now deliver them by hand. I reached for my stapler, just to ensure that the paperwork did not get separated on the way and after making certain that the paper was square and with the stapler in position, I gave it a good thump with the flat of my hand. The stapler embossed a mark in the top sheet where the staple should be but there was no neat staple in place. I had forgotten that it was empty and I knew that there was no refill staples anywhere because it was an ancient stapler and I had searched through my drawers the last time I had tried to use it. Typically, I had then done nothing about sourcing any more staples. I looked around for the next best thing and after lifting up countless heaps of paper that covered my desk I still could not find a single paperclip. There was nothing for it but another long trudge back up to the other end of the building, to the stationery cupboard.

"Where is everything," I said into an empty stationery cupboard, "where's the Sellotape and the post it notes? Where are those nice black rollerball pens that we used to get? Where are any pens? What about the paperclips?"

"Are you conducting a conversation with someone in the stationery cupboard, or should I be paying attention?" said the chap from the other end of the building, whose desk was nearby.

"Where's it all gone?"

"You are behind the times Victor, the cupboard's been bare for a while."

"I just need one paperclip, it's not too much to ask is it?"

"I think that you might be in denial down your end of the building but everyone else in the authority operates a paperless system, so therefore, paperclips are now obsolete."

"And pens?"

"Ditto,"

"But I write stuff down," I said.

"You always were a bit of a dinosaur Victor, nobody writes stuff down anymore, look," said the chap from the other end of the building twisting up his hands, "our fingers have evolved and we couldn't hold a pen even if we wanted to, all we can do is press buttons."

"I'm going to make one," I said.

"A pen? A pen that actually writes?"

"No, a paperclip, it's just bent wire after all."

"My money's definitely on you to survive the apocalypse, what with your home made paperclip, listen," he said lowering his voice, "don't tell the other marauding gangs of desperate survivors out there but there's an old roll of Sellotape and some perished elastic bands behind the empty fish tank in the manager's office, mum's the word, ok?"

When I returned to my office, my mobile phone rang which made me jump and I fumbled to turn it off and then left it on the desk.

I found a short length of wire in the shed and set about making a paperclip but the wire was too thick and it ended up excessively big with a hazardous burr on one end. It was also not very flat but no amount of hammering seemed to make any difference. I had another go but with similar results and I then managed to clout myself on the thumb with the hammer in the process.

I made a cup of tea and looked up "how to make a paperclip" on the internet. After a bit of searching I found "how to make a paperclip sling shot". This would have been ideal for an outbreak of office warfare back in the days of a burgeoning stationery cupboard when you could grab a handful of rubber bands and paper clips and have yourselves a very entertaining Friday afternoon.

There was plenty of guidance on what you could build with paperclips but nothing about actually making a paperclip and it all rather assumed that you had an unlimited supply of the things in the first place.

As well as the right diameter wire I needed the right tools and I rooted about under the passenger seat of my van. My hunch paid off as I eventually located a pair of long nosed pliers that I had not seen for some months and fortuitously, in the search, I also came across a short length of narrow wire that was ideal. A small vice would have been handy but I would have to make do with a pair of conventional pliers in my left hand. With the pliers in action the half formed paper clip then sprung out of my grip and disappeared into the thick boundary hedge beside the shed. No amount of bashing and thrashing of the dense undergrowth with a hazel stick was going to help to recover it and I had to start again. The remaining length of the suitable wire was a bit short but it would have to do.

It was at that moment that the Trust Harrison van clattered into the yard.

"What is you makin'," said Harrison, through the open passenger window of the van.

"Oh, just a little wire thing that I need," I said.

"Cool."

"What are you up to?" I asked, trying to divert attention away from my activity.

"Is you goin' fishin'?" said Harrison.

"No, it's for work, for the office."

Harrison nodded slowly but in a way that suggested that he required more explanation.

"Is you pickin' locks? Is you a burglar, now there ain't no money?"

Dolores and the lads emerged from the van and craned their necks to see what I was doing.

"It's nothing, honestly," I said, "it's just a thing."

"Have you made something out of a paperclip, whatever it is?" said Dolores.

"Does it look like a paperclip?" I said.

"Well, sort of."

"Good, well don't let me take up your valuable volunteer time,"

I said.

"We is finished for today," said Harrison and the gang showed no sign of dispersing or losing interest.

"Look," I said, "I can't explain, I'm too embarrassed to explain and it is all down to an extreme and pernicious starvation of essential resources that prevents us from functioning properly, functioning as we once did. I just want things to be as they were before. I want to open the stationery cupboard and be greeted by an encouraging array of largely boring items, small items, insignificant items that we once deemed essential to enable us to do our jobs. The cupboard is bare and it symbolises the state that we now find ourselves in. I suppose that I knew it was happening insidiously but today opening the stationery cupboard and finding it completely empty, a yawning abyss of nothingness, has brought it all home to me. I think I'm upset and am acting irrationally as I find myself trying to manufacture a once unthinkably, insignificant item."

"You're making a paperclip," said Dolores.

"Yes," I said, "I am rather ashamed to admit it, but that is what I am doing and it has taken up half of the day, so far."

"Haven't we got some fine wire?" said Dolores to Knocker, who frowned fiercely at the thought of issuing anything at all from the well stocked quartermaster store under the seats at the back of the van. As far as Knocker, the self appointed quartermaster, was concerned it was always a one way process of accumulation and any distribution was very much a last resort. Grumbling and cursing, Knocker scrabbled around under the back seats of the van and emerged with a small cardboard box.

"It's a box of paperclips," I said, holding out my hand.

Knocker cagily opened the box and issued me with one paperclip.

"Where did you get these from?" I said.

Dolores gave Knocker a quizzical look.

"You haven't got a couple of black biros and some Sellotape under there as well, by any chance?" I said.

Knocker scowled and it took an assertive nod from Dolores before he returned to the van for some more scurrying around under the seats.

"Thar," said Knocker, flinging a roll of sticky tape and pens in my direction, "n' thas yer tankin' lot."

"These are just the type of pens that we used to stock," I said, "and this is the rather cheap and inferior sticky tape that we had to put up with in the latter years, you could never find the end and it just stretches when you try to tear off a length. Well I never, it's amazing what you've got in that van."

"Yes," said Dolores, looking across at Knocker, who began to pick his nose with some vigour.

"Now you has your fing," said Harrison, "does you want to come wiv us, for a bit?"

"There's something we'd like to show you," said Dolores.

"Oh?" I said, "well, ok."

Still cradling my recently acquired stationery items and home made paper clip I found myself in the back of the Trust Harrison van after Ollie had made his seat available by squeezing in the front with Harrison. Dolores slammed shut the side door and before I knew it we were clattering out of the yard.

"Is it the coppice that we're going to see?" I said, "I've never been to the coppice and I am supposed to be keeping an eye on it as some sort of trustee."

"We ain't goin' to the coppice," said Harrison, over his shoulder.

It was a strange experience travelling in the back of the Trust Harrison van. Nigel slept in his seat whilst Council Peter gave me an occasional sideways glance whilst being careful not to catch my eye. I could sense Knocker's eyes boring into the back of my head, resentful at distributing anything from the quartermaster's store and doubly fuming at the irregularity of me travelling in the back of the van as if I were now one of the gang.

After a few miles we turned off the road and bounced along a track until we came to some old farm buildings. On the concrete hard standing, in front of the buildings was a mass of tangled scrap metal which on closer inspection, as we parked in front of it, I realised was old iron parkland fencing. It was the type of fencing, once coated black, that one used to see regularly in the countryside especially on larger and wealthier estates.

Dolores jumped out and opened up the side door of the van.

"Thank you," I said, "what was it that you wanted to show me?"

She gestured with her arm towards the heap of old iron fencing.

"What do you think?" she said.

"It's a load of scrap metal," I said, "old parkland fencing that has been ripped out of the ground and dumped in a heap."

"Yes and we want to use it," said Dolores.

"What for?"

Harrison emerged from the van and we all walked slowly around the enormous mass of twisted metal.

"Kissing gates," said Dolores, "we want to recycle it. The farmer has said that we can have it but we would have to pay the scrap value."

I studied the heap more closely. It looked old and probably from a quality point of view it would have been decent iron, once produced on a massive scale from some foundry in the Midlands or perhaps South Wales. The rounded bar would have provided the longitudinal sections and the flatter lengths the uprights. Some of it was badly twisted but there was still a lot of straight runs of the rounded bar. Today when you buy galvanised metal kissing gates they seem to be from one central source and you come across exactly the same gates all over the country and as a consequence there is no regional variation as there would have been when local blacksmiths fabricated such things. These modern gates are stock proof, self closing, long lasting but ultimately characterless.

"We want to design our own gates, kissing gates and bridlegates and make them, you know..interesting."

"My bruvver says that he will cut it all up wiv his gear so we has lots of straight bits and we can bend stuff as well," said Harrison.

I had met Harrison's brother Marlon once before and he had exuded the same calm confidence as Harrison and I held no doubt that he could do what he said.

"Someone said that it would be tricky to weld but I'm willing to give it a go," said Dolores, "we could also bolt the bits together if we need to."

"What do you fink?" said Harrison.

"Blimey," I said, "I'm not used to you asking me for my opinion."

"The farmer wants roughly the scrap value," said Dolores, "which he reckons is about two hundred pounds so we'd have to find a way to raise the money, but that's cool. He also said that we could sort it all out here and even make up the gates and there's a power supply in the building and water."

I thought back to earlier in my day, trying to manufacture a paper clip out of some wire. Here was a task on a wholly different scale demonstrating the chasm between the rapidly diminishing local authority vista of vanishing resources, aspirations and vision and the Trust Harrison world of boundless opportunity and unfettered imagination. I wanted to jump ship, to spend endless days travelling around in the back of an old van that made even healthy folk out jogging crave for a bag of chips, to do things in the countryside that everyone would be happy about, to make people's lives better.

"I'll buy it," I said, "I'll pay for the scrap metal."

"No," said Dolores quickly, "no, not at all, that wasn't why we brought you out here. We just wanted to see whether you thought we were mad."

"You're not mad," I said, holding up my half formed paperclip, "you've seen what I've been doing for half the day, if it's madness you're after, then look no further. I would be honoured to buy the scrap metal, to help things along. It is the very least that I can do."

"We can pay you back, maybe when we have sold a few gates? Do you think Nancy would be interested?"

I was taken aback hearing Nancy's name mentioned.

"I don't know..." I said, faltering, before coming to my senses, "of course she'd be interested, she'd love it."

"Thank you," said Dolores who turned to me as though she was going to give me a hug but then stopped short, "your eyes are watering, are you ok Mr Wayland?"

"Oh, it's just the wretched oil seed rape, it happens every year," I said.

We all returned to the van and trundled back to the council yard in silence. Dolores dropped me outside the gate and I walked around to the front door of the office.

"Aha, Victor, we all thought that you had been abducted by aliens?" said the chap from the other end of the building who was just getting ready to lock up.

"No, I haven't been abducted by aliens, people with giant imaginations maybe, but not aliens."

"Giants? No, everyone knows that it is aliens who abduct people, not giants. Giants just stomp around saying fee, fum, fo...fi...I smell the blood of an English...guy, or something like that."

"Yes, that's exactly what they do," I said, "can I just pop in and turn off my computer before you lock up and also get my bits and pieces? Thanks."

"Or is it fe, fi, fum....fo?" said the chap from the other end of the building with the office key poised in his hand as he pushed open the front door to let me by.

7
WILLOW

I STOOD FOR a moment and watched a dog taking three people for a walk. It did not appear to be an exceptional dog and it was displaying normal doggy behaviour but it seemed to have its three followers under close control. Every pause, made by the dog, here and there, caused comment and reaction from the attentive entourage as they padded obediently behind. Meeting another dog caused a babel of canine related dialogue from both sets of subservient humans, whilst those in command sniffed at each other's backsides.

My mobile phone rang and I answered it without thinking.

"Victor?"

"Oh...it's you Nancy."

"For god's sake, I've being trying to get hold of you for ages, why haven't you returned any of my messages?"

"I didn't.. I don't know."

"It's been at least two weeks now, you can't just...not talk to me."

"I'm sorry," I said.

After a pause we then both spoke at the same time.

"Sorry," I said, "you go first."

"No, after you," said Nancy.

"I don't know what to say," I said, "I had this weird dream that you came to the pub quiz at my local."

"You know I hate pub quizzes."

"That's what I thought. That's why I kept thinking that it must be a dream."

"I'm sorry Victor."

"Don't say sorry, it wasn't your fault, we were never going to win."

"Ha, ha."

"Look, you've got nothing to be sorry about."

"No, I know that,"

"I'm glad," I said, "I'm glad for you..glad for you both."

"Thank you Victor, you know that I'm very fond of you, don't you?"

"And those are the five little words that I didn't want to hear."

"So, you didn't answer the phone?" said Nancy, "and made me worry about you."

"I just didn't want to hear you say that you are very fond of me."

"Ok, so let's forget that then. What are you up to today?" said Nancy.

"Oh, you know, bumbling along, providing an inadequate service as usual."

"But that's not your fault Victor, there's so much more we could do if we only had a little bit of a budget."

"People are absolutely besotted with their dogs, aren't they? I'm just watching some dog walkers out on this busy path."

"We're getting a dog," said Nancy.

"You said you couldn't be bothered with dogs?"

"Did I? I was probably just agreeing with you."

"Well, just be careful," I said.

"Thanks Victor,"

"Or you'll end up as a dog slave, talking in doggy speak, like this lot that have just passed me. Harrison's coming in this morning, coming in a bit later for some reason. That's why I'm out and about early looking at stuff. He's going to help me clear some willow trees that are blocking an old ford."

"That's great, I hope you realise how lucky you are to have Harrison and the gang and please return my calls in future," said Nancy, ringing off.

I had forgotten to tell Nancy about the kissing gates made from old parkland fencing and as I wrestled the phone back out of my pocket to call her, it suddenly rang in my hand.

It was the PA to the new director, Jolyon Bellringer, requesting that I should visit Mr X's estate to look at his footpaths, as Mr X was returning to his television work tomorrow.

"That means today then? That's a bit short notice, I'm not.."

"What time shall I say?"

I managed to push the meeting back to three o' clock which at least meant that we could clear the fallen willow trees first.

I nipped back to the office in the hope that I could squeeze in a quick cup of tea before Harrison showed up. Twenty minutes later the Trust Harrison van lurched over the speed hump and pulled up at the bottom of the yard with the engine cutting out. Dolores was quick to open up the bonnet whilst Harrison emerged slowly and then stared at the hedge. Harrison must have said something to Dolores as she came out from under the bonnet to join him in staring at the hedge. I drained my tea as I watched from the office window and then went out into the yard.

I approached stealthily to stand beside them and silently emphasised to Harrison and Dolores that I was all ears.

After a moment Harrison looked at Dolores and she gently nodded.

I looked from one to the other. After half a minute or so Harrison slightly raised a finger and Dolores smiled. I shrugged and shook my head.

"I can't hear anything," I whispered.

"There it goes again," said Dolores.

I listened as hard as I could.

"It's like a wren, wiv a fing on its head," said Harrison.

"It must be very high pitched, what thing on its head, do you mean a crest, is it a goldcrest?"

"It's gone over there," said Harrison, gesturing with a crooked finger.

"It's beautiful," said Dolores.

"I'm glad that you two can hear it. It is obviously out of my deteriorated hearing range. I am now too old to hear a goldcrest, that's great," I said.

"I've got to go," said Dolores, getting back under the bonnet and then jumping into the cab. After a few moments revving the engine she drove out of the yard leaving behind a customary deep fried bouquet.

Within ten minutes Harrison and I were loaded up and on the road.

"It smells like a swimming pool in here," I said, winding down the window.

"That's cos I has been to the swimming pool," said Harrison after a lengthy pause.

"Ok?" I said, "I haven't been to the swimming pool for years, I used to like it but must have got out of the habit. I ought to go again, when can you go?"

"I ain't goin' wiv you."

"No, I don't mean that, it's just that I don't even know when it's open."

I glanced across at Harrison as I sensed that there was more to come.

We continued in silence until we reached our destination.

"Here we go then," I said, as we pulled up just short of a ford where the byway continued across the river with a pedestrian footbridge to one side. A large portion of willow tree had fallen and was blocking the ford with the finer branches resting on the footbridge. The river was fairly shallow and most of the material could be cut and retrieved without having to enter the gently flowing water. Fortunately, there was a fair bit of open ground to one side of the ford where the removed timber could be heaped up and left and not be in the way. If it had been a beech or an ash tree then I would have been very keen to ship some home for my wood burning stove, but not willow. Willow was definitely at the bottom of the list when it came to opportunity.

"That's a shame," I said, as we stood before the blockage, "willow is pretty useless really."

Harrison stepped forward and snapped off a fine, fresh wand of willow and bent it into a circle, interlocking and binding the ends so that it remained fastened as a willow hoop.

Harrison's simple action was a jolt to my complacency. Of course I knew about the worth of willow, the long tradition of very attractive woven baskets for domestic and commercial purposes, hurdles, cricket bats, brake shoes for carts, willow charcoal for gunpowder, clothes pegs, tally sticks and even polo balls.

"I meant as firewood," I said, trying to recover some ground.

Harrison probably could not reel off a list of the traditional uses of willow and osier but he did not need to. He was open to ideas and receptive to opportunities whereas I had stored my knowledge in a box labelled "the past is better than the present" and now complacently valued willow as to whether I could burn it in my stove or not.

I changed into my chainsaw gear and began the process of carving up the fallen trunk into movable lumps. Under heavy ear defenders, I found my mind wandering whilst I continued to work on autopilot. I wondered why willow shopping baskets were not more commonplace, when we use so many disposable plastic bags and why didn't I use one? I moved on from willow. When was the last time that I had looked at a nice straight trunk of timber and thought about all the uses that it could be put to; planked up, stored and seasoned and then planed down when required? Trees and timber are viewed very differently by someone who really appreciates the value of wood, as a material. A village carpenter or a shipbuilder of centuries ago, as he walked amongst woodland, would eye the shapes and potential of mature growing timber, in a way that would be invisible to us today. I jumped when I felt a tap on the shoulder, jerking me back from my isolated reverie. I turned off the chainsaw and looked behind me to where Harrison was now directing my attention towards a large four by four vehicle that had stopped on the byway alongside my van.

"They wants to get through," said Harrison, after I had removed my safety helmet.

"Well they'll just have to wait," I said.

Two large men got out of the vehicle and approached me.

"Can we help?" they said in unison.

"Oh," I said, "I'm afraid you'll need all the safety gear and training before.."

"We've got all that and a chainsaw on board," said one of the men.

"You know what they say, many hands make light work," said the second man, "and apart from that, we want to get through."

"Oh, well, ok then," I said, "thank you."

One of the men returned from the rear of their vehicle clad in much newer safety gear than I possessed with chainsaw and helmet in hand whilst the other donned a fluorescent yellow jacket and another safety helmet.

Before I could say anything he pointed to his safety boots and gave me the thumbs up.

With two chainsaws on the go and with two people dragging away the cut sections of timber the job was completed in less than half the time. I kept my thoughts focussed on the job in hand, keeping track of the other chainsaw. With the tree cleared I thanked the two men who then cheerfully carried on across the ford, causing a bow wave and beeping the horn as they went.

"Well that's good then," I said, "I thought that we might struggle to get this cleared before my meeting this afternoon. Now we can have a bit of lunch and cool off, excellent. Help can arrive from unexpected quarters sometimes."

Harrison had arrived from unexpected quarters nearly a year ago now and Nancy was right to point out that I should not take Harrison and the gang for granted.

"I really appreciate you coming out today and for all the other stuff that you and the gang do."

Harrison frowned.

"Right. Good, so," I said, "now let's put this gear away and have a bit of lunch."

As was generally the rule with Harrison, he never seemed particularly interested in lunch. As I sat in the van, munching away whilst reading yesterday's cricket scores and reports, Harrison had wandered off somewhere. By the time that I had finished and I was standing beside the van brushing off the last remaining crumbs from my lap, Harrison reappeared.

"What's that?" I said, questioning what he was holding in his hand.

Harrison did not answer but proceeded to crouch down by the front passenger wheel that had lost its hub-cap. He offered up a large disc of woven willow wands that he had obviously just constructed and after pressing and pulling the thing about against the wheel rim he stood up and gave it a firm kick. The woven disc sprung into place and Harrison stood back to admire his work.

"How? What?" I said, "that will never stay on there."

Harrison shrugged and opened the van door to slump down into the passenger seat. I bent down and gave the wickerwork hub-cap a pull and a push but somehow it was remaining in place with the exposed stubs of the willow ends slotting neatly into the steel wheel rim.

"I'll give it one hundred yards," I said, "in fact I bet it will float off down the river when we cross the ford."

Harrison made no comment. With everything packed away I revved up before entering the broad but relatively shallow stream. I looked across into the nearside wing mirror but could see no sign of anything bobbing about in the wash of the vehicle. We continued for another mile, bouncing along on unsurfaced tracks and I pulled up before we joined the tarmac road just to ensure that the willow hub-cap had been dislodged somewhere along the way.

"Oh," I said, "it's still there. It's bound to come off when we get a bit of speed up on the road."

I had arranged to rendezvous with Mr X two hundred yards or so down his main drive where there was a fork in the road next to a stable block with one spur continuing up towards the house and the other heading out across his small estate. I had spoken into the intercom at the main gate, stating who I was and that I was meeting with the owner.

"And who is that beside you?" said the responding voice.

"Oh, that will be my assistant."

"Mr X was only expecting you."

"It's ok, his name is Harrison and he is perfectly harmless."

The conversation with the remote gatekeeper ended and after a lengthy pause the double gates slowly opened.

"Sorry," I said to Harrison, "I wasn't expecting Fort Knox and anyway, you are perfectly harmless..aren't you?"

Harrison looked away.

A large shiny black four by four vehicle was parked beside the stable block and a short rotund man in his early to mid fifties was standing beside the vehicle, holding a very small dog in his arms.

Harrison remained in the van as I got out to introduce myself.

"Mr X," said Mr X, holding out a soft pink hand, "you've probably seen the show...but hello anyway."

"Um..well..yes..hello," I said, "Victor Wayland."

"What rough hands you have."

"I'm sorry,"

"No, it's just that everyone I've met in the countryside has such rough hands. Perhaps I will get rough hands if I stay here long enough. Oh yes, may I take this opportunity to thank you for your vigil with the speed camera van after my accident. Your ears must have been burning with all the talk about who was this mystery man, acting on his own initiative?"

"Well..er...it was nothing really," I said, rather glad that Harrison could not hear this part of our conversation, "I just hope that you're fully recovered now?"

"Oh yes, much better, it was all such a horrid shock, no bones broken thank goodness and your director is sorting out a thirty miles an hour speed limit on that nasty fast road, which is very kind of him. What's that?"

"What's what?"

"On the wheel of your van thingy, most strange, you don't see that sort of thing up in town?"

"Oh, it's a hub-cap made from woven willow."

"I see, and who is that sitting in there?"

"That's the maker of the woven willow hub-cap, his name is Harrison. He has only just made the thing this afternoon. I didn't ask him to do it or expect it to stay on for one moment..but somehow it is still there. So, what about these public rights of way then?"

"Is he getting out?"

"I don't know."

"There, there Larry," said Mr X, stroking his small dog, "it's all so exciting isn't it? Footpaths? Well, I'm not happy about it."

"About what?"

"About all those people wandering across my land."

"Are they not sticking to the footpaths?"

"Well, I suppose so but it's the fact that they are in here at all, well..over there."

"I see."

"And if I can see them, they'll be able to see me..and..they've got binoculars."

"It has always been a popular path," I said, "after it leaves your land it enters a nature reserve so I am not surprised that walkers have binoculars with them, they'll be looking at the birds."

"And not at me?"

"Well, no, they may not even know that you live here."

"All my friends warned me about sightseers stalking the place and when they heard that there was a public footpath crossing the estate, well, they thought that I was completely mad. So, you don't think that they are interested in me at all?"

"Well, I don't know about that."

Harrison pushed open the passenger door and got out to lean against the van and Mr X's dog struggled to free himself.

"What is it Larry G?" said Mr X.

I made subtle gestures for Harrison to join us and say hello to Mr X.

"Hi man," said Harrison, staying put.

"So you're the weaver of hubcaps, is that some sort of..what do you call it..local craft?"

Harrison shrugged.

"Can I place an order please? I've got this hideous black monstrosity until mine is replaced and a set of woven twiggy hub-caps would be perfect. I can then go back to London tonight and show all the townies how it is done in the country. How long would it take you?"

"I ain't got time now," said Harrison, who then glanced across at me, "I has to split boss."

Mr X's dog struggled and scratched at its owner to get to Harrison. Mr X relented and crossed over towards my van and offered the yelping Larry G to Harrison.

"There, that's what you've wanted all along," said Mr X.

Harrison took the tiny dog and placed it on the ground where it twisted its neck to look up at Harrison.

"You're not very nice are you?" said Mr X, stooping down to retrieve the dog.

"It has legs," said Harrison.

"Yes, but little tincy wincy legs," said Mr X, nuzzling the rejected pet.

"Can I just return to the issue of the public footpath for a moment," I said, "I still don't quite know how we can help.."

"I'll give the director a call, he always seems very accommodating, I'm sure he'll sort something out."

"But.."

"And he said he would let me erect some Elvis gates at the beginning of the drive, I've always wanted Graceland gates and he said that it would be fine and that he would sort it all out with the planners."

"I think we'd better go," I said, I had heard enough about what the director had promised to sort out for Mr X.

"Yes, and I'm postponing my order for those woven hub-caps young man, until you've done a bit of work on your customer relations. Come on Larry G, let's go and get you your tea. Wave good bye to Mr Wayland.. and good bye to Harrison, although we're not quite sure what to make of you are we?"

Once back in his vehicle, the little dog was placed on the dash board above the steering wheel where it ran backwards and forwards, yapping at Harrison and making manoeuvring difficult.

"That was interesting but mostly a complete waste of time," I said, as the main gates opened automatically to let us out. I also wondered how I could suggest to Harrison that he might be a bit more friendly or polite in certain circumstances when he was at work with me and I was just about to broach the subject.

"Can you drop us at the pool?" said Harrison, interrupting my train of thought.

"Are you going swimming again, twice in one day, that's keen?"

Harrison continued staring ahead.

"Mr X could do with getting some exercise, I mean he drove down from the house to meet us and then back up again, which is less than a couple of hundred yards. And, as for Graceland gates, I'm sure the locals will have something to say about that and the director could end up in hot water if he's not careful. What sort of dog was that?"

"Larry G is the boss," said Harrison, after a long pause.

"You can say that again," I said.

8
THE OUTSIDER

I AM ALWAYS ignoring corporate e-mails about new initiatives and certainly anything that falls into the category of "on line" training. Generally, these splendid new ideas seem to disappear after a while, if you are able to ignore them for long enough. I had obviously missed a recent meeting about a dramatic change in the way that council operations were to be managed. Normally Nancy flags up this sort of stuff and I only have myself to blame for avoiding her calls after the pub quiz, which was ridiculous.

A strange message had been left on my answer machine from another member of staff whose name I did not recognise, which was something to do with a dead animal on the road.

"Oh, hi, it's Victor Wayland here from Rights of Way, is that Sue, Sue Stiffkey?

"Oh, hello Victor and thank you for ringing back. Yes, it's hard not to say what department you were in. I'm in Weights and Measures, sorry, I was in Weights and Measures."

"I'm a bit confused," I said, "your message seemed to suggest that you, in Weights and Measures wanted me, in Rights of Way, to go and pick up a dead animal on the road."

"Yes, that's right, a badger, I believe, isn't that sad?"

After a bit of explanation on Sue's part it seemed as though all members of staff were now supposed to do everything, the only distinction being that there would be inside people and outside people. The scheme is called "first off the rank" and takes its name from how taxis operate. The insider member of staff who receives the communication then transports it to a conclusion. If the problem requires outside participation the first member of staff "off the rank", who is an outsider, then takes up the fare to arrive at a solution, which is the destination.

"I'm afraid I missed that meeting," I said, "it must have been a belter."

"Well, you're an outsider and I thought that you might have a spade."

"Actually, it is a shovel that is required," I said.

"I knew you'd know," said Sue Stiffkey, her voice was soft, "I'm just sending you the details. I have now delivered my fare and can return back to the rank. Thank you...Victor Wayland."

"Don't go," I said, "with all this talk of taxis, I am imagining a movie scene, black and white obviously.."

"We're not supposed to hang around chatting, you know.. with the other.."

"With the other taxi drivers? Yes, cruising the city streets at night in the fog, parking to chat, to kill the dead hours, when suddenly.."

"Ha, ha, it's been a pleasure...goodbye."

"Goodbye Sue, goodbye Sue Stiffkey, until the next time..."

Unbeknown to me Harrison had appeared in my office and sensing a presence, I turned around.

"Oh, hello," I said, reddening slightly at the thought that he had been listening to my conversation, "how long have you been there?"

"Why has you got to pick up that dead fing off the road?" said Harrison.

"So, you heard all that?" I said, "what an absolutely preposterous situation. Apparently I am now an outside person who can be assigned to do anything at all that is outside."

Harrison shrugged.

The location details for the dead badger popped up on my screen.

Harrison wandered across from where he had been leaning against the wall to have a look at the road map on my screen with x marking the spot.

"It's right over in the west," I said, "that's a long way to go to scrape a dead badger off the road."

I then got distracted by another e mail, which actually seemed to be about a rights of way issue.

"That's more like it," I said, turning to look behind me but Harrison had gone and was now passing by my window, heading out towards the main gate.

"I thought that you were coming out for the day with me?" I called out, fruitlessly.

"Ah, Victor, you're not one to normally raise your voice but did I also detect an air of desperation?" said the chap from the other end of the building, as he strode purposefully into my office.

"Hello," I said, "I am not in the best of moods, I must confess."

"I see that you're not displaying your outsider badge?"

I returned to my computer screen to get on with answering the latest rights of way related e-mail but I could sense him loitering behind me.

"Being that you are obviously an outsider," he said, "despite not displaying a badge, it is my duty as an insider to escort you from the building. But, being a reasonable chap, I'll let you finish your tea first, back in five."

I had a meeting to go to anyway and so I gathered up my bits and pieces before heading out.

"I am a public rights of way officer, I am a public rights of way officer, I am a public rights of way officer.." I said, repeating this mantra, over and over again as the contents of my van lifted up and down with a crash as I sped over the speed hump by the depot gate.

I did not get far up the road when I veered off into a gateway to ring Nancy.

"I did try to let you know a couple of weeks ago that there was this big meeting, but you were not picking up my calls."

"I'm sorry," I said, "but who has dreamt up this ridiculous idea? I mean it undermines everyone's professional expertise, we're all specialists in our own field, born out of years of experience."

"I think they specifically quoted that very same phrase, "years of experience" and suggested that it was just baggage and an obstacle to our adaptability."

"Baggage?" I said, "is that what I am?"

"Well not you specifically Victor, the idea is a legacy of the previous director that the Cabinet were particularly keen on implementing, combined with a "can do" attitude amongst the staff, we've all got to pull together in adversity, apparently."

"Oh Christ," I said, repeatedly banging my head on the steering wheel.

"To be honest," said Nancy, "human nature being what it is, I think, out of habit, staff will subversively just carry on with their old roles and try to deal with bizarre requests like fixing street-lights or repairing school guttering or whatever, when they come along."

"Or pick up dead animals from the highway," I said, "as I have been tasked with. I should have taken voluntary redundancy, I really should have, it's all Harrison's fault.."

"You can't blame him Victor, that's not fair, he and the gang are a real asset."

"Well, I've got a proper meeting about a proper rights of way issue to go to and, as it happens, I can check out the dead badger on the way back but with a bit of luck the rooks and the jackdaws will have attended to it by the time I get there."

"Keep your pecker up Victor," said Nancy.

"Thank you," I said, after a short pause.

It was difficult, later on, not just cruising back to the office on automatic pilot. In the afternoon I found myself in a lay-by, purchasing a mug of tea from Josef's burger van.

"And that's another thing," I said, chuntering to myself, "you can stuff your tea money."

"What is that, you not pay?" said Josef in the burger van, sliding the freshly poured mug of tea back towards him on the counter.

"Oh, no, sorry. I was just talking to myself, take no notice, I have the money, the right money in fact. Thank you."

After I left the lay-by I remembered the dead badger and made sure I had high viz, gloves, shovel and a bin liner to hand, as I may have to pull up on the highway with my flashing beacon and hazard lights on.

In the vicinity of the location given I slowed down and switched on the beacon. In the opposite lane, as I crawled along, there was a dark red patch on the road but no carcass. I found nothing in either lane other than the recent bloodstain on the tarmac and so I left it at that but then forgot to turn off my beacon as I headed home. I was a little bit early for a change but hoped that the neighbours did not notice because they love mentioning that they saw my van, either late to leave or early to arrive. Before I turned off the engine I noticed the orange flashing beacon, reflecting in the glass panel on my front door.

"That's great," I said out loud, to myself.

I got into the office extra early the next morning and managed to answer a few e-mails and make a cup of tea before the rest of the depot staff arrived.

"Before you say anything," I said, to the chap from the other end of the building as I bumped into him outside the tea room, "you are obviously taking this ridiculous taxi idea seriously when patently it is all complete nonsense."

"Ah, there speaks the outsider," he said.

"In that case," I said, "let me introduce another metaphor, in addition to that stupid taxi idea. How about the benefits of being outside the tent pissing in as to oppose to being inside the tent and pissing out? Who comes off best in that little scenario?"

"I think I see what you're getting at but as I am a caravan man myself, then it won't affect me."

"Aha, so you're an insider, through and through, even when recreating outside?"

"No, I like the great outdoors and what better way to experience it than touring with a caravan. We've got this lovely old Ace Pioneer and we're off this Thursday and Friday for a long weekend. It's all about the pace of life and when you arrive it is all there for you, no flapping tents or people urinating in through the fly sheet."

"Yes, I've seen the flicker of the cathode ray tube when the sun goes down," I said, "then it's drawbridge up, telly on and home from bloody home."

"Cathode ray tube? I know what you are doing, you're just trying to engage me in a protracted discussion when you should be outside."

Having announced that he would be away on Thursday and Friday I was able to enjoy my old routine and drank plenty of tea that I had no intention of paying for.

The telephone rang and I answered it.

"Oh, hello, you don't know me but it's Wendy Tiptoe here from social housing, no, sorry..not from social housing, oh dear."

"Hello Wendy, don't worry, you must keep that part of you

alive. I am a rights of way officer and you work in social housing."

"You have to be so careful now. There was a revolt over in HR as they did not think that the whole job changing thing was legal and the bin men were sent round to sort them out. Have you got a spade?"

"Is it another dead animal on the road?"

"Well yes, it's a young deer I believe, isn't that a shame?"

"Yes, it is and it will be a shovel that is required."

Just at that minute the Trust Harrison van appeared in the yard.

"Oh yes, a shovel, I suppose there is a difference,"

"Without going into too much gruesome detail the wider, flat bladed shovel would.."

"Yes, I'm sure you know what you are doing."

Harrison and Dolores appeared in the office and I signalled hello. Dolores smiled and raised a hand in response and I then pointed to my telephone which was probably unnecessary.

"I'm curious to know why I keep getting dead animals on the road sent my way when it is supposed to be a first off the rank system, with no specialisation,"

"That's because there's secret handwritten notes being passed around amongst the insiders and on your note it just says spade."

"So, where is this deer?" I said, wanting to wind up the conversation, "ok, on the A472 near the cross roads on the common.. ok..I've got that, goodbye Wendy and don't forget what I said."

"That it's a shovel?"

"No, it doesn't matter, I've got to go."

I turned around and Harrison and Dolores had disappeared with the Trust Harrison van now clattering over the speed ramp. Later on I ventured out and found myself passing the location that Wendy Tiptoe had given me. Again, no carcass and only a dark red stain on the road. I made sure that I turned my beacon off before I continued homewards.

The following week I was back in outsider mode. I began to realise that I was rather enjoying the outsider role, there was an element of the maverick about it, the drifter, cruising about the rights of way network like the Wichita Lineman, out on the definitive line. I realised that my web of connecting roads that I always used had been unchanged for years when in reality there were so many alternatives. I came across footpath signs with directional fingers missing, overgrown stiles, clogged up ditches and I had the time to sort things out, after all I had nowhere else to go. There was no magnet drawing me back to the office where the computer sucked up all my days. How essential was the computer and all those e-mails?

I did have to check my e-mails occasionally and an early start was called for.

"Victor, it may be entirely coincidental," said the chap from the other end of the building, tracking me down, "that I was only discussing my treasured caravan with you last week and returning from our short break, it has now been stolen from outside the house. I'm not saying that..you know, you are in anyway.."

"I'm not even going to respond to that," I said, "I'm off outside, where I belong, but I'm just going to check my e-mails first."

There was another dead badger out there on the road network. I had a look in my tin shed as I knew that I had a really wide shovel that would be perfect for the task, particularly if I was going to get inundated with the same requests. I could not find the wide shovel in the shed and checking in my own van I could not even find my own shovel. I sat in my van and pondered for while and ate a shortbread finger. On a whim I drew a rough road map on a scrap of paper and marked with a cross the location of the dead badger. I put it in a clear plastic bag making sure that you could read Trust Harrison, written in red pen on the paper, before stuffing it under the padlock of my tin shed. There was always a bit of coming and going by the Trust

Harrison gang so they would find this note later on. Sometimes it is best not to try to understand the signs just as long as you recognise them, when they come along.

The outside life carried on and with the odd exception it was always dead animals on the road that came my way. Each time I drew a little plan and placed it in the same place. Every now and again I would check myself but only ever encountered a dark red stain on the tarmac. I was actually getting rather a lot done on the public rights of way network and found that I was able to adapt and was not as institutionalised as I feared.

A decent cup of tea was the only issue and I had tried most of the burger vans with Josef's being the most acceptable but I was not always out in that direction. For a change, a call from an insider flagged up an unlicensed trader in a lay-by in the east of my area and I thought that I could drop by and have a cup of tea before enquiring after their licence.

The lay-by was busy with hardly a space to pull in off the road. A long queue of customers led to a curious looking caravan, crudely adapted into a sort of burger van but painted in various camouflage colours of greens and browns. There was an A board next to the queue that had "The Hunter Scavenger Roadside Cafe" painted roughly in red at the top with a chalked menu underneath that I squinted at to read the irregular writing; "Young wilted nettle, hazelnut mash with wild garlic pesto, grilled very locally sourced tenderised meats, hedgerow salad, tea or coffee with goat's milk, spring water."

A satisfying meaty aroma drifted from the caravan and there was a buzz of expectation amongst the queue that I had now joined.

"Yeah, you've got to be quick," said a chap to his friend, a couple of people ahead of me, "finger's crossed they don't run out."

"Have you got the app?" said a friendly man, directly in front of me, who had turned around to chat.

"I'm sure I ought to know what that means?" I said.

"You know," said the friendly chap, holding up a smart black modern mobile phone, "the app that tells you where they are going to pop up next, they do move around a lot."

"No, not on this thing," I said, holding up my old phone, "anyway, I'm only here for a cup of tea and then I need to inspect their license to trade."

"This guy's going to close 'em down," called out a large red haired man behind me, who had obviously been listening to our conversation.

"NOOOO," said the queue, in unison.

"Anyway," shouted back a man near the front, "it's free so they don't need a licence."

"YEAH," said the queue, in unison.

"Why would it be free?" I said.

"You gives a donation," said another man, calling out from the back of the queue.

I was slowly shuffling forward towards the caravan and side on I could view the hatch but not see inside the caravan. From this angle I could make out a stiff grey beard jutting out of the hatch.

"Oi, you've tankin well forgotten somethin'," said the jutting out grey beard, who was rattling a pot with money in it at a customer who had just been served, "and make it somethin' that don't rattle. Now push off.. you can all tankin' well push off, we're closed."

An old blind was drawn down to close the hatch and the queue disbanded, grumbling to each other as they made their way back to their vehicles.

I walked up to the old caravan and looked behind it where there was a white goat tethered up, eating the grass with a little milking stool next to it.

I knocked on the caravan door but there was no response. There would presumably be a vehicle returning to hitch up the caravan as, despite the tethered goat, it did not look like a permanent fixture.

I left them to it and returned home, rather hungry it has to be said, after experiencing the aromas from The Hunter Scavenger Road Side Cafe.

The next day Nancy rang me.

"Hey Victor, get back to the office and check out the news online, I won't spoil it for you, just do it."

I did what I was told. A national on line paper report stated that;

"A council trialling a scheme to provide a better service to the public has been abandoned, after a traffic warden was buried alive by a child protection officer."

I read the headline again but still it made no sense. Reading on the situation became clearer; "A traffic warden who was just completing digging a grave as part of a council's enterprising "can do" initiative ended up being buried alive by a second member of staff, a child protection officer, who had been appointed with the task of filling the grave back in again. Due to a misunderstanding, the funeral had not yet taken place but the child protection officer recognised the traffic warden at the bottom of the grave from when she had been presented with a parking ticket, quite unfairly in her opinion and she saw red.

"Opportunities like that do not come about very often and I seized it with both hands," said the child protection officer. As a consequence the pioneering "first off the rank" initiative has now been abandoned.

The traffic warden has made a full recovery whilst the child protection officer said that it had been a very therapeutic experience, despite being dismissed for gross professional misconduct and remanded on bail."

The Trust Harrison van appeared in the car park, towing the

camouflaged caravan and blocking up the bottom end of the yard. At the same instant the chap from the other end of the building appeared and I feared the worse when he saw the caravan out in the car park.

"Blimey, someone's butchered an old Paladin Mercury, by the look of it, is that the Sandinistas?" he said, "I think that you would be excluded from most respectable sites having committed that kind of sacrilege. By the way my caravan has been recovered, a member of the owners club spotted it in a yard somewhere, so that's a great relief. And, isn't it time you were back outside Victor?"

"Haven't you heard? It's all over, the first off the rank system has been abandoned. You are no longer an insider and I am no longer an outsider. So, I shall just sit here and while away the morning, catching up with a few of the more interesting e-mails and not a great deal will get achieved."

Secretly I felt a pang of regret that I was no longer an outsider and no more phone calls from Sue Stiffkey or Wendy Tiptoe.

I went out into the yard to speak to Harrison and Dolores.

"So, I've finally caught up with you two. Where did you get this thing from?"

"Hi Mr Wayland, it was dumped up a byway," said Dolores, "so we dragged it out before it got all smashed up. We've adapted it a bit inside."

"You ain't left no more of them notes boss?" said Harrison, nodding towards the tin shed.

"No, that's all finished now," I said

Dolores and Harrison looked at each other.

Harrison went across and opened the passenger door of the van and returned with a plastic bag filled with something heavy and passed it to me.

"What's that?" I said, peering inside, "money? Cash?"

"Yes, there's about eight hundred pounds," said Dolores, "it's for the rights of way, maybe another strimmer, what do you reckon?"

"All from that," I said, gesturing towards the caravan.

Dolores nodded.

"Right," I said, "leave it with me."

I went straight back to my office and rang Sue Stiffkey.

"Well, I'm not dealing with that any more, I'm back doing my normal role now in weights and measures," said Sue Stiffkey, who then paused and lowered her voice to a husky whisper, "but...I've seen handwritten notes being passed between us...between the insiders...so those lines of communication may still be open."

"The future of public rights of way may just depend on it," I said.

"Have you still got your...shovel?"

"Ready and waiting," I said.

9
OPEN DAY

"SO, WHO IS the chef for the Hunter Scavenger Roadside Cafe?" I said, to Harrison.

"You don't know him," said Harrison.

"But Ollie milks Bathsheba the goat," said Dolores, "and when we've got a few tables and chairs out, Knocker is front of house. Peter and Nigel are out with us working on the footpaths and we pick up the caravan on our way back from wherever."

"And it's obviously very popular," I said.

"There was a food reviewer down from a national paper last week," said Dolores, "but Knocker got wind of it and the bloke sort of left quite quickly."

Harrison yawned and got back into the passenger seat of the van.

"Mr Wayland," said Dolores, "can we ask you a favour?"

"Of course," I said.

"Would you like to play some of your records at the coppice open day next Saturday? Mr Sociable says that you play some cool stuff in the van."

"Does he? Do I?"

"Only if you want to, you've got lots of vinyl right? The decks will be set up."

"Decks? Plural? What like a disc jockey? Do people really want to hear Sidney Bechet or Fats Waller?"

"I do, yes, we all do."

"Well, I don't know, it's just something I do on my own, in the evenings or on a Sunday afternoon and then fall asleep."

Dolores did not say anything but just smiled. I tried to think of some plausible excuses but this very odd idea somehow seemed to have become a reality.

"Great," said Dolores, "your first dj set Mr Wayland, what shall we call you on the poster, how about dj Thumbstick?"

"You know my feelings about thumbsticks," I said.

"Yes, but it'll be ironic. Look, we'd better get on and thank you so much Mr Wayland, for agreeing to do it."

A couple of moments later I was left on my own breathing fried food aromas and wondering what on earth I had been talked into. It would be interesting, however, to finally get a chance to see what has been going on inside the heavily defended coppice. The Trust Harrison gang had become interested in coppicing last year and had asked for my help in identifying any landowners who might agree to the gang taking on and managing a coppice themselves. After arranging a meeting with one eccentric landowner, Dolores was able to persuade him that it would be a good idea and she certainly made a compelling case for all the benefits of a well-managed hazel coppice. I had been assigned to keep an eye on the whole thing on behalf of the landowner, but as yet I had not been able to penetrate behind the high security fence.

The dust had barely settled after the "first off the rank" debacle when the new director's pa rang me and then put Jolyon Bellringer on.

"It certainly wasn't my idea," he said, "as I keep telling everyone, it was that previous idiot. But, I need something, I need a positive initiative and I need it quickly. You're a real person Victor and I'm told that you have some interesting contacts out there that seem to get things done but goodness knows how in this financial climate. Anyway, I need someone who has fingers in pies, someone in touch with the zeitgeist."

"That's interesting," I said, "last week I was baggage and now I've got my fingers in some sort of German pie."

"No, no, the zeitgeist is..never mind, it's ideas I need, please Victor."

"Well how about giving rights of way more money and we can provide a better service?"

"No, you're not thinking out of the box," said Jolyon Bellringer.

"Well everyone is always telling us how important public rights of way are and how they provide so much towards our health and wellbeing, there's sustainable access, sustainable tourism, social cohesion through volunteering, doctor's giving patients leaflets with health walks on them, there's rampant obesity, don't you think that public rights of way might just be the saving of us?"

"Yes, yes, I agree but people have heard it all before, it needs to be a thing to catch the public's imagination, it needs the wow factor."

"Well, you're in touch with Mr X," I said.

"Absolutely, we're going up to see the show as guests, backstage afterwards. Of course I want to get Mr X involved, but involved in what is the problem?"

"If anyone needed to lose some weight, then it is Mr X," I said, "he needs to start walking rather than drive two hundred yards from his house to meet me. Honestly though, he even carries his dog around with him so that it doesn't have to walk either. If he can be convinced of the benefits of even short walks and exercise then maybe a few couch potatoes might take some notice. I don't know, I'm sorry that I can't come up with any snappy new ideas and if it is snappy new ideas that you are looking for, then, probably I am not the person you need to be talking to..hello..are you still there?"

Jolyon Bellringer had rung off but I had to go out anyway. I was determined to remain an outsider at heart and had adopted the habit of doing something useful in the afternoons. That would have been a good initiative to tell the new director about, get everybody doing something useful in the afternoons.

Two days later I suddenly remembered that the new director had referred to me as a "real person".

I rang Nancy and told her about the new director calling me a real person and about dj Thumbstick.

"Gina and I will come along," she said, "and it would be great to see what they've been doing in the coppice."

"And listen to my records."

"Yes, of course."

"Apparently Harrison likes the music that I play in the van and I thought that he was just putting up with it."

I then told Nancy all about the Hunter Scavenger Roadside Cafe.

"That's amazing, I'm not sure I could eat it but I'm always seeing plenty of roadkill over this way," she said, "so they are welcome to pitch up here. I'll try and find out who deals with that stuff now that we have reverted back to our abnormal way of working. See you at the weekend then, the very real dj Thumbstick on the wheels of steel."

"You youngsters and your modern rhetoric," I said.

The next morning the Trust Harrison van appeared in the depot and the gang emerged to pick through the remaining wooden posts and bits and pieces of timber which had been always been left behind in the heap in favour of straighter posts and unwarped rails. Now it really was just the odds and ends left but a selection was made and construction began with Harrison hammering in some nails. Curiosity got the better of me and I went out to see what was going on.

"That's my old hammer," I said, "the one that got kicked in the river by that..person...that I swore at and then got into trouble. That's my hammer."

Harrison kept hammering.

"I thought I'd lost it forever, but you must have gone back afterwards to find it, you must have got in the river?"

Harrison continued with his intermittent hammering.

"I suppose that you're claiming salvage rights or something?" I said, "but I don't think salvage rights apply to rivers and non tidal waters."

Harrison appeared unconcerned about the legal details and picked out some more bent nails from a pot of reclaimed nails and staples and straightened them with a few deft taps of my hammer, using a broken kerb stone as an anvil. He then clouted the unbent nails into the timber frame that he was constructing, letting the weight of the hammer do the work.

"Ok," I said, "it's yours, you can have my old hammer now that you have learnt how to use it properly. What are you making anyway?"

"It's a fing," said Harrison, "for the Saturday fing."

"Ah, the coppice open day, apparently it was your suggestion that I played some records after enjoying the music that I play in the van?"

"Old and easy," said Harrison.

"Old and easy?" I said.

"Fanks for the hammer boss," said Harrison.

I returned to my office to answer a difficult e-mail that I had been putting off but the sound of my old hammer echoing about the yard combined with the idea that my favourite music was old and easy, made it hard to concentrate.

"Old and easy," I said, out loud to myself, with my fingers

poised above the computer keyboard, "dj Old and Easy, I think I prefer dj Thumbstick."

"Talking to yourself again Victor," said the chap from the other end of the building as he drifted silently into my office.

"Doesn't everyone?" I said, resuming my difficult e-mail by pummelling out the word "enforcement".

"Well, I don't," he said, "not unless I really am on my own."

"But I was on my own, until you crept in here."

"New shoes, soft soled stealth."

"So you can creep up and listen to people when they think that they're on their own?"

"Anyway," he said, "the depot's being sold and we've all got to move out."

"What?" I said, "You are joking? Why?"

"Fifty four houses apparently. Most of us are packed, well, we haven't got much, but you don't seem to have made a start yet."

"You've only just told me about it. I've been in this room for twenty eight years, I can't pack all this up just like that. Where are we going anyway? This is hopeless."

"Don't shoot the messenger," said the chap from the other end of the building, holding up his arms in surrender before silently backing out of my office.

"I'm going out," I said, raising my voice so that I could be heard, "I'm going out to do something useful in the afternoon, unlike you lot."

There was plenty to think about. Where the hell were we going to be moved to and what should I do with all the stuff in my office? What records was I going to play on Saturday so that I didn't sound predictably old and easy? My head was reeling as I walked unseeing through a lush meadow in search of a problem bridlegate and I then stopped in my tracks. I listened intently, cursing the tinnitus in my ears from all that unprotected bandsawing in my mid forties. It was distant but unmistakable, I had heard a cuckoo. The burden of unreconcilable thoughts fell away and I felt joyful as if all the early summers of my childhood were now gathered together in a timeless moment and nothing else mattered. I recalled hearing a cuckoo with my grandmother in her later life when she counted the calls, saying that it would determine the amount of years that she had left to live. The cuckoo was right as it turned out. I held my breath and waited. There are fewer more distinct and evocative sounds in nature than the two note call of the cuckoo. I was willing the next call and finally drew breath when I heard the cuckoo again and it was much closer this time. I then caught sight of the bird as it changed trees, with its strong fluttering wing beats and a surprisingly long tail. This summer visitor from central Africa, newly arrived, found a perch and then remained obstinately silent before moving on.

"Two years, is that it?" I called out in the direction of the reticent cuckoo, "thanks a bunch. You must be the Harrison of the cuckoo world?" I had moved on from imagining Jim Pringle's hushed tones and was now addressing the birdlife directly.

I wondered whether Harrison had heard a cuckoo yet.

It was dry and sunny on Saturday afternoon and a fair number of people had walked the quarter mile from the nearest parking area to the coppice, following the specially laid out markers directing the way. I was able to drive a bit closer with my van and only had to carry my records fifty yards or so but that took two trips. I was not sure who was going to come today but the first person I bumped into turned out to be the new director.

"Ah Victor, I saw the council van and somebody told me it was you. Jolyon Bellringer, it's good to meet up at last," he said, as we shook hands, "are you being a roadie? Apparently, there's some sort of rustic dj playing this afternoon, which should be a laugh."

"How did you get to hear about this event?" I said, continuing on in through the coppice gate with my record boxes.

"I was invited by the organisers, the something or other Trust and they were very charming, so how could I refuse?"

"That would be Dolores then?" I said.

"No, I think he said his name was..Harrison? Anyway, more importantly Victor, here's the news, Mr X is on board, in principal, he's up for it."

"Up for what?"

"You know, that idea we had, I had, about getting him to do more walking and get healthy, but make a big thing of it, we just need to find a catchy hook. There's that catchphrase thing that he used to do when he came on? It was from a day time tv show, I think it was called "the Energetic Hour" where they were getting old people to move about and Mr X had a slot to shout a lot and wake everyone up, or give them a heart attack, this was even before he was a skinny young pop star."

"Is it the catchphrase that includes the misnomer; "We'll always be together like chalk and cheese?"" I said.

"Yes, that's it, well he needs something else now, something new."

"I'm glad to hear it, that was never going to work, not chalk and cheese," I said, "right, if you'll excuse me, I'd better see where I am playing these records. Nice looking cakes on that stall over there."

"You're not the dj?"

"Yes, I am your rustic dj for the afternoon," I said, leaving the new director negotiating over a flapjack with Knocker on the cake stall.

"Jackflap?" said Knocker, "thas two tankin' quid."

I said hello to Dolores and she showed me where the record

players were set up on the frame that Harrison had been making in the depot, using my old hammer.

"Put your records under there Mr Wayland and you can play in a bit. We're just finishing setting up the PA. Would you like a cup of tea or a maybe a cider?"

"A bit of Dutch courage perhaps," I said.

"Sorry, a Dutch what?" said Dolores, laughing, "it sounds good but I.."

"Oh it's an old..never mind..a small cider please, thank you," I said.

I was pleased to see Nancy and Gina arrive and I confessed to being a little nervous.

"You'll be fine," said Gina, "just enjoy it."

"Joe threatened to come and swap some of your records for his," said Nancy, "you like a bit of techno don't you Victor?"

The PA crackled into life and a couple of test records were being played to check that all was ok. Dolores was standing centrally between the loud speakers to listen to the sound whilst a young man who I had never seen before was putting on a selection of my records.

"Something louder?" said Dolores.

The young man shrugged and played a couple more randomly selected tracks.

"Something with more bass?" said Dolores.

"Er, hem," I said, approaching Dolores, "that young man appears to have one of my records, in his mouth."

"He's freeing up his hands Mr Wayland," said Dolores, "everyone does it when they are on the decks."

"Not with my Joe Venuti and Eddie Lang he doesn't." I said.

Dolores signalled to the young man to put my record away properly in its sleeve.

"I think the sound's ok now Mr Wayland, so we're ready when

you are."

I took my position behind the two very industrial looking record players.

"What are these?" I asked the young man, who had been putting my records in his mouth.

"Technics 1210 mark 2's," he said.

"I like my Garrard," I said.

"You're into garage?"

"No, in my sitting room actually."

"Cool," he said, nodding slowly as he picked up a microphone, "so, give it up for dj Thumbstick on the ones and twos, kicking off with.."

He looked across for confirmation of my first track.

"It is called "Blues my naughty sweetie gives to me" by Sidney Bechet," I said.

"Wicked," said the young man into the microphone, before turning it off and putting it down beside me.

I had to find the next record to play, so that there was not too big a gap between the tracks which I imagined would be frowned upon by any self respecting disc jockey. I selected "the St. Louis Toodle-oo" by Duke Ellington and took a sip of cider. I had a few 45rpm records which I had picked up at the last minute just to bring something a bit more up to date but looking through them now the most recent one was recorded in 1961.

I had been playing quite contently for about three quarters of an hour when the new director edged his way beside me to stand behind the decks.

"Cement mixer," I said, "Slim and Slam."

"This is ..interesting music Victor, it's a nice little side line you've got here. Anything more modern perhaps, you know, just for variety?"

"Ok, I'll play my most modern 45rpm record, I wouldn't say

it's a favourite or anything," I said, "I've got it here somewhere, they won't mind waiting."

"Ah, singles, now you're talking," said the new director, "and, I still need that little missing part of the jigsaw to get this whole Mr X walking again campaign going. We'll be the envy of all the other local authorities, a real coup, it'll open up funding streams, you know, maybe a bit more money in the old rights of way pot?"

"Here it is, I say modern but it came out in 1961, Helen Shapiro, apparently she was fourteen when she recorded this."

"Not quite what I had in mind, no eighties pop?"

"Walking back to Happiness, whoops, wrong side, that's better."

"What did you say?"

"I put the B side on by accident, but I don't think anyone noticed.."

"No, you said walking back to happiness, that's it. Walking... back...to happiness, walking all the way back to happiness, walking back to well-being, walking back to mindfulness, walking back to a world full of thinner people, this is the song, Walking Back to Happiness, it's great, Mr X can record it, this is massive Victor."

In his excitement the new director gave me a few fake punches to the solar plexus and then sang along with gusto and jazz hands for the remaining two and a half minutes of Walking Back to Happiness. In the meantime, I got Nuages by Django Reinhardt lined up and ready.

"I've cracked it Victor," said the new director, as Django began the bluest kind of blues, "I have now found the missing piece of the jigsaw."

He then picked up the microphone that had been placed beside the record players.

"Is this on? Yes, here we go, I've always had a hankering to do this, here we go, it's the "if you go down to the woods today" rap."

The new director turned his baseball cap back to front and began to bob up and down whilst chanting in a tuneless monotone over the majesty of Django's Reinhardt's guitar.

I decided that it was time for me to take a break and retreated to the cake stall.

"It's looking good in the wood," chanted Jolyon Bellringer, "where the butterflies fly and the cider is good.."

"Have you finished Victor?" said the owner of the coppice, through a large mouthful of Victoria sponge.

"Well, I suppose so, I don't honestly mind, the new director has rather taken over. The record is going to finish in a minute and he hasn't got another one ready to put on but I don't suppose he'll notice."

"This is jolly good isn't it?" said the landowner, "I mean the splendid work they have done here in the coppice. I wasn't sure in the beginning but you reassured me that it would all work out and you've sort of kept an eye on things, haven't you?"

"Yes," I said, not letting on that this was my first visit. There was still an inner compound that seemed to be impregnable but the coppicing and management of the main area was very impressive with new growth shooting up from last year's cut hazel stumps.

"Have you tried any of the splendid charcoal that they make here? All profits go to the rights of way fund apparently," said the landowner, "they delivered some to the manor the other day, it really is top drawer."

I had no idea about the charcoal production and it was just another example of the industry of the Trust Harrison gang. The Trust Harrison gang that seemed to have more to it than just a few volunteers going out in an old van running on chip fat to clear a couple of footpaths now and again.

"Nuages" had finished and the new director was now ranting

unaccompanied into the microphone.

"And there goes a bird...bang bang bang...guns in the wood... down in the hood.."

At that point the power went off and I noticed Harrison walking away from the little generator that was tucked behind some straw bales at the back of the clearing. Jolyon Bellringer was looking puzzled and continued to tap on the microphone. This was my first sighting of Harrison today and I left the cake stall to intercept him.

"Hi man," said Harrison, "fanks for the old and easy."

"Is it really old and easy?" I said, "anyway, the coppice looks great, like a village fete in the woods. Is your brother Marlon here today?"

"Maybe later."

"Does it go on later then?"

"Nah, I mean later this afternoon," said Harrison.

I lifted up a corner of a tarpaulin near the record players which seemed to be covering up a large stack of loud speakers and lighting equipment.

"What's all this for?" I asked.

Harrison replaced the tarpaulin.

"That's just in case the one that you was using don't work."

"I see."

"When we has done this bug finding fing for the kids you can play some more?"

"I'd be happy to, oh yes, I've been meaning to ask you, have you heard a cuckoo yet this year?" I said, "because I have."

"Cool," said Harrison, who then walked away to find some bugs whilst I went to find Gina and Nancy.

"Has the cider got to the new director?" said Nancy, "what was that all about?"

"I've no idea, he's being a bit excitable for some reason," I said, "but you'll be pleased to know that I am going to play some more records shortly."

"It's great Victor," said Gina, "it's timeless music."

"Not time wasted then?" I said.

"Ha, ha," said Gina, "not at all."

Dolores came over to say that it all seemed to be going well and that the music was perfect.

"Thank you," I said, "it's been fun."

"You should do it again," said Nancy, "it might broaden your horizons a bit. You're never going to meet your future partner down the local, are you?"

"Who could resist a rights of way dj? We'll try to arrange some more gigs, get the ladies dancin' and you never know?" said Dolores, laughing.

"I'm glad my status as a single man is the cause of so much public concern and amusement," I said.

"Oh, don't be like that Victor," said Nancy, "you know that you want to meet someone nice."

"Well, we'll see what we can do about it then," said Dolores, giving Nancy a wink.

"That's quite enough," I said, "I think it's about time that I played some more music."

The afternoon really had been very pleasurable and thankfully the new director had disappeared by the time that I returned to the two record players. The last of the visitors began to drift away by five o clock but I could not help feeling that events were going to take on a different complexion with the arrival of Marlon and some other faces that I did not recognise. Once the huge alternative amplification and lighting equipment under the tarpaulin had replaced the rather small public address system that I had been using then I imagined that the coppice would be transformed into something else altogether.

A few days later and Harrison was again accompanying me out in the van and we managed to finish replacing a stile by lunchtime. The van smelled of swimming pools and to shelter from a rather fierce midday sun I sat in the shade of a large oak tree to eat my lunch whilst Harrison had wandered off somewhere. I was just biting into a cheese and pickle sandwich when I heard a cuckoo. I stopped chewing and listened intently, counting the calls. I felt hugely reassured after the previous cuckoo disappointment of last week and I even mentally sketched out plans for a long and pleasant retirement involving things like trout fishing in North West Scotland. Also, perhaps dj Old and Easy could find a niche somewhere, at village fetes or playing at ancient birthday celebrations? I did not care any more about the depot closing, there were always rumours like that flying about, often with no foundation or outcome. It simply did not matter. I suddenly felt more positive about life in general, I was finding my way back towards happiness, with the help of a garrulous cuckoo. Harrison reappeared as I was standing under the oak tree, brushing away a few breadcrumbs after my lunch.

"You must have heard that?" I said, "that was amazing, I heard thirty or more cuckoo calls. That means I've got thirty or so years left to live."

I explained about the old superstition when the number of cuckoo calls that you hear at one time, for older people anyway, equated to years left to live.

"I'm not superstitious normally but that'll do me at my age," I said, "if you believe in all that stuff that is."

Harrison shrugged.

I turned to put my lunch bag in the cab and unmistakably I heard the cuckoo again but this time it was very close, in fact it sounded like it was directly behind me. I turned around sharply to look at Harrison who remained impassive with his hands in his pockets.

10

THE MENDING

I HAD BEEN doing something useful in the afternoon, as per my new policy and was now inspecting a deeply sunken lane with its rocky, water eroded surface shrouded under a canopy of oak, ash and holly trees, making it a very dark and evocative place. It was my favourite path for imagining the past and those who had walked and ridden this route over centuries, passing unseen between the surrounding fields along this incised passageway in the landscape. Rather irritatingly there was a walker about fifty yards behind me when I really wanted to be on my own amidst the faintest possibility of ghosts. I had spied the walker about ten minutes before and I cursed when I looked back to see that I had not managed to shake him off and what was worse, he seemed to be gaining on me.

"Bugger off," I muttered to myself, feeling at odds with my role of opening up the countryside to all, "why can't you just ..go somewhere else?"

Ahead of me a long strand of thick creeper dangled down at head height and when I reached it, I instinctively gave it a tug. There was a crisp snapping noise from up above in the higher branches and the length of creeper dropped before me like a falling rope. Normally these long and twisted vines are very strong and I was surprised how easily the thick creeper had become detached and perhaps that snapping sound had something to do with it. Things then got a bit confusing.

"Hello, my name is Hywel, um..and I am a first aider..um..oh crap, what do I do now?"

"You give my shoulders a gentle shake," I said with my eyes still closed, "and ask whether I can hear you. If you get no response then move on to the ABC, airway, breathing and circulation."

"Ok, that's very helpful, thanks," said Hywel the first aider, giving my shoulders a persistent shake, "can you hear me? It's so different when it's for real, isn't it?"

"Yes, I can hear you," I said, opening my eyes to look up at the walker that I had been trying to get away from, "and you can stop shaking my shoulders now."

"Oh, sorry," said Hywel, the first aider, "it's a good job that I was right behind you, wasn't it?"

"Yes," I said, heaving myself up into a sitting position.

I looked around at the dead branch beside me that had snapped off when I yanked on the dangling vine. It was not that large but had fallen a sufficient distance to gain momentum before striking me cleanly on the head.

"Now what happens?" said Hywel the first aider.

I felt the top of my head and checked the palm of my hand. There was no blood and a lump had quickly formed.

"I think I'm ok," I said, "there's a bump but that's ok, better a lump forming on the outside than some hidden bleeding on the brain. Thanks for your help but I think I'll be alright now, you go on, I'll be fine."

"I can't just leave you here."

"Well no, I'm going to carry on, I'm not staying here."

"We can walk together."

Hywel the first aider helped me to my feet. I did not think that I was concussed as I could remember everything that happened and I still hankered to be on my own. No amount of encouragement on my part was going to make him go on ahead and so I listened to how he had fainted at the sight of fake blood on his first aid course.

As it turned out we had parked fairly close to each other and Hywel walked me back to my van. Once I had explained, as briefly as I could, about the unusual woven willow hubcap that Harrison had made, I was ready to drive away. As an afterthought Hywel suggested that I should not really drive, so soon after a bang on the head.

"I'm fine," I said, "I just need some painkillers, for the headache."

"No, I will drive you home," said Hywel, "it would be poor first aid otherwise."

I had begun to feel a bit nauseous and so I agreed. My van was parked next to a garage near the edge of the village with a couple of houses overlooking it so I hoped that it would be safe enough left where it was in the short term.

After trying to give this unwelcome walker the slip in the old sunken lane, I now found myself being driven home by him and I did not feel like talking very much.

Hywel commented on a load of flytipping that he had encountered earlier on his walk and described where it was. I stated blandly that it had been a flytipping hot spot for a number of years.

"Two questions," said Hywel, taking one hand from the steering wheel to gesticulate and emphasize his strength of feeling on the matter, "why take all your rubbish to a beauty spot and dump it there to spoil it for everyone else? What sort of a person would do that? And, secondly, why is it that everything seems to be designed with a very limited life span, everything from light bulbs to frying pans to... this bloody car that I am driving. There is a very real and damaging cost to cheapness and built in obsolescence. I firmly believe that there has to be a fundamental shift to ensure that things last for as long as possible, probably like they used to before we were steered towards such a consumerist society."

I felt excused from responding to these very reasonable concerns and gave a Harrison style shrug instead. We continued in silence for the remainder of the journey

"Is there someone at home?" said Hywel, as we pulled up outside my house, "you know, someone who can keep an eye on you?"

"There's Leadbelly," I said, "Leadbelly is a cat and he'll need feeding."

Hywel followed me to my front door and Leadbelly appeared but quickly disappeared at the sight of a stranger. As I opened the front door, I felt that I ought to invite Hywel in but instead, I kept him on the doorstep and asked him what he did for a living.

"I'm a jazz musician, old school, you know big band stuff, I'm off to New Orleans in the morning in fact, I've played over in the States a few times."

"Have you?" I said, trying to imagine playing jazz in New Orleans.

"Yep, anyway, as long as you think you're ok?"

"So, what do you play? Come in, if you want to."

"I play clarinet," said Hywel, "I'm afraid that I have to go, are you sure you're going to be alright?"

"Clarinet?" I said.

"Yes, I've got to get my stuff together for tomorrow, so.. um.. goodbye...that's not very good for a first aider is it, I haven't even established what your name is?"

"Victor. Victor Wayland."

"Please ring someone then Victor, just to tell them what happened to you, just so that they are aware, promise me you'll do that?"

"I promise and thank you for your very diligent first aid, much appreciated, and....New Orleans," I said.

"Bye," said Hywel.

Leadbelly reappeared and kept winding himself around my legs until I fed him and then he went out.

I forgot to ring anyone and woke up in the morning with a headache and did not feel like going to work. Around mid morning I put a bag of frozen peas on my head and rang Nancy to tell her what had happened.

"Oh Victor, what are we going to do with you?"

"I don't know," I said, "it's nothing serious."

"You will get some medical help though won't you, if you feel worse?"

"Yes, yes, the first aider who happened to be right behind me when it happened plays clarinet in a big band and is just off to New Orleans to play jazz."

"Wow, so you two had plenty to talk about then. You will fill in the accident book, won't you, when you do go into work? Don't forget."

I thanked Nancy and then took some more painkillers.

Nancy rang me back at the end of the day, just to check that I was ok. I did not have very much to say but I thanked her for calling. It was not until tea time that I realised that I had missed the whole of the last day of a test match and not turned the radio on once. England had managed to hold out for a draw and I was annoyed that I had forgotten about all about it.

In the end I had two days off work and then suddenly remembered that my van was still parked where I had left it before the branch had fallen on my head. I rang Wayne, my old pub quiz team member before I jumped ship and he agreed to come round at the end of the day and give me a lift to retrieve the van. I would have forgotten my van keys if Wayne had not reminded me but I was relieved to find the van still intact. I thanked Wayne for his trouble when he dropped me off.

"No problem," said Wayne, "quiz Monday, we can call ourselves the amnesiacs?"

"Ha, ha," I said, "maybe next month, if I remember."

I wanted a quiet return back to work and even found and filled in the accident book without anyone noticing. The headaches were diminishing but everything felt a bit strange, a bit dream like.

"Nice break Victor?" said the chap from the other end of the building, when I bumped into him outside the kitchen. I recalled the sound of the breaking branch and then found myself flinching in anticipation.

"Yes, I did a lot of relaxing thank you," I said, which was true.

"Great," he said, without prying further.

Later on, Harrison appeared in the office, seemingly for a chat, which was a new and strange experience but punctuated with the same customary long silences. He told me how the Hunter Scavenger Roadside Cafe had made enough cash to buy two strimmers and get an MOT for the van and get it serviced. He mentioned a couple of paths that had been cleared and were now being used by some grateful horse riders. He described a small bird with a white rump that kept flying on a short way ahead of him up the path to find a perch before flying on again when he caught up with it. I suggested that it might be a wheatear and he then pointed to my old broken clock on the wall.

"That clock is fixed," said Harrison.

I looked up at the clock on the wall and the hands pointed to twenty past eight. I checked the time on my computer.

"It's thirteen minutes passed eleven," I said.

"You has to wind it up," said Harrison.

"It's a battery operated clock."

"It ain't now."

I lifted down the clock and sure enough there was now a homespun winding mechanism fitted into the back. I wound up the winder and set the time before placing it back up on the wall.

"I can hear it ticking," I said to Harrison, but he had already left.

Every now and again I glanced up from my computer screen to check the progress of the clock hands and the wound up time and digital time remained in accord. The following morning it was still keeping good time but needed winding up again and I was careful not to overwind it. I was just drinking my second cup of tea of the morning when there was a knock at the window. A man a bit younger than me was struggling with a microwave oven.

"Open the window," he called out, breathlessly.

I opened the window and he balanced the microwave oven between us on the sill.

"Cor, that's heavier than it looks, I'm not too late am I?" said the man, puffing out his cheeks. At that moment the Trust Harrison van entered the yard and Harrison nipped out of the passenger side to intercept the microwave oven as the man attempted to pass it in to me through the open window.

"Fanks," said Harrison, receiving the microwave oven, "they is fixin' fings in the shed."

Harrison hurriedly carried it away towards the old tin shed in the corner of the yard as the man called after him.

"Yesterday it completely nuked a chicken Kiev, it must be the timer or the pinger or something."

The man then pushed closed my office window and walked back out through the depot gate.

My telephone rang at that moment and I conducted a conversation with a member of the public whilst scanning the yard to see who was in my old tin shed. I also wanted to catch the Trust Harrison van before it departed to find out what was going on and why I was being handed a broken microwave oven through the office window. I made my apologies to the caller and scribbled down their number with a promise to call them back as I could see the gang mustering to depart. I went out into the yard and flagged down the accelerating van before walking around to talk to Harrison through the open passenger window.

"Hi Mr Wayland," said Dolores, from behind the wheel.

I said hello to Dolores and then asked Harrison what was going on in my old tin shed.

"That's Fido," said Harrison, "he is fixin' fings. You weren't using that shed."

"No, but it is still my shed."

"Yeah."

"And there's no electricity down there, no lights or anything."

"There is now, he has put a solar fing on the roof and he has a genny for weldin'."

"Fido wants to repair things rather than throw stuff away," said Dolores, "we all know it's crazy just burying everything in holes in the ground and he's been doing something about it."

"We has to go boss," said Harrison.

The Trust Harrison van carried on out of the yard as a bright blue flash emanated from the partially open door of my old tin shed.

"Cooee, is this the right place? I hope they haven't gone yet?" said a voice from behind me and a lady appeared at the depot gates, as the old chip fat aromas lingered.

"Ooh that smells nice, are you doing takeaways as well?" said the lady who then entered the yard and offered me a toaster that she was carrying in a large plastic bag, "it doesn't pop up any more and keeps setting off the smoke alarm. I would be very grateful if you could get it to pop up again, it is a pop up toaster after all and it would be a shame just to throw it away, thank you. My telephone number is on that label there and it's Mrs Briars."

A loud bang and a puff of smoke emanated from the old tin shed.

"Ooh dear," said Mrs Briars, "that made me jump."

"Excuse me," I said, "I had better go and see what is going on."

"Yes and I've got to go to the chemist, goodbye," said Mrs Briars.

Carrying the broken toaster I walked to the bottom of the yard to find out who was making explosions on council premises.

"Hello," I called out, over the sound of a diesel generator and then knocked on the partially opened door of the tin shed.

The door opened and a man with a welding mask and a lit welding torch emerged. He then pulled off the mask to reveal his very dark curly hair and a contrasting thick bright red beard.

"A toaster," said the black and tan man, over the sound of the generator, "have you put your name on it?"

"It's not my toaster."

"I bet it doesn't pop up any more and it's setting off your smoke alarm?"

"It's not my toaster and it is setting off someone else's smoke alarm," I said, "on the other hand, this happens to be my shed and Harrison didn't ask whether you could commandeer it to fix toasters."

"It's not only toasters, oh deary me no."

The black and tan man cast open the door of the shed and inside was an Aladdin's cave of kitchen equipment, worn shoes, broken tools, a heap of electrical components, old wiring and all manner of plastic junk. The tin shed seemed to have expanded inside to accommodate all these broken goods and appliances.

"I fixed your clock," said the black and tan man.

"Yes, thank you," I said.

"You'll have to remember to wind it up, let's have your toaster."

The man took the toaster and disappeared back into the shed

and closed the door behind him.

I looked back at the Highways end of the office and no one had seemed to notice the smoke or explosions or the bright flashes coming from my shed. I had to go out to a meeting so I decided to deal with the situation when I got back.

Events dictated that I was out and about a fair bit for the next couple of days. I was still getting headaches and I took the odd painkiller when required but generally I was feeling better even if everything still seemed a bit odd. It was as though I was experiencing a slightly different kind of normal.

Towards the end of the week I had forgotten about what was going on in my tin shed. As I crossed the top of the yard to get my lunch from the van I heard a burst of mechanical coughing followed by fierce revving and my cumbersome old flail mower burst out of the tin shed, dragging the black and tan man behind it.

"Good grief," I said, "that hasn't been running for years."

"It's a beast and that's for sure," he called out, "can you find another home for it, it's getting a bit short of room in here? I'll leave it running, it's had a slug of special jollop, it'll settle down in a minute."

The black and tan man disappeared again and closed the shed door behind him.

I left the flail mower chugging away at the bottom of the yard for the time being and went to make a cup of tea and found the office kettle in the bin. The chap from the other end of the building popped into the kitchen to take his sandwich box from the fridge.

"Yes, disaster for the tea addict Victor, actually I'm off out to get another kettle when I've eaten my sandwich. They're just less than a tenner so it will be about a quid each? Cheap as chips, sort of disposable really."

"What about getting it fixed?" I said.

"The kettle? Fixed? It's broken, kaput.."

"I'll get it fixed," I said.

"Are you expecting the itinerant kettle mender to come around, door to door, as he does every year, on the appointed day?"

I took the kettle and its lead out of the bin.

"In a manner of speaking, yes," I said.

I did not want to draw attention to the fact there was a man with an extraordinary hair and beard combination fixing things in my old corrugated tin shed so I smuggled the kettle into the van and reversed down to the end of the yard. I knocked on the door of the shed and the man called Fido appeared with an old barrel shaped vacuum cleaner in his arms. It had a tartan pattern on it and it triggered a memory from my earlier childhood of trying to get away from a similar vacuum cleaner.

"I don't suppose you could fix the office kettle could you?" I said, "they were going to throw it away and buy another one for a tenner."

"Whoa, we can't be having that, hey Boxer, grab this kettle from the gentleman, they're all gasping for a cuppa next door."

A second man appeared from the tin shed who was short and squat and flat faced. He snatched the kettle and lead from my hands and scampered back into the shed. Moments later there was an ear splitting ringing of hammer on anvil and Fido tapped his nose and gave me a wink.

I reversed back up to the other end of the yard as I did not wish my hearing to become even more impaired than it already was. I made a couple of calls and had just put the phone down when the chap from the other end of the building wandered into my office.

"You'll be relieved to know Victor, that the kettle is working again."

"Did he bring it back?"

"Did who bring it back? It just started working again for some reason, so it's panic over. By the way, the big wigs are coming down tomorrow morning to look around the depot with the developers so I would definitely keep your merry band of revolutionaries out of the way as questions could be asked."

When I left for home I wandered back down to the bottom of the yard and the tin shed had the combination lock back in place.

"We're closed for a bit of shut eye," said a gruff voice from within.

"Oh," I said, "but thanks for mending the kettle."

There was no reply and the chap from the other end of the building appeared in the yard.

"Is your clock running slow Victor?" he called out, "you're the last one here so don't forget to lock the gate."

"Ok," I said, and I gave him a cursory wave as his wife drove into the yard to pick him up and I waited until they had left.

"I've got to lock the depot gate up now," I said, to the closed and padlocked corrugated tin door, "but then you seem to have locked yourselves in from the outside. Um, there's a bit of a problem, you really cannot be here, mending things, in the morning as the bosses are inspecting the depot. I appreciate what you are trying to do but I might get into a bit of trouble over it. I'm not ruling it out in the future, maybe give me a ring sometime?"

I thought that I could detect a faint snoring coming from within the shed so my words may have fallen on deaf ears.

The next morning when I arrived at work there was a small gathering of smartly dressed people in the yard all with new fluorescent yellow tabards on. Once in my office I watched from my window as they were conducted on a slow excursion around the yard, pointing at this and that. When I returned with my brimming mug of tea they had moved down by my tin shed and one even pushed at the door and rattled the padlock. The small group moved on and eventually got into various large cars and drove away. I finished my tea and walked down to the tin shed and tapped on the corrugated tin door.

"Hello, the coast is clear," I said, but there was no answer.

The Trust Harrison van then appeared, which was fortuitous timing and I waited for Dolores and Harrison to disembark and then raised the subject of the occupancy of my tin shed. Harrison shrugged and went over to the shed, unlocked the combination padlock and pulled the doors wide open. The tin shed was empty, apart from my old flail mower. Gone were the old kitchen appliances and everything else. There was no trace of Fido, the black and tan man, or Boxer.

"We is going to take that fing out today on your trailer," said Harrison, gesturing towards the old flail mower, "the paths is getting bad out there."

"Where have they gone, your friends and all that stuff, that shed was rammed full yesterday?" I said.

Harrison shrugged.

"Fixing stuff," he said.

"Have they set up somewhere else?"

"I guess," said Harrison.

"Look, let Fido have my phone number," I said, "I suggested that he should give me a ring sometime and perhaps they could come back, you know, for another mending session? I'm sure we can organise something."

"Ok boss," said Harrison.

I had not told Dolores or Harrison about the depot being sold off for housing as it was such a gloriously sunny day and I did not want to think about it. The Trust Harrison gang were now a resilient force that would not be perturbed by such things and they would find a way. I, on the other hand, felt like I was part of a crumbling institution and it was inconceivable that I could be moved or even want to carry on doing my job if everything changed. I saw it as the end.

The old flail mower was loaded up on my trailer and the volunteer gang set off to undertake some much needed path clearance, out there somewhere on the public rights of way network.

11

JOHNNY SWIFT

IT WAS THE Trust Harrison van but the person getting out from behind the steering wheel to talk to a tractor driver was definitely not Dolores, or Harrison for that matter. I pulled in on the opposite side of the road and I could assess the problem in an instant, the Trust Harrison van was blocking a field access and the farmer wanted to drive into the field. I approached and waited for an opportunity to intervene.

A slightly shambolic looking man, perhaps in his mid fifties although it was a bit hard to gauge, was now leaning on the rusty wheel arch of the ancient red tractor, talking very loudly to the old farmer over the sound of the chuntering engine.

"Ha, ha, I'm dreadfully sorry but you're speaking pure farmer and I simply can't understand a word of it. Ha, ha, what a perfectly ridiculous situation. Anyway, the name's Johnny Swift, how do you do?"

The old farmer ignored the outstretched hand and the large welcoming smile and was clearly running out of patience.

"Oi zed, move thic vaaan, zo'us can paaass wi me trata."

"No, sorry, I'm still not getting any of that, ah hello," said Johnny Swift as he noticed me standing beside them, "perhaps you can help, I'd be so very grateful, we need a translator here. The name's Johnny Swift."

We shook hands and I shouted to introduce myself whilst the old farmer and the ancient tractor engine chuntered away in unison.

"He wants you to move the van so that he can get into the field," I shouted.

"Ah, brilliant," said Johnny Swift, "you've obviously got the lingo, so you can tell him from me, of course my dear old chap I would be delighted to cooperate and I will move the van forthwith."

As the farmer chuntered off into the field, Johnny Swift parked up the van so that it was not blocking the field access and then strolled across to thank me for my assistance.

"My word, without your help we could have been there for hours," he said.

"Er, I just stopped because I saw the van," I said, "and then saw that it wasn't Dolores driving it so I came across to be nosey."

"So, you know Harry and Dolly? How wonderful, I'm just here for a few days at most."

"Are you covering for them? I mean are they away and you're taking the lads out?"

"I think "covering" might be overstretching it a bit," said Johnny Swift, "keeping half an eye is more like it. It'll probably kill me, I'm not a worker at heart. To be frank, I'm not even a fan of the countryside but I expect you're all very proud of these interminable rolling downs, rolling down into your gloomy vales. No, I'm definitely a city or coast man."

"So, if you don't mind me asking, how do you know... er Harry and er hem..Dolly?"

"Harry and Dolly? I was living in a tent at the time, somewhere out there in your dismal countryside, waiting for an old aunt to pop off so that I could commandeer her car but she was a tough old stick and kept us waiting for weeks. Harry and Dolly must have thought that I was some sort of tramp at first and brought me food and clothes and things but very soon we were as thick as thieves. Never did get that car."

"I see," I said, not really knowing how to respond.

"I must say, I do like this whole volunteering malarkey," said Johnny Swift, "especially as you don't actually have to do it, you can just not do it and that's that."

"Yes," I said.

The lads seemed to have adopted the same relaxed approach to volunteering and showed no signs of getting out of the van.

"So, where are you working today?" I said, "I mean, not that you have to be working at all, as you say."

"Well, we've done a bit here and bit there and, you never know, we may even do a little bit more later on."

"And you didn't say where..Harrison and Dolores had gone, while you're keeping half an eye on things?"

"No, I didn't did I? Aren't they a delightful couple?"

"Yes, but they're not ..you know.. an actual couple?"

"What do you mean not an actual couple? They're married and that's pretty coupley in my book. You obviously weren't at the wedding then? Listen, my dear old Vickers, I'd hate to keep a busy man from his work and it is now way beyond my siesta time."

We shook hands again and Johnny Swift thanked me profusely before ambling back towards the van and I drove away in a daze. When did Harrison and Dolores get married? And who was Johhny Swift?

Two days later I caught sight of the Trust Harrison van and they were delivering charcoal to a local shop. I looked out for Johnny Swift and found him in the shop, squinting at a newspaper from the stand.

"Ah, Vickers," he said, lowering the tabloid briefly "just checking the nags."

I bought a soft flapjack and ate it outside the shop. The lads were getting back into the van and I gave them a wave. It was really good that the Trust Harrison charcoal was getting distributed and sold in local shops. In the process the lads had managed to get themselves covered in charcoal dust and once in the van all I could see were the whites of their eyes peering out.

Johnny Swift emerged from the shop without a newspaper.

"That's the chores done then," he said, "fancy a swift one Vickers? Bit early?"

"Well I can't really," I said, "is everything ok, with the volunteering on the public rights of way front? I mean, do you need any help with finding anywhere?"

"As a matter of fact I do, your arcadian world here lacks some very essential facilities, a bookies and a fried chicken shop, for starters."

"I see, in that case you will have to go to town, where you'll no doubt drop the van off before you go and..you didn't tell me where..Harry and Dolly had gone, are they having a short break or something?"

"Oh, they're just taking a few days, they've not had any time to themselves, you know, since Harry's fall from grace a few months back."

"What fall from grace?" I said.

"Harry's fall from grace, you didn't hear about it? I must say Vickers you're not particularly well informed are you? You do know, at least, that he was a stuntman on a film set in Venice?"

"Venice? Well, I did hear Italy. He came back because he didn't want to eat any more pizza or pasta, apparently."

"No more pizza and pasta? Yes, that's very good and partly true actually. No, the reason he came back is that when he was doing a particularly tricky stunt, he slipped and fell into a canal, swallowing some rather filthy canal water whilst he was about it and picked up a rotten tummy bug. I understand that he was bad at both ends for some considerable time. But, that wasn't the problem. The problem was that he couldn't swim, well he can do a sort of doggie paddle but it looks for all the world like he can't swim. The film industry had never encountered a stuntman who couldn't swim apparently and so he got the boot."

"That explains a lot," I said, "Harry.. Harrison, has been going to the swimming baths a lot recently. He must be learning to swim?"

"I've no idea. Listen, Vickers, you're tremendously busy and I'm getting thirsty, let's meet again. I tell you what, I'll pop in to see you at your place of work whilst I'm sculling about over the next few days, the lads can show me where you are."

Johnny Swift waved as he ambled across the road towards the van and I went back into the shop and bought some charcoal before returning to the office.

The next morning Nancy rang me.

"How are you Victor, have you recovered and what's happening with your new jazz friend?"

"My new jazz friend? I believe his name is Hywel, as in Bennett."

"Alan?"

"What?"

"I'm sorry Victor, let me start again. Have you kept in touch with ..Hywel..your jazz friend, since the incident?"

"Well no, he's in America and I don't have any contact details for him, or even know what his surname is."

"I thought you said it was Bennett?"

"No, I don't expect it is. He was an inexperienced first aider but he took his responsibilities very seriously by insisting on driving me home, which was very good of him. It's just that I don't think that I was very welcoming when we got back to my house, which on reflection..."

"He sounds nice. Gina's asked me to marry her."

"What? I thought you'd rung me up to ask me how I was?"

"I don't know what to do and I didn't know who else to talk to about it."

"Well, I'm... flattered, but what about Joe?"

"I'm not sure what I think myself, so I can't tell him anything yet."

"Well I'm hardly an expert when it comes to relationships, as you well know."

"We're happy as we are, something like this could make it different or change things."

"Gina's not hanging around, no procrastination there then."

"Maybe she thinks that I will change my mind about the whole thing."

"The whole thing?"

"Well, you know, anyway, forget I mentioned it."

"No, you obviously wanted to share it with someone and I should be congratulating you. You sound like you need to blow your nose."

"Thank you Victor,"

"That's better," I said, "look, it's all a bit of a surprise, but it's not really any of my business, is it?"

"But you won't go all funny on me again?" said Nancy.

"No, no of course not."

"I'm going to be over in your area this afternoon, I'm off today but I've got to pick up a bit of furniture in the works van, you know how it is? So, if you see me flitting by on the road and looking sheepish you'll know why."

"Mum's the word," I said.

I was going to tell Nancy about Johnny Swift but I had been

thrown by the wedding proposal bombshell.

In the early afternoon, the Trust Harrison van crept very slowly into the yard and stopped at the end, next to my shed. I kept an eye on it but after twenty minutes no one had emerged and so I walked down to see what was going on.

Everyone appeared to be asleep inside and so I backed away but managed to knock over an upended wheelbarrow in the process which clattered down onto the tarmac and woke everyone up, with the exception of Nigel. Johnny Swift smiled and waved, I could see the soles of his shoes up on the dashboard, displaying large holes that had been patched internally with what looked like pub beermats. He got out of the van to stretch and yawn and roll himself a rather detailed cigarette before lighting it and coughing a great deal. I looked around to check that no-one was observing this transgression of the rules about smoking in a place of work.

"Vickers...I seem to have woken up feeling all nostalgic," said Johnny Swift, through a bout of coughing, "just out of idle curiosity... where do you stand...on pornography?"

"What?"

"Don't tell me you're a high definition, bald pudenda square in the face sort of a chap?"

"Well.. no," I said.

"Then we are peas from the same pod, my dear old Vickers. We are traditionalists and our porn films have to be hairy and the film all grainy and at least fifty years old. You can even call it erotica, if you have a mind to."

"I suppose you can," I said, cautiously.

"I mean, where is life's mystery otherwise? It's all changed since our day Vickers, do you remember those innocent fumbles, not knowing what you were going to encounter? That's all gone now, all gone."

There was something endearingly shameless about Johnny Swift as he moved on from erotica and the excitement of teenage trysts to tell me about his decades of sofa surfing and how all his friends were reluctant to invest in new sofas. There had been money, there may yet be money. I was intrigued by his appearance, the frayed shirt collar and cuffs and a swipe of hair across a thinning crown. He gave every indication of not having a care in the world whilst belonging to a former time and class where any brush with hardship equated to adventure rather than the cold slap of destitution. His warm and carefree, confessional attitude emboldened me towards contributing something, something of myself to his world.

"I've got a friend," I said, "and she's going to marry another woman."

"Do go on," said Johnny Swift, enjoying the very end of his rolled cigarette whilst trying not to burn his lips.

"Well, she's only just discovered, only in the last few months really, that she's..you know?"

"A lesbian?"

"Yes, I suppose so."

"And reading between the lines, you rather fancied your own chances before the whole lesbian thing blew up in your face?"

"Well I wouldn't put it like that..but..I just want her to be sure that she is doing the right thing."

"Listen, Vickers, I've got a friend who is a professional lesbian breaker, he gets called in when there's any doubt in such cases, lovely fellow, he's as gay as a fruit scone but he plays the charmer to perfection and he's simply irresistible to women. I'll give him a call now," said Johnny Swift, producing an ancient brick of a mobile phone from his pocket, "where are we, Jeremy, Jeremy, Jeremy...ah here we are."

"No, no please don't do that," I said.

"He'll be down in a flash."

"No, I wish I hadn't mentioned it, please forget it, I'm sure it will all sort itself out."

Just at that moment a van entered the yard and drove on down to where we were standing.

"Hi Victor," said Nancy, calling out through the open driver's window, "I just thought I'd call in and say hello as I was passing by the yard, it would have been very rude not to wouldn't it? I'm going to pick up a table in a minute, just down the road from here."

"Nancy?" I said, with a rising sense of alarm.

Nancy got out of the van and walked over towards us.

"Hello," said Nancy to Johnny Swift.

"Johnny Swift," said Johnny Swift, shaking hands with a broad welcoming smile and smiling eyes, "I'm delighted to meet you Nancy."

"Johnny's been taking the lads out while Harry and Dolly, I mean Harrison and Dolores are away, but I think he was just leaving."

"No, I'm not going anywhere. Dear old Vickers here has been filling me in on the situation."

"And what situation is that?" said Nancy.

"The situation we are in," I said, feeling very hot around the collar and blurting out words before Johnny Swift could say anything else, "the situation where we haven't got enough help, I was saying that your area is only slightly smaller than mine and that you would love a team of volunteers. I am very lucky in having the services of... Harrison and Dolores...and..you are not so fortunate.."

"Ha, ha, well done Vickers," said Johnny Swift, "as I can see by the panic in your eyes, this is one of those priceless situations where the person we were just talking about turns up out of the blue and what was a few moments ago a rather hypothetical conversation suddenly becomes far more personal and interesting."

"Honestly Nancy, we were just talking about the volunteer

situation."

"No, we weren't," said Johnny Swift, "actually, we were talking about you Nancy, getting married to another woman, presumably also a lesbian, otherwise the thing wouldn't work would it and old Vickers here was wondering where he stood in all this?"

"I see Victor," said Nancy, "so you have you been talking about me and Gina, about private stuff to someone who I have never met before?"

"No," I said, "well, yes. Oh god, I just wanted to talk to someone about it, like when you rang me up, wanting to talk about it..I just didn't expect you to turn up mid conversation."

"Well, you can just bloody well carry on with your conversation because I'm leaving," said Nancy.

"No, no, no, please don't do that Nancy" said Johnny Swift, "that won't help at all, in the long run. Do you love her, your partner? You said her name was Gina?"

"Yes, her name is Gina," said Nancy, addressing Johnny Swift but glowering at me, "and yes I do..I do love Gina."

"But you haven't been a lesbian for very long and it's all sort of come out of the blue?"

"Well yes, sort of. But it's complicated and deep rooted and there are other factors, like the men you're unfortunate enough to get involved with. Anyway, it just feels..right."

"So," said Johnny Swift, slowly rubbing his hands together, "there is always one question raised when a wedding is imminent. Should these two people get married or can everyone see that it is simply a ludicrous idea and someone ought to take responsibility and kidnap one or both of them to prevent such an absurd union? Everyone can see that it is a nonsense and friends and family should just put a stop to it, that's how things work in our family anyway. My brother woke up in the Faroe Islands when he should have been at a church in

Camberley. Of course, we had to drug him to stop all that kicking and screaming but he's eternally grateful now."

"Is that what you're planning then, my dear old Vickers?" said Nancy, "drugging me and hauling me off to the Faroe Islands, where are the Faroe Islands? It doesn't matter."

"But," said Johnny Swift, "here in your situation, not only is it the right person, but are they the right gender? I know that it is hard for our dear old friend here as I fancy that he has long held his candle for you Nancy, but now, well for him anyway, everything's shot up in flames. What do you think Vickers, as you're the one that's going to be doing the kidnapping?"

"I'm not kidnapping anyone," I said, "I really like Gina. Nancy and Gina seem to be very happy when they are together..and Nancy's happiness is very important to me, as a good friend, as my best friend in fact."

"So, Nancy and Gina rub along pretty well together, oh please, do excuse me?" said Johnny Swift.

"Yes, they rub..they seem to get on very well," I said.

"Well, I'd better cancel the lesbian breaker then," said Johnny Swift.

"The what?" said Nancy.

"He is only joking," I said, "that's a bit of nonsense."

"I can assure you that it isn't, by the by," said Johnny Swift, as he concluded rolling another intricate cigarette and then lit it, inhaling deeply.

"I only popped in to say hello," said Nancy, "and this is the sort of frank discussion that Victor and I would never have had, if it was just left up to us."

"Well, what is the point of dear old Vickers here, clinging on to some forlorn hope, raising his expectations and then forever beating around the bush?" said Johnny Swift, "oh, do listen to me, I am dreadfully sorry, I keep trotting out these very second rate double entendres which nobody wants to hear, including myself, I really must apologise."

Nancy made a choking sound that quickly turned into a full blown giggle that then transmitted into near hysteria for the three of us. Tears were rolling down my face and I could not look at the other two for fear of losing control again. This helpless situation seemed to go on for an eternity before we all came up for air.

"Oh, dear," said Nancy wiping her eyes, "I feel a lot better now after that. That was a really good laugh and, in the process, I have actually made my decision, I am going to accept, I am going to say yes. I must tell Gina and Joe, he's my son."

"Well, that calls for a celebration," I said, "shall I make a cup of tea?"

"Vickers, please, a cup of tea is not a celebration. Listen, there's a very cosy back street cider pub in town, frequented by some purple nosed gentlemen and I'm actually popping over there right now, if you fancy it?"

Nancy made her excuses that she had to drive back across the county and I muttered something about the working day.

"Well, enjoy your cup of tea Vickers," said Johnny Swift, shaking my hand before giving Nancy a kiss on both cheeks, "and congrats for the future, I'm delighted to have met you Nancy and I'm very much looking forward to meeting Gina one day."

With more beaming smiles, Johnny Swift returned to the van and after a crunching of the gears, the Trust Harrison van rattled out of the gate.

Nancy put her arms around my middle and gave me a big hug and I squeezed her in return.

"Pancake rolls," said Nancy.

"Nice of you to mention it, I know that I've spread a bit over my waistband."

"No, I meant from the van, silly. The exhaust smells of pancake rolls."

"That could have all gone very badly wrong," I said, "when you turned up."

"Well, I'm glad I did, I haven't laughed like that for ages."

"You must pass on my congratulations to Gina," I said, as we let go of each other, "and if you fancy any music at the wedding, a nice bit of old and easy perhaps, mates rates?"

"If it's a choice between that and Joe's techno then you might be getting a call. Thank you for being such a caring friend Victor, I'd better go and pick up this table and we'll celebrate another day. I really liked Johnny Swift, what was he putting in his roll ups? It smelled rather nice actually."

"I've no idea and he shouldn't be smoking anything in the yard anyway but other people's rules don't seem to apply to Johnny Swift."

On the Tuesday of the following week the Trust Harrison van clattered into the yard and normal service seemed to have been restored as Dolores was back under the bonnet, fiddling with the engine. The lads got out and loaded a couple of old and hard bags of cement into the van, from my shed.

"Good morning," I said, as I approached, "did you both have a good break?"

"Good morning Mr Wayland," said Dolores, wiping her hands on an oily rag. "yeah it was great, I went to a film festival in Ireland, I'm not sure what Mr Chatterbox here got up to."

Harrison yawned through the open passenger window.

"Oh, I thought you'd gone off somewhere together?" I said, "I bumped into your friend Johnny Swift, he was interesting, but I'm not sure how much work got done. Will he...you know, be coming back this way again?"

"Maybe, you're never quite sure with Johnny. He was planning on stowing away on a friend's, or rather a friend of a friend's old sailing ship, that's heading across to the West Indies for a couple of months. He might even have left by now, if he hasn't been rumbled."

"I think we could all learn a thing or two from Johnny Swift," I said.

"Yeah, he's pretty zen, is Johnny," said Dolores.

"He kept referring to you both as Harry and Dolly and he told me about your wedding. You kept that quiet then?"

Harrison smiled whilst Dolores shook her head.

"Yeah, Johnny's cool," said Harrison, "best man."

Dolores threw her head back and roared with laughter and she was still laughing when she got back into the van and drove away.

12

BLOOD ON THE MAP

THE CHAP FROM the other end of the building wandered into my office holding aloft a post card.

"Victor, apparently you have a friend visiting New Orleans, a musical friend and he is wishing you well."

"Really?" I said, "show me."

"Ah, ah," he said, holding the postcard beyond my seated reach, "not so fast, it also seems as though you've had a bang on the head recently, whilst at work and here.. is the evidence."

"Give me my postcard," I said, firmly.

"It's a bit dogeared as it has been doing the rounds, it's very rare that we get a postcard delivered to the office these days."

"But it's my bloody postcard," I said, standing up and snatching it from his hand, "and it is clearly intended for me, look, it says; Victor Wayland the footpath man. It is my post card."

"So, as duty dictates, I have checked the on-line accident book and it appears Victor that you have not recorded the incident, as you are required to do by law. Therefore, I may have to take this up with the Health and Safety Executive."

"Just you wait there a moment," I said, leaving my office to return with the old accident book from its dusty location on a shelf in the corridor, "there. It says accident book on the front and inside, immediately underneath my entry from 1992, when I got bitten by a poodle, it gives a full account of my recent accident when I got hit on the head by a dead branch. Satisfied?"

I thrust the old accident book in his face, flicking through the pages as I did so.

"That old thing? Pah.." he said, coughing at the dispersal of dust from the pages of the slender book, ".. it's all done on line now Victor, pah..that, is a relic."

"Well, it's my relic and I'm going to keep it here from now on, with all my other relics. Now, if you'll excuse me, I would like to read my postcard, that is clearly addressed to me and not to Uncle Tom Cobley and all."

"I'm leaving, I'm leaving," he said, "and he says that he's going to drop you a line when he is next playing in the vicinity, so if you need a plus one..."

"Goodbye," I said.

I read the postcard through and then looked at the old photograph on the front which showed Bourbon Street in New Orleans, teeming with monochrome life and I could almost hear the music and excitement drifting from the old wooden buildings. I flipped it over and read it through once more. Hywel concluded by saying "keep up the good work on the paths, you really do have the best job in the world." I studied the old photograph again and then took the postcard with me when I left the office to go out on my rounds.

On my way to a prearranged meeting after lunch, I undertook a couple of inspections beneath lowering skies. Rain was forecast but it was holding off for now as I checked an old wall that formed the boundary of a public footpath in the village of Makepeace. The report had stated that the public were in danger from the unsafe wall next to the footpath but I could see as I approached that it was leaning away from the path and only really presented a danger to whatever was on the far side of the old wall. On tiptoes I peered over the crumbling red brick wall, being careful not to dislodge anything. Half a dozen sheep were nestled along the underside of the toppling wall and it was obviously a favoured spot as the grass had been worn bare, with skeins of dirty wool hanging from some thistles.

"Hello there," I said, with a fair degree of civility, "I don't believe you realise the peril that you are in."

The sheep pricked up their ears but remained in the danger zone.

I looked around at the small grass field and realised that it had once been an orchard, with two very old apple trees remaining at one end. I tried to visualise the orchard in its prime, with spacious rows of various strains of apple tree ranging from cider apples, cooking apples, eaters and perhaps even pear trees. Geese, ducks and chickens would have roamed freely with sheep drifting through periodically although they could nibble the bark from the standard trees if left for too long. As it was, the patchy grass had a few crude pony jumps strewn about the place and it all looked rather sorry and neglected. The fine red brick wall would have been built by local or estate bricklayers with the bricks also made locally. They ranged in hue through warm oranges and reds with blemishes and inclusions from the firing process giving each brick its own individual character.

"It's falling down," said a voice from behind me and I turned around to see a man on the footpath walking a small dog.

"Yes, it's a shame," I said, "shame about the wall and shame about the orchard as well."

"It's a danger," said the man, "it needs to come down."

"Well, it's falling away from the path and into the field, so the only thing in danger are those dozy sheep on the other side. Sheep are very stupid but I suppose we can't expect them to be structural engineers?"

"I've complained to the council," said the man with the small dog.

"Yes," I said, "I'm here from the council."

"And you're not going to do anything about it?"

"Well no, as I say, it's going to fall away from the path and not into it."

"So, you don't care if I get crushed and my dog gets crushed?"

"You and your dog are not going to get crushed."

"Oh, what's the point," said the man, heading off up the path, tugging at the small dog's lead as it arched its back and then slid along on its quivering back legs, leaving behind a skinny trail of faeces on the footpath.

"Excuse me," I said, "I think you've forgotten something."

The dog walker responded by holding up two fingers behind him.

"That'll be an eighty pounds fixed penalty notice then, for dog fouling," I called out.

"Take it out of my council tax," said the man, without looking back.

I shook my head and took a photograph looking along the wall and another one square on to the wall from as far back as I could get, leaning into a barbed wire fence on the opposite side of the path. I would try to establish who owned the wall and then notify them of its condition and the potential danger that it presented, to the sheep.

I moved on from the leaning orchard wall to check a flight of wooden steps at the end of a lane that I had installed myself over ten years ago. The public had struggled to climb a steep section of footpath and an obvious solution was to construct a simple run of wooden steps, held in place by wooden pegs. Now the pegs were failing and one or two wooden uprights had disappeared altogether and to make it safe the whole thing needed replacing. It certainly did not seem like ten years ago that I had constructed the steps and it was rather nightmarish now to view this wear and decay and I wondered where on earth that decade had gone. I had no resource now to purchase more timber and so the path would soon revert to the slippery slope that it had been before I built the steps. I would have to have a chat with Dolores and Harrison to see if they could help. Realistically I should remove all the remaining steps and pegs before they gave way and a member of the public got hurt and then we would be facing a claim of failing to maintain a structure on a public right of way. I took a photograph and drove away but soon pulled into a layby to eat my lunch and stare at the image on the front of the postcard again as the sky darkened and the first wave of rain finally arrived, pounding upon the roof of the van. The rain soon tailed off and the sun emerged in brilliant and blinding contrast but it felt short lived and I got out of the van to brush away the bread crumbs before the next downpour. I continued on my way, splashing along narrow lanes to my arranged meeting on a farm where I had received a number of recent but separate accounts of rights of way issues. It seemed as though there were paths obstructed by barbed wire fencing and in one case a confrontation between the farmer and a walker when the walker had been trying to assert their right to walk the legal line of a public footpath. In the neighbouring county there had been a lot of recent development where a huge new housing estate had been built on the outskirts of a moderately sized town. The new residents had very quickly taken to recreating in the countryside across the border which had created a new demand on some paths in my area that had seen little use before these new habitations had appeared.

The next batch of rain coincided with me arriving in the farm yard and I grabbed my coat and an old A4 plan of the public rights of way in the immediate area that I had found in my filing cabinet. I knocked on the front door hoping for quick refuge from the rain but then struggled to put my waterproof coat on, stuffing the paper plan in my pocket to try to keep it dry. After knocking again, a dog barked and the front door was finally yanked opened.

"Mr Wayland?" said a lady, holding back a sheep dog by its collar.

"Mrs Friendly?"

"Yes, it's Liz, come in and you can go outside," said Liz Friendly, hauling the dog to one side and then pushing it out into the heavy rain shower before slamming the front door behind me, "don't worry about your boots, come on through to the kitchen."

"I'm Victor, by the way," I said, following behind and dripping rainwater on the worn quarry tiles.

"That's quite a name to live up to."

"Is it?" I said.

"Well, it sounds as though you have to be victorious about something, the victor, plunging your rights of way sword into the breast of the footpath obstructer."

"I see...I haven't tried that approach yet," I said, "Victor was my grandfather's name."

"That's a coincidence, Elizabeth was my grandmother's name."

"Elizabeth and Victor," I said, "a pair of good old fashioned names."

The large kitchen had small windows making it dark but it was warm and there was a little washing drying in front of an ancient Rayburn. A family sized and much marked wooden table had one dining chair on either side of it and I sensed that we were alone in house. I mentioned when her husband Roy and I had met fifteen or so years ago and we had made some progress with sorting out the rights of way that crossed the farm. One field edge footpath served as a good connecting path between parishes and it was decided that he would fence it off from the rest of the field to keep the public and the sheep segregated.

"Roy died two years ago," she said.

"Oh, I'm sorry."

I must have shown my surprise as I thought that it was her husband that I had arranged to meet.

"No, I'm using the farm internet address which still has Roy's name on it, sorry if you thought that he was going to stroll in through the front door and whisk you off to show you what your dear old public are up to on our land."

"They're not my public," I said, after a lengthening pause, "I just look after the paths."

"That's a moot point, and I suppose you've had complaints about me?"

"Well, they mentioned the landowner which, in error, I did automatically assume was your husband and I'm very sorry to hear that he has passed away."

"Anyway, what do you want to do about it? Shall we go and take a look and if we're still on speaking terms when we come back, I'll make you a cup of tea?"

"I've got a plan of the paths," I said, taking the folded A4 paper map from my coat pocket, "which is now a bit damp."

A cup of tea after our meeting seemed an unlikely prospect when I knew I had to put some pressure on the landowner to accommodate the hoards from across the border by opening up some obstructed public footpaths. The remaining two paths on the farm that I had ignored fifteen or so years ago had both ended in cul-de-sacs on the county boundary with no continuations and therefore contributed little to the public rights of way network. It is an old adage muttered by experienced sages in such matters that public rights of way never go away, they just lay dormant for a while and then rise up and bite you on the backside when you are not expecting it. Those little paths to nowhere had now become the conduit for the hoards of cross border dog walkers from the new housing estate, turning the quiet sheep fields into an open access area. I learnt recently that the planners in the neighbouring county, with not so much as a by-your-leave, had cunningly married up the old cul de sac paths so that there could be direct access to the countryside from the new developments. As a consequence, any resulting rights of way issues were now conveniently shovelled over the border for me to deal with.

We left the farmhouse as the sun burst through the clouds and I had to shield my eyes briefly from the glare after emerging from the dimly lit kitchen. I took off my raincoat and gave it a good shake. It was far too warm, even for my thin waterproof but another heavy downpour was not very far away and so I draped it over my arm for the time being.

"Let's walk," said Liz Friendly, "and we can dodge the showers, I don't need a coat. What's that on the wheel of your van, very rustic?"

I explained about the hazel hubcap that had been made by a young volunteer.

"Lucky you," she said, "I get a bit of help at lambing time but they're not volunteers."

The sheep dog slunk beside us and we set off on a route that I had walked with her husband fifteen years before.

As we passed through the first field gate, I noticed that she had a bloody tissue clenched in her left hand.

"Have you cut yourself?" I said.

"Oh, that, I was opening a stupid sardine tin, it cut me on the fleshy bit of the palm, it will stop bleeding in a minute."

"Do you want me to put a plaster on it, I've got a first aid kit back in the van?"

"No, it'll be fine, I remember my father wandering around the farm with a six inch nail through his welly boot until my mother wrenched it out after dinner. Do you know anything about sheep Mr Wayland?"

"Please do call me Victor. No, not much apart from the fact that they seem to keel over and die at the slightest opportunity and to put it politely, they're a bit dim."

"You don't have to be polite about sheep, they're fucking stupid creatures and you're right about them dying all the time. We, I mean, I am constantly getting people ringing up and being very concerned that there's a dead sheep next to the footpath. After the third or fourth person has rung I say "yes it's still dead, it was dead this morning and I expect it will still be dead by the time that I have the time to go and pick it up." Honestly, I know that they're only trying to be helpful but this is a sheep farm not a bloody petting zoo."

We strolled on across the gently sloping downland and it was all very much as I remembered it.

"It's a nice open, undulating landscape," I said, "but it's always a surprise when you get over the brow of the hill and you can see across the vale to Elsbury which all looks a bit industrial with those old tall brick chimneys poking up above the trees."

"Across the vale?" said Liz Friendly, "you'll be lucky. You obviously haven't been over this way for a while, I think you might be in for a bit of a shock."

We continued the gentle climb across the sheep field, following a worn sheep trail towards a water trough. The sheep were scattered evenly about the field with this year's lambs now plump and mature.

"Christ," I said, as we reached the brow and I stopped to take in a completely different vista from fifteen years ago. There was no vale, no distant brick chimneys, no middle distance, nothing but a continuous band of new houses, the colour of mass produced brick and tile with a fibre glass imitation chimney popped on top. The town of Elsbury had expanded right up to the county boundary.

"When they were building it.. I had too much else to deal with and I couldn't think about the impact it would have on the farm. It's going to rain again," she said, "let's go over to that tree."

We continued in the direction of the new houses and the county boundary towards a lone sycamore tree that stood in the sheep field, fifty or so paces in from the fenceline. The rain suddenly swept in and we broke into a trot to reach the shelter of the spreading tree. Because of the direction of the rain, the far side of the trunk was the most sheltered spot but as I nipped behind the tree, stepping over the exposed roots I did not see a piece of old bent wrought iron fencing that was protruding from the ground and I banged my shin on it.

"Ow," I said, "that hurt."

I reached down and pulled up my right trouser leg and I had knocked off a large scab that had been slow to heal after a laden wheelbarrow of topsoil had tipped back and scraped down my shin a couple of weeks ago when I had been shifting soil in the garden. It started to bleed immediately and I looked for something to dab it with but could find nothing in my pockets and so I wiped it off with my fingers.

"Are you ok?"

"Yes, it's nothing, it's just an old scab but it will probably take a while to stop bleeding. We both seem to be in the wars today."

"I think that's a bit of an exaggeration. The rain's easing off now, you can see it slanting as it drifts away."

As we emerged from beneath the tree a large patch of sunlight slid across the contours of the downland, illuminating the sheep and it quickly enveloped us in its brilliance.

"Right," said Liz Friendly, shielding her eyes to look at me, "now you tell me what I can do about these wretched paths, it's hopeless, I'm fighting a losing battle here, you can see for yourself those old chewed tennis balls where they've been throwing them for the dogs to fetch. Every time I come up here I keep finding all sorts of rubbish, broken glass, plastic bags and look, there's some more dog shit over there."

We walked on down towards the wall of housing on the county boundary, to where the tarmac estate footpath emerged from between two houses and then stopped at the barbed wire fence. The fence was slack at that point where it had been clambered over repeatedly and here was the obstruction that had been reported to me.

"Let me have a look at the plan," I said, retrieving the damp paper carefully from my pocket and immediately getting a bloody thumb print in the middle of it, "this map is likely to fall apart if we're not careful. It's a copy of a section of map from the nineteen twenties at a one to two thousand five hundred scale. The boundaries are well surveyed and the paths will be marked. Actually, I think it's the very same bit of paper that I brought out when I met your husband. The quality of the photocopy paper was much better in those days."

Liz Friendly held out her left hand to rest the map on and immediately the blood from her cut bloomed out in the centre of the A4 sheet.

"Oh, god, I'm sorry," she said, manoeuvring around so that she could place her other hand under the map to support it, "it's all a bit of a mess, our blood is mingling."

"Now I need my reading glasses," I said fumbling again in my pocket and putting them on. Without thinking I then reached down to scratch the itch on my shin that was now seeping blood. With my glasses on I could see that the map was upside down and I turned it around on Liz Friendly's palm and in doing so introduced more blood from my fingers into the wet fabric of the paper.

"We'll be lucky if we can see anything in a minute," she said.

As I studied the map and looked about for any old reference points she pointed across to the parallel path one hundred yards or so across the field where a dog walker had emerged from between the houses with the dog immediately fouling on the grass and the walker continued without picking it up.

"That's what I'm up against," she said, "bloody ignorant people who don't realise the problems that un-wormed dogs cause to my sheep. Do you ever prosecute offenders? I bet you don't. Go and prosecute him, it's as plain as day, you saw it happen, we're both witness to it."

"Hang on," I said, "sorry, I've just realised something."

I looked back towards the sycamore tree and where the old metal fence remnant had caught my shin.

"And meanwhile he gets away scot free, you're very quick to rattle your rights of way sword at me but what about the public?" she said.

I pointed to the blood soaked sheet of A4.

"I think they've put their tarmac path in the wrong place. This isn't where the footpath comes up to on your side of the boundary. That sycamore tree must have started life in an old hedge line at one time and that metal thing that I scraped my shin on was part of an old fence. You can even see a slight mark in the field where that hedge or fence line was. Your footpath is a good thirty or so yards from the link that the developers have created."

I paced out along the fence line to where I believed the footpath met the county boundary.

"Here's where your path ends," I said.

On the opposite side of the fence was the wall of a pocket handkerchief sized garden with no gap or provision for a pedestrian link.

"So, they've put their gap in the wrong place?" she said.

"Yes, I think they have, if you look at the evidence on the ground."

"What does it mean?"

"Well, it means that they've got it wrong and because the houses and gardens are all set out now, they can't access directly onto the legal line of the public footpath, onto your land. I checked this old plan against our definitive map before I left the office this morning and I'm pretty sure that these paths are shown correctly on here."

"Let's look at the other path?" she said, with some excitement in her voice.

We walked along the fence line until we reached the next gap in the houses and I squinted again at the bloodied map and then looked about for similar signs and points of reference.

"Yes, I think they've done the same here, you can see a change in levels over there where a fence line used to be, probably caused by ploughing on one side and pushing up the soil towards the old field edge over many years. The old plan shows that the path should be the other side of that now removed field boundary and they've got their access at least thirty paces to the west. They really should have consulted with me first and I could have put them right."

"I'm very glad they didn't. I certainly don't remember these old field boundaries, they must have been removed before my father bought the farm. So, what now?"

"Well, on the face of it, you have not obstructed these two paths and they have now made it impossible to link up with your paths on the legal line. The public won't care about that and they'll just keep coming through where they do at the moment."

"But they'll be trespassing?"

"Well yes, I suppose they would."

"So, I could build a big fuck off wall on my side to keep the buggers out?"

"In theory, yes but there might be planning issues with building a high wall."

"I could kiss you Victor, can I keep this blood soaked map? It's our blood, it's like a pact and I'm going to dry it out and keep it."

As we walked back to the farm, Liz Friendly linked arms and

told me that she had been at her wits end and now it seemed that there was some hope at least.

I explained that is was normally my job to facilitate access not to prevent it, so it was a strange situation and it made me feel a bit odd.

"But the neighbouring county tried to pull a fast one by not telling you about their plan, it's their fault. Come on Victor, I think you've done a really good job by helping me today."

"It's the best job in the world, apparently," I said, "I've got a friend in New Orleans at the moment, playing in a jazz band. He's just sent me a postcard telling me that I've got the best job in the world but playing jazz in New Orleans seems like a pretty good job to me."

"Yes, well, the grass is always greener, I wanted to be an actress or a dancer but I'm still here being a widowed sheep farmer. Are you married Victor?"

"Er, no," I said, "no, I'm not married."

We continued in thoughtful silence until we reached the farm and after crossing the yard Liz Friendly had to shoulder open the front door of the farmhouse.

"I think the door must have swollen with the rain. You haven't got to rush off have you? I'll make that cup of tea I promised you as we're still on speaking terms and well, our blood has already mingled hasn't it? I think that must be a portent, come on inside."

The sheep dog that had silently accompanied us on our walk suddenly began to bark.

"What's up Jack, don't you want me inviting strange men into the house, for what could be a fun afternoon? What's up? Shut up a minute."

She walked back out into the yard to listen.

"There's a loose dog in with the sheep," she said, dashing into the house and returned a few moments later with a shotgun and a handful of cartridges and then ran off to an out house where a quad bike was parked. With gun broken open across her lap, Liz Friendly accelerated out of the yard with her sheep dog sprinting behind. I stood in the yard listening to the engine whine and as it faded I could hear a dog barking in the distance and the collective panic of the sheep flock. I realised that I was now holding my breath, to eliminate the sound of my own breathing but I was left with the tinnitus ringing in my ears. After what seemed like an eternity, I gave a large gasp for air as I heard a gun shot. Two gun shots and finally a third shot and then nothing.

I looked around the empty yard, empty of people as farmyards always seem to be these days. I walked back towards the farmhouse as I could not drive away leaving the front door of the farmhouse wide open. The blood soaked A4 paper map lay on the door mat where Liz Friendly must have dropped it and I picked it up between thumb and forefinger before slamming shut the rain swollen front door.

13
AGINCOURT

"HAS YOU EVER bin' married boss?" said Harrison, after I had picked him up from the swimming pool in town one morning to come out and help me for the day.

I must have paused for longer than Harrison was prepared to wait for an answer.

"Don't you remember?" he said.

"Well yes, I do remember," I said, "it's just..."

"Never mind, forget it boss. It don't matter."

Liz Friendly, the sheep farmer had asked me a similar question last week, but actually it was more specific. She had asked me whether I was married. It was as if she wanted to establish my status, was I single or in a relationship? Very briefly our two worlds had touched, we had touched when she linked arms and our blood had mingled, which she considered significant. Perhaps the rain soaked and bloodied map was the evidence of a bloodstock union that defied conventional human husbandry; a public rights of way officer and a sheep farmer?

It was the recollection of those three gun shots that haunted my thoughts. I had not been back in touch with Liz Friendly and neither had she contacted me. The bloody map had disintegrated and I had thrown it in the bin when I got home. I had heard a report on the local news that a family's golden retriever dog had slipped out of the house and run amok. It is a shock to realise that someone's pet could turn sheep killer with such raw and innate instincts so close to the surface, no longer a pet but a wild beast. It was no surprise that the sheep farmer would protect her flock, her own innate instincts of defence surfacing in an instant. My reaction was to drive away and leave her to it, which now bothered me a little. The cold facts are that an enormous housing estate being built immediately adjacent to a large sheep farm was a disastrous situation, whether the connecting paths had been legally lined up properly or not. The lure of desirable open space was there and the public would spill out onto it regardless. There could only be one winner in the longer term with Liz Friendly a lone frontierswoman, shotgun in hand.

"So, in answer to your question," I said.

"It don't matter," said Harrison.

"Well, I'm going to tell you anyway. Yes, I was married once, unsuccessfully, as it turned out. There were dogs involved, which may interest you, lots of dogs. I've never kept a dog since, a couple of cats though. It was a long time ago. No children, in case you were wondering."

"I weren't wondering boss."

"Why did you ask?"

"Dolores said somefink about it, women need to know stuff like that."

"Well, there you go," I said.

"What sort of dogs?"

"Big ones, very big ones, Newfoundlanders, as big as a small horse."

"Cool," said Harrison.

I opened the window to let out the smell of the chlorine from the swimming pool.

On the subject of dogs, I thought I would tell Harrison about the dog being shot for attacking sheep but I then suddenly realised that

I had not established with the landowner the code for the barrier that we needed to pass through, to get to site this morning.

"I bet there's no signal down there in the valley," I said, "I'd better ring the landowner before we get there."

I pulled over whilst still on the ridge and I was relieved when he answered.

"Ah Victor, yes you need to... code for...it's..."

"I'm afraid you're breaking up, please can you repeat that?"

"There's no bloody sig...it's useless..the code is.."

"No, sorry, I still didn't get that?"

"..Agincourt..."

"Pardon?"

"...you know your hist...Victor...battle.."

"But the code?" I said, with some desperation.

"...ancestors, my great... great... great.."

"Hello? hello?"

The line went dead and I tried to ring again but with no success.

"That's great," I said, "the code for the barrier seems to be an historical date but unfortunately the landowner has rather overestimated my depth of knowledge regarding the dates of various battles. Agincourt, Agincourt. It was probably during the One Hundred Years war."

"How could someone fight a war for one hundred years, they would be dead way before the end?" said Harrison.

I continued on down the hill to the valley and then turned into the gateway. We sat for a moment starring at the locked barrier.

"The first digit is bound to be a one," I said, "and the second digit is either a four or a three or it could even be a five. I saw the film again not that long ago and I have an image of Laurence Olivier in my head, giving a stirring speech to his army whilst wearing a pair of close fitting, armoured trousers, but that's not really helping very much. It was Henry the Fifth, one of Shakespeare's histories so it could have been set a century or two before he wrote it. Have you got a phone with a signal?"

"I ain't got no phone boss."

"Right," I said, ensuring that my phone did not have a signal, "I'm going to have to admit defeat and go back up onto the ridge and ring someone. I'll ring Nancy and she can look it up if she's in the office. If not, I'll ring my mate Wayne from my old quiz team, he's normally good with dates."

Harrison yawned and then got out of the van to perform a more expansive stretch. He made no move to get back in the van and instead wandered across and leant against the locked barrier. I reversed back out onto the road and retraced my tracks up to the top of the hill. There were not even any houses around, although it would be an odd request to knock on a stranger's door to establish the date of the battle of Agincourt.

Nancy answered but was not in her office. She said that she could try ringing Gina, who may know or at least she could look it up. I told her that I might try my old quiz mate Wayne first and test his general knowledge.

"It's phone a friend, is it?" said Wayne, "well, let me see.."

Wayne had a think and seemed to summon up the same image of Laurence Olivier giving a rousing speech in his tight metal trousers.

"Did we watch that film together?" I said, "that's all I could come up with as well."

"No, I haven't watched it for years but Larry's armoured legs must have made an impression on both of us."

"So, any ideas?"

"It's fourteen something...it was on St Crispin's day, I can remember that much."

"You don't know do you?" I said.

"How annoying, that is why we never won any quizzes, you need to be able to pluck these dates out of thin air. I'll look it up and text you back, sorry mate."

I ate a small handful on nuts and raisins whilst I waited for my phone to ping.

When I arrived back down in the valley, Harrison was leaning against the open barrier.

"How did that happen?" I said, "did someone from the estate come by and open it?"

Harrison shook his head.

"So, you opened it?"

Harrison nodded.

"So, you knew the date all along? And you let me drive back up the hill and I nearly got taken out by that wretched library van coming back down that was careering around a bend on the wrong side of the road, bloody maniac. You'd better lock it back up once we're inside."

Once we had passed through Harrison slammed shut the barrier and re-attached the combination lock.

"We're in, so that's the main thing," I said, once Harrison had slumped back down in the passenger seat, "and you can let me know how you opened the barrier, all in good time, no rush."

We drove along some farm access tracks until we intercepted the public bridleway.

"Well, since you haven't asked," I said, "we're replacing a couple of bridlegates today. The old ones have finally collapsed and the local bridleway group have done a couple of sponsored rides and raised enough money for two new metal gates on this path and some other stuff just over the border in Nancy's area. They've been really positive which is great. I told them where to order the gates from and I said we'd erect them. I had to load them all onto the back of the van along with all the other stuff we are going to need, on my own this morning."

Harrison did not respond.

"Anyway, the landowner is claiming poverty, it's one of the oldest families in the county, well they've been around since before the Battle of Agincourt, which we now know is 1415. They own plenty of land but he's always muttering something about death duties and inheritance tax and like all authentic aristocrats, his cuffs and shirt collars are always threadbare to the point of non-existent. He's been very good in agreeing a few official permissive paths on his land and he turns a blind eye to plenty of unofficial public inundations. I think he believes that this makes it quid pro quo, or tit for tat, when it comes to replacing gates and what not. Actually, he does have a blind eye come to think of it. He's also got a proper suit of armour in the hallway of his ancient manor house, imagine wearing something like that?"

"That is why they lost," said Harrison.

"Why who lost?"

"Them French."

"At Agincourt?"

"Yeah, the princes and all the important dudes wearing them suits, they got stuck in the mud. Some was walking and some was on horses."

"Ok?" I said.

"Their army was massive and they fort that it would be a piece of piss but they all got shot at wiv millions of arrows. Them horses went nuts and loads of the metal men drowned in the mud."

"Blimey, and didn't the French surrender? I think I can remember that much."

"Yeah, but the England king.."

"Henry the Fifth?"

"Yeah, he said kill all the prisoners, that was bad shit man."

"I remember that aspect from the film, now you mention it,

well the film of Shakespeare's play, not quite in those words though. Do you know anything about any other battles? Is it battles that you are interested in? I know that some people are. There's Naseby or the battle of Worcester? What about Passchendaele or even the first Iraqi war?"

"Why is history all done in crap battles? Why don't good fings get remembered, history is all about nutters and wars? I don't fink we learn nuffin' from history, it don't change us."

"And they say history repeats itself," I said glibly.

"Then repeat good history," said Harrison, shaking his head, "happy stuff, not wars and shit."

"Good news doesn't make headlines, it seems," I said, "oh well, let's crack on, we've got plenty to do today."

Harrison did seem to have a smattering of information about the actual battle of Agincourt which was rather mystifying. I concluded that somehow he must have remembered the date after all, despite not being into battles, or history for that matter.

We worked in relative silence, apart from the odd curse from me or a request to pass this or that. It had been an overcast morning but the skies were clearing and the sun revealed itself just before lunchtime. These days Harrison had a much better understanding of how tools worked and had begun to display an easy rhythm that comes with experience and the familiarity of using hand tools on a regular basis. I watched with some satisfaction as he twisted, tensioned and stapled the barbed wire from the old fence line to a couple of sweet chestnut posts that we had inserted alongside the new metal gate. Once he had finished it was time for lunch and I said that we would tackle the second gate in the afternoon. Harrison rarely bought any lunch these days and generally refused anything that I offered him. He had drunk half of a large plastic bottle of water during the morning but I had not seen him eat anything.

"No fanks boss," said Harrison, when I held up a cheese and tomato sandwich.

"I'd have thought you'd be hungry after all that swimming this morning and now digging holes?"

He got out of the van and wandered away towards an extremely large poplar plantation that these days would have very little commercial value. As Harrison disappeared in amongst the regularly planted ruler straight trunks of the poplar trees, I closed my eyes for a moment and savoured the silence of this place. I heard the yaffle of a green woodpecker in the distance through the open van window and the sun felt pleasantly warm on my face.

The next thing I became aware of was Harrison nudging me awake.

"Boss, wake up boss, I has seen the golden bird, for sure."

"Eh? What?" I said, blinking and trying to focus.

"The golden bird, in them woods. Has you got any bins man? Quick boss."

"What golden bird?" I said, rubbing my eyes, "what a finch? Not an eagle surely? No, don't be silly Victor, er..binoculars, yes... somewhere in here..."

"Quick boss."

I rummaged behind the passenger seat and pulled out old maps, cd's that I had forgotten about and eventually a small pair of binoculars that were covered in breadcrumbs.

Harrison snatched the binoculars from my hand and wiped the lenses on his T shirt.

"Come," said Harrison with a sense of urgency that was as rare as the burst of excitement that he had displayed a moment before.

After heaving myself out of the van, I stumbled after Harrison, towards the poplar plantation.

"Shh," said Harrison as he beckoned for me to keep up and

then pointed at the ground, "mind them dry sticks cos they makes a noise."

In amongst the fresh bed of nettles and young growth were the white and desiccated stalks of last year's nettles and umbelliferous plants. I did my best to step between them but also keep up with Harrison's pace.

The old poplars were well passed their best and many tops had snapped off and were wedged in between neighbouring trees.

"These poplar trees were planted for match making," I said in a whisper, "but never got harvested after the bottom fell out of the match industry."

"Shh," said Harrison.

"Nobody uses matches anymore."

"Shh."

"They all use cigarette lighters and now there's those vaping things as well."

"Shh."

"How do they work anyway?"

Harrison stopped and turned around to give me a stony-faced look.

I nodded to indicate that I was going to keep quiet from now on.

After I few more minutes of creeping in amongst the regular formation of the old poplar plantation, Harrison indicated that we should crouch down. As I lowered myself, my knees gave out and I sat down with an audible crushing of old dead vegetation.

"Shh."

"I am shushed," I said.

"We wait," whispered Harrison.

"Are you sure it's not a green woodpecker, I heard one earlier."

"It ain't," said Harrison, "and shh."

Waiting silently is difficult and I could feel my bottom getting damper by the minute. There were also the new fresh nettles to keep away from exposed skin and then there was the hemlock water dropwort with its large developing fronds all about us.

"That's highly poisonous," I whispered, pointing at one emerging domed floret near my face.

"Shh."

I surrendered to the cause and remained silent for what seemed like an eternity of discomfort and decided that I probably was not the right material for special forces operations or even serious ornithology.

As my mind began to wander towards whether the next test match started today, as it should traditionally do on a Thursday, or whether it started tomorrow on a Friday, which never seemed right, Harrison held up his hand. At first I didn't know whether to look or listen but then we heard a brief burst of a deep fluted whistle. Harrison quickly raised the binoculars and I could sense his taut and braced body beside me as he scanned the canopy above. I looked up to where Harrison's attention was focussed. All of a sudden there was a flash of yellow as a bird passed between two high branches.

"Is that it?" I whispered.

Harrison did not respond at first and then handed me the binoculars and pointed. The binoculars needed readjusting for my eyesight and as I looked down, Harrison touched my arm.

"There is goes," he said very quietly.

"Damn, I was just fiddling with these as you've changed them from my setting."

With the focus adjusted, I looked again but could find no burst of bright yellow in the tree canopy.

"That's it boss, I fink it's gone."

"Well, I saw something yellow.."

"It was the golden bird for sure, black wings and a red beak, it was the male."

Harrison raised himself up easily from his crouched position whilst I searched around for something to cling on to, to haul myself up.

"You'll have to give me a hand up," I said, as Harrison had begun to wander away.

Harrison returned and pulled me to my feet.

"Thank you," I said, "I was a bit stuck down there and now I've got a wet backside."

"That was really cool," said Harrison.

"I could be wrong but it may be called a golden oriole, but only because I've read the name somewhere, not that I could identify it or anything. Actually, all I saw of it was a flash of yellow. What will you do now, will you report it?"

"I guess," said Harrison.

"Perhaps other people have spotted it as well and that would really confirm it. It must be a pretty rare summer visitor?"

"It was the golden bird, for sure boss," said Harrison, with some finality.

We walked back in silence to the van and then moved on to the site where we were going to replace the second bridle gate. After fiddling with the radio for a moment and satisfying myself that the test match must be starting tomorrow, we again worked in silence but it was a thoughtful silence. Harrison's demeanour had changed from his normal ambiguous silence where I had no idea what he was thinking to a more satisfied and contented silence. I imagined that he was replaying the sighting of the golden oriole in his mind.

By the time that we had finished erecting the second bridlegate I had not given any more thought to how Harrison had summoned up the date of the battle of Agincourt along with a few scant details of the battle itself. When I stopped the van in front of the locked barrier, without prompting Harrison nipped out and unlocked the padlock, swinging open the barrier and then locking it again as we passed through. As I waited by the road junction Harrison did not immediately return to the van and I looked in the rear-view mirrors to see what he was up to. I turned off the engine and got out and he was looking back down the track towards the poplar plantation which spread across the near horizon.

"I is coming back early in the morning boss, to see if the golden bird has gone."

"How will you get here?" I said.

"I dunno, walk? Maybe borrow a bike from my bruvver?"

"I suppose I could get up really early and come out as well and then I could give you a lift?"

"Nah, it's ok boss, but fanks anyway, can you drop us at the swimming pool in town?"

"Yes, of course, swimming again? You ought to eat something first, do you want a banana?"

As we returned to the van the library van that I had narrowly avoided on the road earlier that morning, was careering back down the hill.

"Watch out," I said, "there's Stirling Moss in the library van. Look, he's just stuck the V's up to us, bloody cheek."

Harrison waved back.

"Why are you waving? Do you know him or something?" I said, "wait a minute, wait a minute. He must have passed by when I went off to ring Nancy this morning?"

Harrison remained impassive.

"But he wouldn't have stopped here, there's no houses. Did you flag him down?"

A smile broke out on Harrison's face.

"Yeah, he skidded a bit on the road," said Harrison.

"You leapt out in front of that maniac?"

"Yeah, he knew all about the Agin fing and didn't 'ave to look it up in no book. He's cool, you needs 'im in your pub quiz gang, if you wants to win. Them two fingers is what the guys wiv the long bows did to show that they still had their fingers to shoot wiv, I fink the French wanted to chop 'em off."

"I see, a veritable fountain of knowledge then?" I said.

"Yeah, and he said that if you is real lucky, you can see the golden bird in them woods that we went in, when they has flown over from Africa for the summer. We was real lucky today boss."

"Well, he was right on all counts then," I said, "even if he does drive like a lunatic."

"It's banana time," said Harrison, giving me a wink as he opened the passenger door of the van.

"Actually I quite fancy it myself now," I said, slowly lowering myself into my seat, "but you've got to go and do all that swimming. Anyway, I think you've probably earn't it, risking life and limb in the cause of volunteering on the rights of way by holding up a runaway library van to establish the date of the battle of Agincourt."

Harrison ate the banana and as we drove back up towards the ridge, my mobile phone pinged as a couple of messages came through, now that we were back in signal. I thought about asking Harrison to read them out to me but I still had not established whether he could read or not and my thoughts then drifted to thinking about Liz Friendly and her situation. Before I knew it, we were outside the swimming pool in town.

I thanked Harrison for his help today and he nodded as he grabbed the plastic bag with his still wet towel and trunks in it, from his morning swim.

"You could have hung your swimming stuff out to dry when we were working," I said.

Harrison shrugged.

"And you saw, well we both saw the golden oriole and that must be a rare event?" I said.

Harrison nodded as he pushed open the passenger door of the van.

"And don't forget to tell Dolores about, you know, me being married once, you said that she wanted to know, apparently."

Harrison frowned and then sprung out of his seat and onto the pavement in one movement.

"And I hope that you see the golden bird early tomorrow morning."

"Fanks boss," said Harrison, slamming shut the van door and walking away towards the entrance to the swimming pool with those short urgent paces.

14

THE CRICKET MATCH

"THAT'S OUTRAGEOUS," I said, out loud to myself in the office, "they can't do that, they can't build houses on a cricket pitch."

I rang the planning office immediately to protest. The planning proposal had been sent to me via e-mail as there was a public footpath in the vicinity and all planning proposals that could potentially affect a public right of way get flagged up for my attention. It was not the potential alterations to the public footpath that raised my hackles but the fact that a cricket pitch was going to disappear altogether.

"Apparently nobody uses it any more," said the appointed planning officer on the telephone, "there used to be a team but they folded a while ago. It is council owned land and quite frankly we need the money. Anyway, there's no demand for it as a cricket pitch."

"Oh yes there is," I said, hastily, "I'm going to make sure of it and we're going to be playing on it, very soon."

I had no idea who the "we" were that I had referred to and I could not think of a single person who now played cricket, including me.

That evening I rummaged about in the loft for my old cricket bag and dragged the dusty thing down into the bedroom. Just to be on the safe side I decided to try on my old cricket trousers as it had been a few years since I had last played and I did not want to discover in the changing room on the day of the match that the zip had broken. I was mortified to catch sight of this hopeless and half mast struggle in the full length mirror on the wardrobe. What had happened? It did not seem that long ago that here stood a village cricketer in his prime and full of medium pace aspiration. Delving further into my cricket bag it was all rather yellowing and crystallized but I salvaged my old jumper, boots and cricket pads. I had no idea what had happened to my bat. There would have to be some expenditure on my part if my ridiculous notion of a cricket match was to go ahead but more worryingly, at this stage, I had no idea who was going take part.

Something told me that the new director would be a cricket nut, the last one certainly was and perhaps it came with the territory. We needed some high profile involvement if the cricket pitch was to be saved and Jolyon Bellringer would be a good start. As soon as I arrived at work the next morning I sent a carefully worded invitation to his PA describing the prestigious forthcoming cricket match, mentioning that there would be celebrities present. A positive response pinged back immediately. Various names from the world of entertainment were cited and the prospect of playing on hallowed turf was keenly anticipated. I wrote the new director's name down on a blank sheet of paper and then added my own at the top of what would hopefully become a team sheet. As to hallowed turf then the dog toilet pitch and ramshackle pavilion next to Little Shits Wood, on the periphery of the large council estate in town would have to suffice. Last year there was a lot of trouble in this area and particularly in the adjacent woodland, with an outbreak of vandalism. The activities of the "Little Shits", as the perpetrators were referred to, then ceased abruptly in mysterious circumstances and the Trust Harrison gang were somehow involved in sorting this out. Anyway, there was no further trouble but I now referred to this area as Little Shits Wood.

At this stage I decided not to inform Jolyon Bellinger about the campaign to save a cricket pitch from a housing development by the local authority, of which he was the corporate director.

"Have you ever played cricket?" I said to Harrison, the next time the Trust Harrison van appeared in the yard.

Harrison shook his head slowly.

"Did somebody mention cricket?" said an unfamiliar voice from the other side of the van. I thought that I had detected cigarette smoke over the fast food aromas of the Trust Harrison van. I wondered whether Johnny Swift would appear but it was a short man, perhaps in his late sixties that stepped into view and gave me a salute.

"New recruit, Major Jennings at your service, bowled chinamen for the regiment but now got more tin in my legs than Robbie the Robot."

Major Jennings finished his cigarette and looked about him, wondering what to do with the stub and then appeared to put it in his Harris tweed jacket pocket.

"Still keen as mustard though, even if it's just a bit of umpiring."

I was surprised to encounter a new member of the Trust Harrison gang and introduced myself.

"How did...you..?" I said to Major Jennings but was really addressing Harrison or Dolores, as she emerged from under the bonnet of the van.

"Major Jennings came out and joined us when we were working in one of the parishes and has been helping out, on and off, ever since," said Dolores, "Knocker and Major Jennings are best buddies in the back there, they've been chuckling away together non-stop all week. A chatty van is a happy van as far as I'm concerned, and when you've got Marcel Marceau as a co-pilot, it makes a welcome change."

Harrison remained silent.

I explained that I had rather rashly stated that there would be a cricket match up at Little Shits Wood to try to save the old unloved pitch from becoming a housing estate.

"That's a rum do," said Major Jennings rubbing his chin, "no, we can't let that pass without a fight. Count me in."

"I can certainly do with an umpire," I said, "in fact I need an opposition to play against and another nine players in my team."

"Wait a mo," said Major Jennings, as he scurried back into the van and returned with an old safety glove.

"There you go," he said, handing it to Harrison.

Harrison frowned but accepted the glove, holding it limply between thumb and forefinger.

"Now toss it down at his feet," said Major Jennings, pointing at my walking boots.

Harrison let go of the glove and it flopped down onto the tarmac in front of me.

"There, he's thrown down the gauntlet. Now, do you accept the challenge Mr Wayland? Come on, what are you waiting for, let's shake on it."

Major Jennings grabbed Harrison's wrist and held out his hand. I took Harrison's limp hand and shook it.

"I accept the challenge," I said, as Harrison looked on impassively.

"There, now you have an opposition," said Major Jennings, rubbing his hands together in anticipation of a game of cricket.

"You'd better get practising mate," said Dolores to Harrison, "but in the meantime, we've got some clearance to do."

"Jolly good, jolly good," said Major Jennings returning to his seat in the back of the van to continue chuckling with Knocker about the old days whilst Harrison gave me a blank stare.

"There's no going back on a challenge," I said, "it's a gentleman's agreement."

Harrison yawned as the chip fat fuelled engine coughed into

action.

"You guys are history," I said, trying to inject a bit of competitive spirit into the proceedings.

"No man, the council is history," said Harrison, opening the front passenger door and swinging up into his seat.

I now found it impossible to think about anything else other than the forthcoming cricket match and back at my desk I jotted down a list of potential team names. I underlined "The Past v The Future," which seemed appropriate with "The Past", as Harrison had kindly intimated being the local authority, soon to be a thing of the past and "The Future", representing the volunteer workforce which was expected to replace all council services. I would have to dress this up a bit for the sake of the new director and sell it as tradition and heritage play the promise of the next generation, well Harrison and Dolores, if she agreed to play.

I rang and left a message, inviting Mr X to the cricket match as I had promised the new director that there would be celebrities present and having left the message, I then realised that I had not stated when or where the match was going to take place.

I thought that I ought to swing by and have a look at the cricket pitch when time permitted in my working day and fifteen minutes later I found myself parked near Little Shits Wood wondering what on earth I had been thinking of. In light drizzle I looked out upon the badly overgrown pitch and the dilapidated pavilion with its lengths of missing lapboard planking and the inevitable graffiti daubed across it.

Later on that day I managed to get a key to the pavilion from a chap in ground's maintenance who informed me that it was at least three years ago since the last game of cricket had been played on the ground. There was now no manpower or contractors engaged to undertake the maintenance work and he himself was retiring in a week's time. He beckoned for me to follow him and in a leaky shed he showed me an old gang mower that had been used to cut the council's various sports fields in the past.

"Got a trailer?" he said, "borrow it, in fact, have it for all I care. You'll be doing them a favour by taking it away."

Returning with a trailer I picked up the old gang mower, hauling it onto my trailer with the winch on the front of my van and I then left it behind the cricket pavilion under an old tarpaulin. Grown into the edge of the encroaching woodland I spotted an old ride on roller that would have been used to roll the wicket flat at some point in the past. If there was a man who could breathe life back into these old rusting and silent mechanical relics then it was Fido.

When I next caught up with the Trust Harrison gang in the yard I took the opportunity of mentioning the old mower and roller.

"Well," said Dolores, "let's ask Fido, he likes a challenge."

"That's what I hoped you'd say, that's great, thank you," I said.

I asked them how their preparations were going for the forthcoming cricket match and again it was Dolores who answered, with Harrison staring down at his feet.

"So how many people are there in a team thing?"

"Eleven and the match is three weeks on Sunday," I said, having now settled on a date.

"Hmm," said Dolores, thoughtfully, "we'll be away and flat out for the next two weekends but maybe it would be good to do something different after that?"

Harrison shrugged.

Major Jennings strolled into view from behind the van, cupping his cigarette behind his back, more in the manner of a private on patrol than a ranking officer.

"All in hand old boy, I'll knock 'em into shape, three weeks you say?"

I had no such confidence in finding nine more players and

having started the appeal in my local pub at the weekend, I had now decided to ask anyone at all regardless of age, gender or experience. A packet of cigarettes had been left in the tea room and I placed them out of sight, on the first aid kit. I did not have to wait long for a reaction. The smoker had evidently been going from room to room, quizzing staff about the whereabouts of his cigarettes and very soon arrived at my door.

"Oh, hello, do you fancy playing in a cricket match that I am organising?" I said.

"Have you seen my cigarettes?" said the smoker, ignoring my request.

"Well, let me see...I'm sure I have seen them somewhere, now where was it? What about this game of cricket then?"

"Well, I used to play a bit, but not for years...I'm sure I put them down in the kitchen?"

"I am trying to think," I said, "they were somewhere that you would not expect to see a packet of cigarettes. The game is a fortnight on Saturday?"

"Yeah, ok, whatever, are you sure you can't remember where you saw them?"

"Great, you're in the team. I've now remembered where I saw your cigarettes, for some reason they were on the top of the first aid kit, in the kitchen," I said and then called out after him, "and try and get a bit of practice in before the match."

The chap from the other end of the building's wife drove into the yard at the end of the day and I popped out swiftly to have a quick chat and I mentioned in passing the forthcoming game of cricket. Being from somewhere up north, I thought that she might be supportive.

"So, we've got this game of cricket coming up," I said, "and we're a bit short of players."

"Well, he'll play for a start," she said nodding towards her husband as he approached the car.

"Play what?" he said, looking concerned.

I waved goodbye and let them discuss the matter as they drove away.

I also sent out a few e-mails to work colleagues and whether it was through persistence or pity, I managed to cobble up three quarters of a team.

"I've got eight and a half players," I said in a message to the new director, "any suggestions?"

I was informed later that day that Jolyon Bellringer was away on annual leave and it seemed that he would return only a short time before the match.

"He's expecting celebrities," said his PA, "Jolyon's very excited."

Fido came up trumps and worked his magic on the old machinery and with Major Jenning's supervision, miraculously the outfield and square actually looked fit for a game of cricket. I swept out the pavilion and slapped some black paint over the worst of the graffiti and I even managed to jog a couple of slow laps around the pitch as a gesture towards my own physical preparation.

I happened to have Harrison in tow for a day in the week leading up to the cricket match and I parked in town at lunchtime with a note in the windscreen proclaiming that I was on council business.

I guided Harrison towards the old sports shop and I was distraught to find that it was having a closing down sale.

"That's terrible," I said, to the owner who had been part of my cricketing past by renewing the rubber grip on my bat handles and giving teams a ten percent discount on their kit.

"It's the internet," said the sports shop owner, wheezing unhealthily, "that and the big sports chains, can't compete."

The upside was that I managed to pick up all the bits and pieces I needed at fifty percent discount. I tried out a couple of bats and demonstrated to Harrison a few classic shots; the off-drive, the pull, the square cut and my bread and butter shot, the nurdle around the corner on the leg side to get me off strike.

Harrison looked on impassively.

"Ah, a new cricket ball," I said, picking out and holding up a new leather ball that was a lovely deep cherry red colour, nice and small in the hand and with a proud seam, "now there's a bowler's ball if ever there was one. Without a cricket ball then there is no contest and battle cannot commence. Here is the missile to destroy the batsman's castle, the three stumps with the bails across the top, which he must protect at all costs with his bat. Here also is the ammunition for the batsman to put the fielding opposition to the sword, flaying their attack all around the field of battle, cutting them to shreds with the ball. Cricket is war. Are you sure there's nothing you need for the game on Sunday? I don't mind..you know..helping out?"

"Nah," said Harrison.

I conducted my last ever transaction with the sports shop owner and when we got back to the van I was relieved to find that I did not have a parking ticket.

"What do you mean you've only got eight and a half players? What sort of cricket match is this?" said the new director on the eve of the game, "I'm not messing around here, we've got to win this Victor."

I was pleased that the new director's competitive instincts had taken the focus away from the portrayal of the rather grand event that I had painted initially.

"Mr X is on board," I said, making a mental note to ring him again and inform Mr X that the game was in two day's time.

"Look," said Jolyon Bellringer, "I'll commandeer three players and a scorer from this end, you can't have half a player anyway, that's nonsense. Send over the location details and I'll see you there. I've been running three miles every day along the beach in hot sun, my body is a svelte machine, I'm really up for this."

On the morning of the cricket match, the sun was shining. There was not much for me to do in the way of final preparations as the chap from the other end of the building's wife had kindly agreed to make the cricket teas. I had borrowed a water boiler from my local pub, stopped for some toilet rolls from the community shop and went around with a spade to pick up all the dog faeces from the playing area. I hauled out the old wooden cricket scoreboard and stood it up on the grass, in front of the pavilion. It seemed like all the numbers were there to hang on the board, as the score progressed. Now all we needed was people.

An old council minibus pulled up in the parking area, driven by Phil Smailes whom I had encountered last year and I recalled that he occasionally broke out into a whispered generic gangster accent, I assumed for his own entertainment.

"Thanks for driving them all here and for playing, that's great," I said.

"Dat's ok buddy, I got the hardware under the seat, right here, if it gets nasty, ok?" said Phil Smailes, who then broke out into song, "I don't like cricket, I love it...come on you lucky people..you have reached your destination."

The new director's county hall recruits disembarked with some uncertainty from the old minibus and with a bit of encouragement I managed to usher them into the old pavilion.

I had realised that as there were two teams with both women and men playing then there would have to be a separate men's and a women's changing rooms, irrespective of whose side you were on.

"Women, to the left please and men to the right, any questions?" I said as the respective genders shuffled silently into their musty accommodation.

Nancy and Gina Rosabella appeared at the open pavilion door.

"Hi Victor," said Nancy, "this is fun, I used to enjoy rounders, is it anything like rounders?"

"I actually used to play cricket," said Gina, "I opened the batting for my university, but that was a good while ago."

"That's really good news," I said, "do you fancy opening today?"

"I'll give it a go," said Gina, "ah, that smell."

"Um, everyone..can I have your attention please," I said, pointing to a heap of cricket gear on the floor of the pavilion, "I found this kit in a locker, it's all a bit ..old, but it should be ok, help yourselves, there's pads, gloves, a couple of bats that have scored a few runs by the look of them, wicket keeping gear and...stumps..and bails. So, it's game on."

I left everyone to get on with it and took the stumps out into the middle to set them up. Major Jennings had done a clear job marking out the pitch with a bright white that smelled of gloss paint. With the stumps in place I felt that old tingle of nostalgic excitement and I tried a couple of bowling dummy runs, which didn't feel too bad.

The new director had arrived independent of his co-opted team mates and was straight out to the middle to express his surprise at the venue for what he took to be a very prestigious cricket match.

"This isn't what I imagined at all," said Jolyon Bellringer.

"It's one of the oldest grounds in the district, apparently," I said.

"Is it?" said the new director, surveying the adjacent sprawling council housing estate.

"Yes, it's steeped in history," I said, "as befits our team. We represent the heritage and tradition of the past, our opponents today are brimming with youth and anticipation for everything that is to come and that is why our team is "The Past" and they are "The Future.""

"I see," said the new director, glowering at the old pavilion, "I know bullshit when I smell it..but I am also a fierce protector of our traditions as you know and cricket is cricket, after all. I can't pretend that I am not a little disappointed Victor, but now I'm here, you'd better introduce your captain to the team."

"Actually, I'm the skipper today," I said, "and anyway, it's only a bit of fun."

"Fun?" said Jolyon Bellringer, blinking and looking confused.

The Trust Harrison van coughed itself to a halt, briefly enticing the office workers out of the pavilion to investigate the source of the fried food aromas.

Eventually everyone who was participating in the day had arrived. I was impatient to get on with it and so I chivvied Harrison out into the middle for the all important toss.

"Not changed into your whites yet skip?" I said, with coin in hand, ready to flip, "heads or tails?"

Harrison frowned. After a while of explaining that coins had a head on one side and a tail on the other side, even though there was no actual tail depicted on the coin, Harrison picked the coin up and looked at it.

I tossed it again and Harrison rubbed his chin.

"Well?" I said.

"Why?" said Harrison eventually.

"Ok," I said, "we'll field and your team can have a bat, ok? Otherwise we'll be here all day at this rate."

I delivered the news to our team that we were fielding and clapped my hands enthusiastically to encourage them from the sanctuary of the pavilion.

Taking to the field to play cricket is a pleasure that I never thought I would experience again. Some fielders jog, others sprint whilst some just stroll out exuding calmness and confidence, under the eyes of the opposition. Our team, The Past, took to the field as though they were dutifully exercising a fire drill after having to vacate the building and were now mustering uncertainly, awaiting the all clear. I clapped my hands again and then produced a spare cricket ball from my trouser pocket and tossed it to Dave Barlow from comms. The ball was then passed between them in a very health and safety conscious sort of a way until the new director got hold of it and hurled the ball aggressively at Phil Smailes who managed to duck out of the way.

"Ok buddy, if you're gonna play hard ball then you'd bedda watchya back from now on," muttered Phil Smailes, under his breath and then raised his hand and called out politely, "I'll go," as he trotted after the ball to retrieve it.

Still smarting from being denied the captaincy, Jolyon Bellringer was insistent that he was going to open the bowling. I reluctantly handed over my new ball and after trying to explain the fielding positions to our team and receiving plenty of blank looks in return, I asked them all just to spread out.

Major Jennings was to stand as umpire at both ends and we were eventually underway. Gina Bellarosa was doing a fine job keeping wicket as there were plenty of balls being bowled high, wide and handsome and she managed to stop most of them. We had settled on five overs maximum per bowler so that most people could get the opportunity to bowl and after all, this was supposed to be a friendly match where the participants were either very rusty, like me, or had never played cricket before in their life.

The game ticked along with extras leading the scoring and the unlikely sights of Ollie, Knocker and Council Peter all attired in whitish clothing and swinging the bat, which in Council Peter's case, was one handed.

Nigel was a revelation and strode purposefully to the wicket, after Fido had been dismissed walking back onto his own stumps. Nigel began with deft touches, calling Dolores through for ones and twos. With ease he managed to dominate the strike, protecting his inexperienced partner so that they could build a decent partnership. When he was into his thirties he began expanding his strokeplay with a series of glorious shots all around the wicket. I brought the new director back on for his last two overs and he was immediately dispatched for a succession of straight sixes, back over his head. Nigel acknowledged his fifty and when he got to seventy two he then fell asleep, leaning on his bat and was gleefully run out by the chap from the other end of the building as Dolores called Nigel through for a leg bye.

I was keeping my bowling powder dry for when Harrison appeared at the crease and after a considerable wait he eventually emerged from the pavilion, after the fall of Nigel's wicket.

"Skipper in, team," I called out to the fielding side and we all clapped the new batsman in.

Harrison wandered slowly out to the middle, dragging his bat behind him and wearing what appeared to be a karate suit, barefooted and with no pads or gloves. He looked about him, at the stumps, the wicket keeper and the white lines and made no preparatory effort to face the bowler.

"Are you ready batsman?" said Major Jennings, "do you want a guard?"

Harrison gave the umpire a quizzical look.

"No man," he said, eventually.

"He hasn't got any protection," I said to the umpire, "I mean nothing, no shoes or anything and I bet he isn't even wearing a box, I asked him in the sports shop if he needed any kit and here he is wearing some sort of martial arts outfit."

"Play," said Major Jennings loudly, dismissing my concerns.

It is very disconcerting for the bowler when the batsman is just standing nonchalantly, holding his bat as if it were an unfamiliar curiosity and more importantly, not even looking in the bowler's direction.

"Just aim for the stumps Victor," I told myself, as I prepared to run up and bowl.

I used to love the pause before the moment of bowling, as the fielders prepared to walk in, it was the ultimate focussing of attention on the movement of the batsman, on the action that was about to unfold, on the ball about to be bowled. Cricket is a feast of inactivity for most of the time. When you drive by a cricket match in progress, despite craning your neck to take in the action, there is seldom any action. It is either between overs or the ball is being lobbed slowly between the fielders on its way back to the bowler who then polishes it madly on his groin. In that time you will have driven by and the game is out of sight and nothing will have happened.

The act of bowling is the trigger for something to happen, a burst of action with the ball now in play. As a bowler lets go of the ball, you tend to know when it feels right. As part of a bowling spell you know when you are in good rhythm, whether you are in control, whether the pitch is helping to deviate the ball or whether the batsman is more bent on survival than attack. In this instance, before I had bowled a single ball, I had no such feelings. The ball seemed alien in my hand with no muscle memory that I could draw upon. Neither were there any signals coming back from the batsman, no indication in his stance, no twitch to betray him advancing down the wicket, no look of intent in his eye, that old unnerving gunslinger's stare, you move first and I'm going to shoot you dead. Nothing. It was as though in such passive circumstances and with Harrison just standing there, there was nothing to attack, no duel. Consequently, I did not let go of the cricket ball and stumbled in my follow through, to end up in a heap on the cut strip.

"Are you ok Victor?" said Nancy, skipping up from mid-off.

"Yes, yes," I said, clambering up onto all fours and dusting myself off before heaving myself up to trudge back to my mark to start all over again.

The umpire signalled "dead ball" and nothing had happened.

On my second attempt I released the ball with Harrison seemingly looking elsewhere but at the very last moment, just before the ball clattered into the stumps, the bat somehow intervened, slicing through the air with the flourish of a musketeer's rapier. It all happened so quickly that nobody knew where the ball had ended up before a dog walker near the pavilion tossed it back to the nearest fielder.

Major Jennings wafted his arm back and forth to indicate the boundary. I told myself that this was surely a fluke but by the end of the over Harrison had successfully defended his wicket and had scored twelve runs. With all the reactions of an uncatchable house fly, Harrison seemed to have invented a new martial art and no amount of my lumbering in with a cricket ball was going to endanger his wicket or inconvenience him in any way. On a number of occasions he did not look in my direction at all or move a muscle as the ball simply drifted slowly by into the gloves of the wicket keeper. It was a great surprise when Harrison gently guided a ball straight into the hands of the smoker who was fielding at point and then walked off with his characteristic short urgent paces, having scored thirty eight runs.

The remainder of the innings comprised three of the Little Shits, who up until last year had been terrorising the locals in the neighbouring wood and vandalising the pavilion but now seemed very enthusiastic about playing cricket. The three lads scored another fifty runs between them and the eventual total for The Futures on the old scoreboard was one hundred and ninety three runs.

"Well," I said to my team as we wandered from the field, "that's a decent total. Anyway, let's enjoy our tea first before we worry about that."

I was about to wake Nigel up and congratulate him on his fine knock when the chap from the other end of the building beckoned me over into a corner.

"Psst, Victor," he said, "it's vegan, the cricket tea is vegan, don't ask me why, I had no idea until this morning. My youngest daughter came along and high-jacked the whole thing, the worst of it is I think my wife might have become radicalised. Anyway, my daughter's now refusing to stay and help after I said that I was looking forward to hearing the sound of leather on willow. You can't veganise cricket can you?"

"I see," I said, not knowing quite what to say.

"Listen, between you and me, I bought a couple of tins of spam from the garage and I've got them in the boot of the car. I'll let you have the key and then you can go and devour it somewhere."

"That's nice," I said, "slobbering over a tin of processed meat behind the pavilion like some self conscious hyaena. What about the normal cricket tea sandwiches, you know like cheese and pickle, egg and cress or ham and tomato?"

"There's keen-wah apparently, whatever that is and you're going to have to eat it out of a cup with a tea spoon. Look out, here's the wife now, appear pleased for christsakes."

"Oh, hello," I said, "thank you so much for going to all this trouble."

"It's no trouble pet, if you're anything like him, you'll eat any old muck but we couldn't be having that now could we? Oh yes, I've brought some tea towels."

"Thanks," I said, "that's very kind, you'll have to let me know how much it has all cost you and I'll settle up."

The scorer, who was the council's chief finance officer by day, then approached me to say that they had never scored at a cricket match before and did I have a spreadsheet that she could use instead of the cricket score book. Whilst I went through the scoring procedure and rectified a few details in the book, the cricket tea was being served. By the time that I picked up a paper plate and with some trepidation, approached the trestle table, there was very little left.

"I've managed to save you a couple of sandwiches and a scone, pet," said the chap from the other end of the building's wife, "I'm afraid they wolfed up the quinoa salad but there's hummus and cucumber in the sandwiches and there's fruit compote and some coconut cream for the scone."

"Thank you very much," I said, accepting a cup of tea as well with something in it that looked milky but was not milk, "er..that's great, much appreciated."

I sat down next to Dolores and Harrison.

"That vegan tea was amazing," said Dolores.

"Yes, I remain to be convinced about a vegan cricket tea I'm afraid, some things are just too sacred to be messed about with, but everyone seems to have tucked in," I said, between mouthfuls of sandwich, "mmm.. and well batted you two, by the way."

"I enjoyed it, it was fun," said Dolores, "and what about Nige, he's a bit of a dark horse isn't he?"

"Absolutely, fabulous batting and so light on his feet. What about you skip," I said, looking across at Harrison, "you rather gave your wicket away?"

Harrison scratched the top of his head in a passable Stan Laurel impersonation, although he probably did not realise it.

After thoroughly enjoying the two heavily laden halves of my scone I suddenly remembered that I had intended to do a team photo after tea and between us we carried the long wooden benches from inside the pavilion and placed them end to end on the grass. Without prompting, the new director sat down at the front, in the middle and everyone else either sat wherever they could or stood behind.

"What could be better than sitting between two lovely ladies?"

said Major Jennings, squeezing in between Nancy and Gina Rosabella.

Once we were all arranged then there was nobody to take the photograph and so Dave Barlow from comms hailed a passing dog walker and handed him my digital camera.

"Say cheese," said the dog walker, aiming the camera, "why is you all pointing at me?"

"It's your wretched dog, behind you," said the new director, "it's crapping on our pitch."

"I'll get a spade," I called out, from the end of the bench, "just please take the photo, thank you."

After the photo had been taken, I quickly followed up with my spade as I was keen to get the second innings underway.

Gina Rosabella made a confident start and a couple of wickets fell at the other end. The new director stated that he always batted at four and jamming his old university cap on his head, he then strode purposefully out to the middle. For a while the game assumed the atmosphere of cricket as I remembered it, slow, steady with unruffled progress by the batsman amidst the odd appeal by the bowler. The click of bat on ball and the mild, absorbing tension sensed in an ambient way by all the participants of the game amidst the acres of inactivity. The new director then ran Gina Rosabella out when she was on forty nine, refusing to run an easy two as it would get him off strike for the beginning of the next over.

We all clapped Gina Rosabella back in.

"Brilliant," I said, as I passed Gina on my way out into the middle.

Council Peter was now bowling and having run a three off the first ball of the over it took me a while to get my breath back.

I took guard and batting suddenly seemed very unfamiliar. I could not remember how I used to stand but told myself over and again just to watch the ball.

Council Peter lobbed the ball up and it landed half way down the wicket, coming to a halt before it reached me. I was about to step out of my crease and toss it back to the bowler who was obviously not really a bowler.

"Hit it man," shrieked the new director, from twenty two yards away, "just smash it."

Perhaps it was my lack of a killer instinct that had kept me languishing in the lower ranks whilst the new director had clawed his way to the top, winning at all costs and thinking nothing of smashing a sedentary cricket ball bowled by a one armed man in a friendly cricket match.

"Christ Wayland, if you don't club that ball to kingdom come then I'm going to make your.."

My instinct was to toss the ball back but somehow the raw moment now took hold of me and with the new director still screaming insensibly I stepped out and hit the ball with all my might. Like a golfer teeing off but without the elevation, the ball fizzed back towards the bowler.

"Yes," yelled the new director in full battle cry, leaving his crease and beginning his charge up the wicket.

Council Peter did not move as the ball hurtled towards him, striking his left hand that was not a left hand but a stainless steel hook and deflecting dramatically to clatter into the wickets at the bowler's end.

"Howzat?" shouted one of the Little Shits from the boundary.

The umpire nodded and raised his finger. The new director stopped in his tracks, marooned in the centre of the pitch. I was very relieved that Council Peter had not suffered an injury as he rubbed his hook with his good hand.

"You're out sir," said Major Jennings, "on your way batsman."

"But I can't be out," said the new director.

"The bowler deflected the ball onto the stumps."

"Yes, but not with his hand, it was with that metal hook thing, that's not a hand. It's an appendage, I'm definitely not out."

"Look batsman, I am the umpire and I have given you out. You're out."

"What does it say in the rules then?" said the new director.

"I haven't got a blasted rule book with me man but when the umpire gives you out, you're damn well out and I don't need a rule book to know that."

"Bring me my phone," shouted Jolyon Bellringer to his PA on the boundary, "I'm not leaving the wicket until I have some clarification."

There is nothing like a long halt in proceedings to kick the stuffing out of a day with players wandering from the field in search of fags or beer or just to sit down. In the end the new director was pacing about on his own, out in the middle with his mobile phone, trying to get hold of anyone who could tell him what he wanted to hear.

The umpire called for the drawing of the stumps and that was game over.

"It's a draw," said Major Jennings, shaking his head, "a fine example to set the young 'uns, I'm sure. Grisly business, the chap's a bounder and no mistake."

It was not at all a satisfactory conclusion to events but everyone seemed to have enjoyed the day. I thanked everyone who had participated and expressed particular thanks for the cricket tea which received a hearty round of applause. I stated that we had achieved what I hoped we could do, which was to make a point by playing a game of cricket on this old pitch to ensure that cricket had returned.

"Three cheers for cricket," said Major Jennings, raising his old regimental cap, "hip, hip.."

"HOORAY", shouted out one and all and twice more.

"Well played skip," I said to Harrison, as we shook hands, "we should do this again next year, what do you say, we've got to use this pitch to have any chance of saving it, the Past versus the Future?"

Harrison thought about this for a moment and then nodded slowly.

"Yeah, maybe." he said, "nuffin' happens, but that's cool."

Mr X had not made an appearance and I wondered whether I had rung the right number, but it did not matter anyway. After clearing up and with the prospect of stiff muscles in the morning, I drove home to feed my cat and was looking forward to soaking in a nice deep bath. Everyone else had drifted away, apart from the new director who was still talking on his mobile phone, whilst pacing up and down the twenty two yard strip, amidst the exercising dogs from the adjacent housing estate.

15
DOG DAYS

"YOU'VE GOT A very red face Victor," said the chap from the other end of the building when I encountered him in the kitchen, waiting for the kettle to boil.

"Have I?" I said.

"Yes, you've caught the sun."

"Now you come to mention it, my face does feel a bit tight."

"I wouldn't say that it was tight, exactly."

"Thanks, I said it feels tight. I have been outside all morning and I was out working in the garden for most of the weekend."

"No sun cream?"

"Well, no, actually."

"Hat?"

"No, I guess I didn't realise how strong the sun was."

"Tut, tut, you ought to know better Victor."

"Anyway, what's the matter with you?" I said, "you keep grimacing and rubbing your stomach."

"Oh, it's been making all sorts of strange noises this morning. Something's going on."

I went into the gents to look at myself in the mirror and my face was quite red.

"I'm not following you, honestly," said the chap from the other end of the building as he thrust open the gents toilet door, edging past me as I stood in front of the mirror and he then hurried into a cubicle, locking it behind him, "I seem to be a bit out of kilter, I think it must be the heat. I read in the paper this morning that these are the dog days, when Sirius, the dog star, ascends before dawn ..excuse me.. and dogs and men flop around the place, whilst the women become aroused.."

"That's fascinating, but I'd better get on," I said, nipping back out into the corridor.

I returned to my desk to answer some e-mails and the old electric fan that I had only just plugged in when I returned to the office after lunch, had now stopped working.

"That's great," I said out loud, "come back Fido, all is forgiven, I bet you'd fix it in a jiffy."

Certainly the summer had suddenly burst into life over the last few days but it was an oppressive heat that made you feel sweaty and lethargic.

I think that I must have closed my eyes for a moment and lolled forward in my chair as the ringing phone made me jump.

"Hi, Victor? It's Liz Friendly, remember me, the dog murderer?"

"Oh, er..hello," I said, trying to wake myself up and be coherent, "I wouldn't say that, I mean you were just protecting your flock."

"Well, that's what I've been called by your charming public, a dog murderer."

"They're not my public," I said, "I just look after.."

"Anyway, you pushed off pretty quick on that day?"

"Well, er..I don't know.. I didn't know what I could do really, you'd just shot a dog and.."

"And you just shot off in your van."

"Well..yes...I suppose I did," I said.

"And we had some unfinished business."

"Oh," I said, "it's very hot and humid isn't it?"

"What's the weather got to do with it? What I want to know is what the hell do I do now? I can't shoot all the dogs on the new housing estate, can I?"

"No, not really," I said.

"Look, please call back round to the farm, when you're passing next and I'll make you that cup of tea I promised you. Oh yes and I couldn't find that map, you know, the one with our blood on it?"

"I don't.. um.. I haven't.."

"Anyway, I'll see you very soon, ok Victor?"

"Yes, I'll call in, I will call in."

After I put the phone down I was pleased to hear the Trust Harrison van clatter into the yard and I went to see what they were up to.

"I've got something for you Mr Wayland," said Dolores, as she got out from behind the wheel, "there you go, that's the money you lent us to buy the old scrap parkland fencing. We've now made up some gates and sold a few, so, thanks very much."

Dolores handed over two hundred pounds in twenty pound notes.

"Blimey," I said, "thank you, are you sure that you don't need it..for anything..?"

"The Hunter Scavenger Café has opened up again for a couple of days a week, so we're doing ok thanks, but that was really helpful to get us started with the gates."

Harrison nodded and yawned simultaneously from the passenger seat of the van.

"It's hot isn't it?" I said, "you know, a bit close? Where are you working at the moment?"

"All over," said Dolores, "when old Rip Van Winkle there manages to stay awake."

Harrison closed his eyes and sank down further into his seat.

"Actually, I could do with his help one day this week?" I said.

"What day?" said Harrison, after a long pause, with his eyes still closed.

"Is Thursday ok?"

"Pick us up from the pool, same time."

"Great, thanks," I said.

Dolores smiled.

"Good, well that's it, we just wanted to sort out the money," said Dolores, who then gave me a kiss on the cheek, "thanks Mr Wayland."

"Yeah, fanks," said Harrison, opening one eye.

"I must dig out my Cuban cap, obviously they look a lot better on you," I said, "but I seem to have got a sun burnt face and a cap with a peak might be a good idea."

"You're looking good Mr Wayland, healthy, tanned and handsome, watch out all you ladies of the countryside," said Dolores.

"Yeah, watch out," said Harrison, with his eyes closed again.

"Right," I said, backing away across the yard as Dolores gave me a little wave before returning to the van and driving off.

A trip to the pub the night before invariably means a nocturnal visit to the bathroom and as I was stumbling about before dawn I caught sight of a conspicuous star through the open bathroom window. It was low in the sky and bright but also flickering and fiery. It had been a warm night and after returning to bed I slept skittishly until the alarm clock woke me at seven. Harrison was coming out with me today and so I packed an extra banana in my lunchbox.

Before I picked up Harrison from outside the swimming pool I spent an hour in the office and was about to leave when the new director's PA rang up to tell me that Mr X wanted to see me at his house this afternoon.

"Why can't he just ring me up himself like any normal person?" I said.

"Jolyon wants to do it this way, he wants to be kept in the loop, so, I'll say you'll get there about three o' clock, shall I?"

"Well," I said, "I suppose so, but it'll probably be a waste of .."

"OK, goodbye," said Jolyon Bellringer's PA.

I could probably still get the work done that I had in mind with Harrison's help, before I went to meet Mr X.

Harrison was yawning as he walked towards the van from the swimming pool entrance. The plastic bag containing his wet swimming stuff was chucked into the passenger floor well, along with a large bottle of water and he slumped down into his seat.

"Thanks for coming out today," I said.

Harrison yawned again.

As we drove away, Harrison muttered something and I resisted the temptation to ask him to repeat it and instead tried to work it out for myself.

"My hearing isn't brilliant but it sounded like you said "for a while, I has to be dog" but as that is rather unlikely, I'll plump for you saying that "for a while, you has to bring a dog"? Was I close?"

"It don't matter boss," said Harrison.

"Well, you haven't brought a dog, so..? Anyway, we're working in a field with cattle present so bringing a dog would not have been a good idea."

"Cows don't like me, that ain't going to work," said Harrison, with a hint of animation in his voice.

"But they'll lose interest, they always do."

"Nah, they'll go nuts, trust me boss," said Harrison, glancing across at me to emphasize his statement.

We continued to the site where we were going to be working and I pulled up beside the track next to the first of the two old stiles in the fencing that we were going to be replacing.

"Well, there are cattle in the field," I said, "cows with calves, by the look of it."

"Bad idea," said Harrison, "I can't go in that field."

"Why not? Obviously I realise that you have to be very cautious when there are cows with calves but we don't have to cross the field or anything."

"Ok, you watch."

Harrison got out and jumped over the old wobbly stile whilst I observed through the open window.

"First you watches out for the one who is boss," said Harrison, "she'll be hidden in the middle of them cows, yeah, there she is, she has already sussed us out. They has probably smelled us before they has seen us. The rest will wait to see what she does."

Harrison walked further out into the field.

"Her head is down and her ears is forward."

"Which one is she, I can't tell the difference?"

"She has some space around her, her tail is flying about and she is shittin' like a good 'un. They is the signs, 'ere we go."

Suddenly the cattle broke into a run, bellowing as they thundered across the dry ground towards us.

Harrison hopped back over the stile and walked back towards the van.

The cattle managed to stop their charge just before the stile but were now pressed up against the fence, stamping the ground and raising dust with their heads all turned towards Harrison. The calves had hung back but the bulk of the herd was intent on making their feelings known in no uncertain terms.

"There you goes boss," shouted Harrison, above the sound of the agitated cattle.

"Ok, but why is that? They're sort of behaving as if you have a dog with you, or something?"

Harrison nodded.

The only way that this was going to work was if Harrison caused a distraction across the other side of the field and I could then get on and replace the stile.

"I was rather hoping that you would give me a hand, but..."

Harrison walked off along the outside of the fence and the mob of incensed cows pursued him closely, uninhibited in their vocal protest.

I had no choice but to replace the old stile myself. The noise from the other side of the field was unrelenting and I got on with the work as quickly as I could.

Once I had finished I waved with both arms to indicate to Harrison that he could now return. On his way back, the herd rampaged around the perimeter of the field and once Harrison was in the van I drove a good distance away from the cattle field so that we could eat our lunch in peace.

"That was hot work" I said, "working on my own."

Harrison drank deeply from his bottle of water and then slid down into his seat, closing his eyes.

After lunch, the second stile was replaced in identical fashion, with me sweating profusely and Harrison getting bellowed at as he distracted the cattle.

The last thing I felt like doing after that was going to meet Mr X about whatever it was that was bothering him. There was no way that I could drop Harrison off first so he had to accompany me to the meeting at three o clock and I informed him of this as we left site.

"Sorry about this, but the director's PA has arranged it."

Harrison shrugged and if he was annoyed at being made late for his afternoon swim, he did not show it.

I had arranged to rendezvous with Mr X in the same place as

last time, next to the stable block, two hundred yards or so down his main drive from the house. I stated who I was into the intercom at the gate and that I was meeting with the owner.

"And who is that beside you?" said the responding voice.

"This happened the last time I came," I said, "that will be my assistant."

"Mr X was only expecting you."

"It's ok, his name is Harrison and he is perfectly harmless."

The conversation with the remote gatekeeper ended and after a lengthy pause the double gates slowly opened.

"Sorry," I said to Harrison, "I don't know why we have to go through this rigmarole."

Mr X was waiting beside the stable block, his pearl white 4x4 had obviously now been repaired.

"Mr Wayland," said Mr X, "thank you so much for coming out. Who is that sitting in the van?"

"That is Harrison, I think you've met him before?"

"We certainly have, haven't we Larry G?" said Mr X, addressing the very small dog in his arms, "Harrison is the maker of the woven hubcap, which I see is still in place incidentally, but we don't really know what to make of him do we?"

Harrison got out of the van and raised a hand slightly, in acknowledgement.

"Yes, and hello to you too, Harrison the silent one."

"So, um," I said, "how can I help?"

"Well, isn't it hot? It's so hot all the time. Anyway, I've had a bit of a scare and this is strictly confidential you understand, cover your ears Harrison. My doctor has told me that I am morbidly obese, well I said, does that mean that I am dead as well as fat? Anyway, he was being very serious and said that I might well...just die... if I don't lose a lot of weight. So, I've got to change my diet completely and take lots of regular exercise, which is where you come in."

"Well, there's plenty of places to walk, just get a map of the local area. You could start walking from here, from your own land."

"There you are, that's why I've asked you to come, you know these things."

"You just need to...take your dog for a walk, like everybody else does."

"But Mr Wayland, look at Larry G.. look at his tincy wincy legs, he gets tired just walking across the kitchen and I couldn't follow a map."

Harrison stopped leaning against the van and walked up to Mr X with his right hand held out.

"So, now you want to say hello and shake my hand, do you young man?"

"No," said Harrison, "give us the dog,"

"Well, I don't know about that, but Larry seems keen, what are you going to do with him? There you are then, but be careful with him, he's only got little bones."

Harrison took the dog and placed it on the ground.

"Oh dear, Larry doesn't really like grass," said Mr X.

Harrison walked away and kept walking towards a small dense copse of bushes and then disappeared from view.

"Where's he gone?" said Mr X.

Larry G ran off towards the small copse, in pursuit of Harrison and then disappeared.

Mr X stood open mouthed, alternately looking between me and the small copse.

"Do something," said Mr X, eventually.

At that moment the small dog re-emerged from the small copse and walked back towards us. When it got within a few feet it sat down and stared at Mr X.

Mr X stooped down to retrieve the dog but it got up and sat down again, just out of reach.

"What has that nasty Harrison done to you Larry G? You've gone all blank and unfriendly. Look, Mr Wayland, this is all very upsetting and I'm going to take him home."

The small dog got up and trotted away from us, in the direction of the fields and the footpaths. He then stopped to look back at Mr X.

"He's waiting for me, he wants me to come, he wants me to go for a walk, he wants to save my life. I'm coming Larry G. Goodbye Mr Wayland."

As Mr X retreated into the distance, in pursuit of a very small dog, I wandered over towards the small copse. There was no sign of Harrison. I sat in the van and waited for a while but Harrison did not reappear. I beeped the horn a couple of times before I decided that Harrison must have just wandered off, or walked back to his house, wherever that was. I drove away, reassuring myself that I had no choice, I couldn't wait there forever, for him to return. Harrison had gone, that much was clear.

I had no way of communicating with Harrison, as he claimed not to own a mobile phone and Dolores always came up number withheld if she ever rang me. All I could do was wait for the Trust Harrison van to appear in the yard and hopefully Harrison would be sitting asleep in the passenger seat. It was the following Monday morning when the Trust Harrison van clattered into the yard.

"I haven't seen him since last week," said Dolores, "I dunno where he is. God, it's been hot and steamy, it's hard to sleep isn't it? I've only got a sheet on my bed at the moment and I have to throw that off during the night and then you try and do something during the day and you end up sweating like a right ...sweaty thing."

"Um, yes," I said, "it's like most weather extremes, we're not really used to it, are we? Anyway, I suppose I'd better get back to my desk and answer a few e-mails, but do you think you could let me know if, or rather when, he turns up again?"

At home I gave Harrison's swimming trunks and towel a wash, making sure that I put some fabric conditioner in with the towel. I then stowed them in the van, in case I should bump in to Harrison at some point.

As the days passed I got on with other stuff. Dolores came and went with the lads in the van but she just shrugged when I enquired about Harrison.

One morning I woke up wondering, at what stage do you submit a missing persons report? It rather depended on who was supposedly missing, which in this case was Harrison and as he was so unpredictable, it was hard to gauge. Dolores was a means to gauge any concern but after a couple of weeks, even she had begun to ask me whether I had heard anything of Harrison's whereabouts. On a Monday morning, I was just looking up how to file a missing person's report, when the phone rang. It was the new director's PA asking me to call in to see Mr X in the afternoon.

"Look," I said, "I can't help Mr X, he just wants to see me when there is anything remotely relating to the countryside, I seem to be his go to contact when he's bored and he then drives the two hundred yards or so down from his house to meet me and tell me that he needs some exercise."

"Shall we say three pm?" said the new director's PA.

"I suppose so," I said.

The weather had cooled a little after a crashing thunderstorm the night before which now made working life more bearable. Just before 3 'o clock I arrived at the gates to Mr X's house and was let in with no inquisition. Mr X was waiting in the usual spot but this time there was no pearl white 4x4 parked by the stable block and Larry G was trotting around on the grass.

"Mr Wayland, I'm going to call you Victor from now on, good afternoon, no Harrison today?"

"No, not today," I said, I refrained from telling Mr X that I had not seen Harrison since my last visit, "so, how can I help?"

"Well, I think you have helped enormously, look at me, I've lost almost a stone and I've nearly worn out a pair of boots already. Larry G here has taken my condition very seriously and has been unrelenting, unrelenting I say, in getting me to walk absolutely everywhere. I've even been walking around London, no cabs for me and Larry G. I just wanted to thank you in person Victor, you're probably wondering what all the fuss is about and I'm sure it's all very obvious to you, you know... the great miracle of walking."

"Well... that's good," I said, "I'm really glad that you've discovered walking. I suppose I do take it a bit for granted and I'm just doing my job, really."

"Oh, look out, Larry G is off. He's going over to those bushes again, you haven't got Harrison lurking in there have you?"

The little dog disappeared into the small copse. A moment later it re-emerged barking and trotting and running up to Mr X, pawing at his shins.

"You're barking again Larry, I haven't heard your little voice for weeks. No, I'm not picking you up, it's all about walking now isn't it? We love walking don't we, it makes us happy."

"Well, if that's everything?" I said.

"Yes, I just wanted to say thank you, thank you for doing your wonderful job and I think it must be the best job in the whole wide world?"

"Some would say so," I said.

"I've got lots of maps now and the director has given me some special maps of your footpaths on great big sheets of paper."

"That would be the individual parish maps, parts of the county's definitive map."

"The definitive map, listen to us Larry G, we're talking about the definitive map, who'd have thought it? Until the next time then ..Victor.. and I'll tell you all about my walking plans...and...there'll be an important announcement very soon, but it's all very exciting and hush hush."

Mr X turned and began to walk back to his house whilst the little dog yapped at his heels.

I returned to my van and on the way back home I was wondering again about Harrison and decided that I really must do something formal about alerting the authorities. He was a person and he was missing, so something ought to be done about it. I then saw a figure, walking along the road ahead of me, holding out their thumb in an unexpectant kind of a way. I had not picked up a hitchhiker for years but something made me slow down and then stop, to offer them a lift. I reached across, stretching to wind down the window and looking up at the hitchhiker, I then realised that it was Harrison.

"Oh, hello, that's a surprise," I said, "long time no see?"

"Hi, man," said Harrison.

"Well, I was just thinking that I hadn't picked up a hitchhiker for years and when I do, it turns out to be you. Where have you been, I was almost getting worried about you? The last time I saw you, you disappeared after walking into some bushes?"

"Yeah, I walked a long way after that."

"Ok, so do you want a lift, or...not?"

Harrison paused, and then opened the passenger door to slump down into the seat.

"You can wind up the window, if you want, it's a bit cooler now after that thunderstorm last night," I said, as I set off.

"It's ok," said Harrison.

"So, you've been away somewhere, was it a walking holiday?"

Harrison nodded.

"Yeah, I bin' to loads of places," he said, after a pause, "can you drop us in town?"

"I've got your swimming stuff here, all washed and dried. I could drop you at the swimming baths, you know, if you wanted to have a swim?"

Harrison thought about this for a moment.

"Yeah, the pool is cool."

No more information was forthcoming and I pulled up outside the swimming pool in town.

"There's your stuff, I expect you're looking forward to that swim? Oh yes, and here's a banana."

Harrison nodded and then got out of the van.

"Fanks for the lift.. and the banana and stuff," he said, holding up the plastic bag with his swimming trunks and towel in it.

I watched him walk away and his pace was measured and less urgent than normal but I felt a sense of relief that I did not have to report him as a missing person.

I popped down the pub later on that evening but stayed a bit longer than I intended. In the night, before dawn, I got up to go to the bathroom but I could not see the fiery and flickering star, the dog star Sirius, that had been low on the horizon, the last few times that I had been stumbling about in the early morning.

16

IRON IN THE FIRE

IT ALL STARTED a few weeks ago, back before Harrison's unexplained disappearance. Actually, you could say that it all began with the dissatisfied parents Jupiter and Juno, casting their ugly red faced new born, named Vulcan, from the top of Mount Olympus. How far back do you want to go as it could quite reasonably be suggested that it all started with the formation of planet Earth?

"Has you one of them geo fingy maps?" said Harrison, when he had called into my office one morning, a few weeks ago.

"A geological map?"

Harrison nodded slowly.

"Of this area?"

Harrison nodded again.

"I think I've got one in the loft, it's probably at least twenty five years old but then I don't expect the geology will have changed much since then. I'll dig it out. Old joke?"

Harrison nodded slowly and left.

A couple of days later when the Trust Harrison van had called into the yard, I had wandered down with the geological map and posted in through the open passenger door window to Harrison. There had been no explanation given and I thought no more about it.

The morning after Harrison's return, when I had picked him up in the afternoon hitchhiking, he arrived in the yard with Dolores.

"Good morning Mr Wayland," said Dolores, from under the bonnet of the van, "we're just dropping off a few bits and pieces and we'll be in and out over the next couple of days. We'll make sure that we're not in the way."

"Ok," I said, "no lads today?"

"No, just me and the boy wonder, at the moment."

"Any...you know...information forthcoming?" I said, nodding towards Harrison.

Harrison was standing beside the van with his eyes closed and his ear plugs in, listening to something and swaying gently.

"Look at him," said Dolores, "he doesn't give a ..hoot..that he's just dodged a load of hard graft when we've been getting everything together for this."

"Together for what?" I said, "or shouldn't I ask?"

"It'll be fine Mr Wayland, but it's good that it's cooled down a bit, it's been tough working in that heat."

"Yes, so you said, do you need a hand with anything?" I said.

"No, but thanks anyway, actually we've got a bit of help arriving shortly," said Dolores, slamming shut the bonnet of the van and wiping her hands on an oily rag.

"Ok, I'll leave you to it then," I said.

I had not long returned to my desk to answer some e-mails, when a large motorbike crept slowly into the yard with a pillion rider on the back. When they had parked up down the end and taken off their helmets, I could see that it was Harrison's brother Marlon and Fido, with his unmistakable black hair and tan beard combination. After periodically looking up from my computer screen, I got the impression that there was plenty of stuff being manoeuvred from the side door of the Trust Harrison van.

"Good morning," I said.

"Good morning Mr Wayland," said Marlon, politely.

Fido was evidently too busy thinking to say hello.

"Can I offer anyone a cup of tea?" I said, "obviously it's just an excuse to come out here and see what you're all up to, but it is a genuine offer nonetheless."

Only Harrison declined and Marlon answered for Fido. Five minutes later I returned with four mugs of tea on an old tray, a teaspoon and another mug with some sugar in it.

"You can sort your own sugar requirements," I said, placing the tray down on the tarmac and picking up my own mug.

Marlon bent down and took a mug of hot tea and then poured most of it into the mug that I had quarter filled with sugar. He then stirred the resulting sugar sludge with the tea spoon a couple of times, before handing it to Fido who then drank it down in one go.

"Ok," I said, sipping my tea, "I think I might burn my throat if I attempted that."

"Fido thrives on heat," said Dolores.

"And sugar, by the look of it," I said.

I had become increasingly fascinated by Fido after having observed him more closely at the cricket match. His heavy limp had become more apparent during the game, as he dragged one foot along the ground, but to prevent his boot from wearing through he had rivetted a thick portion of car tyre to the sole. His dragging foot in no way impeded the speed that he was able to operate, with his limp foot just following behind in the wake of his determined and ferocious activity. His face was red and sorrowful but that could change dramatically when a smile broke out and then it was as if his head had suddenly been turned upside down and gravity had taken over. His upwards, smiling head would not be in response to a joke, or some humorous remark but to things working out as planned. His interests seemed very specific and focussed and he was obviously in charge of the day's proceedings, whatever they were. There were many clear plastic sacks containing large balls of wet clay with what looked like hay mixed in with it, two plastic barrels of water and a bucket of water, a multitude of heavy iron tools, an anvil, lots of bags of charcoal, a huge log, a couple of sheaths of stiff water read and a few buckets of a crumbled, rust coloured stone.

After thinking things through Fido then suddenly began hauling stuff around, pointing and barking instructions and events were underway.

"Oh, Mr Wayland," said Dolores, "whilst you're here, could you just test the clay for us, it needs someone with clean hands?"

"Ok," I said.

Dolores took a large ball of clay from one of the sacks.

"Dip your hand in that water first and just stick your fingers straight in there."

"Like this?" I said.

"That's it, all the way, yes that looks fine, don't you think?" said Dolores, looking around towards the others.

"Perfect," said Marlon, "the clay's got sheep dung in it as well, so you might want to wash that off."

"Right," I said, instinctively sniffing my hand.

"Thanks Mr Wayland," said Dolores.

"Fido is just doin' what you asked for," said Harrison, collecting up the drained cups and handing them back to me on the tray, "fanks boss."

"Thank you," I said.

I returned the cups to the kitchen and then scrubbed my fingers clean before washing up the cups, all the while wondering what it was that I had asked Fido for.

I had not spoken to Nancy for a while and so I gave her a ring.

"I've no idea what they are up to," I said, after describing the activities in the yard, "but they're building something with lots of clay and it involves fire, by the look of it. Apparently, they are doing what I asked for but I can't recall asking for anything, I think that I'm just going to ignore it. Luckily there's hardly anyone around here in the office at the moment as most of them are away on annual leave."

"When are you taking your holiday then Victor?" said Nancy.

"Me?"

"Yes you, you must have loads of leave to take?"

"Oh, I don't know, I'll think of something. Maybe go on a walking holiday in another county and then complain about the state of their rights of way, that might be therapeutic."

"You've been saying that ever since I started, ten or so years ago."

"Have I? God how boring. What about you?"

"We're off to Italy for two weeks in September, you know, Florence and then Rome and after that we'll be walking in the heel of Italy for a few days, right down South. Gina's got some relations in Puglia."

"Great, that sounds fun."

I wanted to tell Nancy about Harrison's unexplained disappearance but as the only conclusion that I could come to was so outlandish and in no way plausible, I could not bring myself to give it any credence by putting it into words. Harrison could not have actually transformed himself into a small dog, even for a couple of weeks. There had to be another explanation.

"It's been so hot hasn't it?" said Nancy, "thank goodness it's cooled down a bit now."

"It was the dog days, apparently, when Sirius, the dog star, ascends before dawn and dogs and men flop around the place.....and the women..."

"And the women just get on with it as usual?" said Nancy.

"Something like that."

"Well, take care then Victor and sort out a holiday, better still, sort out someone to go on holiday with?"

"I have got one iron, vaguely pointing in the direction of the fire, but it's very early days."

"Well, that sounds encouraging Victor, do it, just go for it, life is passing you by. Dive in, you have to start somewhere."

"We'll see," I said.

"Bye then Victor and thanks for ringing."

I stared at Liz Friendly's phone number on my note pad and then went out to inspect a missing drain cover on a byway.

The next day, things really were taking shape at the bottom of the yard but until later in the afternoon, there was no sign of the Trust Harrison gang.

"What's that thing down the bottom of the car park?" said the chap from the other end of the building, as we passed in the corridor, "is that something to do with Che Guevara and his crew?"

"Yes, I think that they must be making bread, or something," I said, vaguely.

"Well, they'll have done a full safety audit and a risk assessment, I imagine?"

"Oh yes, probably," I said, "it's all in hand."

"Should we be informing the fire safety officer?"

"I don't think there's any need for that," I said.

"You realise that I am effectively in charge this week, whilst everyone's away, so bear that in mind when the loaves are being handed out."

"Right," I said, "I've always had you singled out as someone ripe for more responsibility, combined with your obvious integrity."

"Thank you," he said, as he returned back to the other end of the building.

The Trust Harrison van appeared late on in the afternoon and Dolores dropped Harrison off before driving back out again. I watched from my office window as Harrison pulled out the long sheaf of stiff reed from the top of the tall clay chimney.

"I'm going to stay on and lock up," I said to the chap from the other end of the building, as he entered my office to find out why I had not gone home yet.

"You've planned it this way, haven't you?" he said, pointing out of my window towards the bottom of the yard, where plumes of smoke were now billowing out of the clay chimney, "and now I'm going to miss out on the bread?"

"Your loaf is secure," I said.

In the event of there not being any bread baked on the premises, I would just buy him some sort of rustic loaf from the bakery in town and that would keep him quiet. After his wife had picked him up and they had driven back out of the yard, I walked down to see Harrison.

"We has to dry it out first, wiv a small fire," said Harrison.

"Ok," I said.

I had the words formed in my mind to ask him about his unexplained disappearance, as it seemed like the perfect opportunity, but instead I found myself asking Harrison something entirely different. Perhaps it was the thing that was uppermost in my mind. Harrison had returned after all and I would find out, in time, what it was that Fido was making me, that I could not remember asking for.

"You know when I told you that I had been married before?" I said, cautiously, as the swirling smoke briefly enveloped Harrison, "it's sort of picking up that same conversation, which you actually started incidentally, where it left off, a few weeks ago, if you remember?"

Harrison poked at the small fire of dry brushwood that he was controlling at the base of the drying clay chimney.

"Anyway, I got married, years ago and it was a bad decision," I said, "I just didn't know it, at the time. But, how do you know? How can you be sure, that you're making the right decision?"

"Is you seeing someone?" said Harrison, eventually.

"Well, no, but it's sort of hanging in the air and I feel that it is up to me, to make the next move? That's the decision that I have to make. I am at a crossroads and which way do I go?"

I do not know why I thought that a young man of twenty three or four years of age would have gained enough life experience to answer this conundrum, but I felt better just voicing these thoughts. Harrison was resourceful and that was reason enough to ask.

"Is it that dog shootin' woman?" said Harrison.

"What?" I said, "how the..how did you know?"

"We has done some stuff on her farm."

"You've spoken to her, about me?"

"I ain't," said Harrison.

"Somebody has?"

"She had big problems," said Harrison.

"Yes, problems that I am unable to help her with. You just said "had""?

"Yeah, she has sold it already and she gets rid of her sheep at the next market."

"The big sheep fairs in September? She has already sold the farm?"

"Maybe three months ago."

"That would be before my visit and the dog shooting incident?"

In the ensuing silence, Harrison added a little more dried hazel brushwood to the fire. I stared at the small conflagration for quite a while, absorbing this new information.

"I is goin' to be a couple more hours boss," said Harrison, interrupting my thoughts.

"Sorry," I said, "I'll leave you to it, please just make sure that you snap shut the lock on the main gate when you go?"

I drove home with the realisation that Dolores must have acted as a kind of matchmaker in all this and I was stunned that Harrison had known all about it anyway. Being resourceful is one thing, but all-knowing is something entirely different.

"Today's the day, Mr Wayland," said Dolores, when I walked down to the bottom of the yard, hoping to talk to her about her matchmaking activities, but it was all a bit busy. Fido had his upside down head on with a look of wild excitement in his eye.

"Ok, is it a significant day?" I said, "what is the date today anyway?"

"August the twenty third," said Marlon, "today, we make iron."

"They were speculating in the office that you were making bread, but I knew all along that the oven was the wrong shape," I said.

"It's not an oven, it's a furnace," said Marlon, "we'll be pushing fourteen hundred degrees C later on."

"Wow, and what's that rusty looking stuff in the buckets?"

"That's iron ore, we collected that from one of your footpaths," said Marlon.

"So that's why Harrison wanted the geological map a few weeks back?"

"Yep, we worked out where the right geological areas were, where surface iron ore might exist. It took us a couple of weeks of hunting but we found it. We've roasted the ore and crushed it a bit and we then add that with plenty of the charcoal that we've made in the coppice. We've got an old hairdryer that we can plug into the cigarette lighter in the van and that's our bellows, our air supply, it's been modified it a bit."

"Apparently you're making something that I asked Fido for?"

"Ah, yes," said Marlon, with a smile, "all being well, but there's a lot to do before we get to that stage. We need iron first."

"Well, I'll leave you to it," I said, thinking that I would approach Dolores when things were a little less hectic.

"No bread yet," said the chap from the other end of the building, popping his head around the office door, after I had returned to my desk.

"No, not yet, you'll have to be patient, these are artisans at work. Any idea what's significant about today's date, August the twenty third?"

"Well that's simple, it's Geoff Capes' birthday, shotputter, strongman but more significantly, he was president of the budgerigar society, a bit of a hero of mine."

"I see, well that'll probably be it then." I said.

"So, don't forget my loaf Victor? By the way, the selling of the depot for housing has been put on hold for some reason, so you can stop packing up for now."

"Ok, thanks," I said, not having packed anything anyway.

I got on with answering some e-mails and resisted going back down to the furnace until I saw the smoker deviate from his well trodden route to the front gate, being drawn instead to the conspicuous conflagration in the car park. I hurried down to the bottom of the yard to catch up with him.

"Is it another strike?" he said, lighting a cigarette.

"No, just a sort of experiment," I said, vaguely.

Nobody paid much attention to our presence until the smoker, having finished his cigarette, was about to pop it down the flaming chimney.

"No," said Fido, gripping his arm.

"Oh?" said the smoker.

"No," said Fido again, his grip unrelenting.

"Ok," said the smoker, who was then released to stub out his cigarette on the tarmac and he wandered back to the office with the extinguished butt in his hand.

I stayed on to have a better look at proceedings. The furnace was now humming with the intense heat generated and the combustion gases were acrid and unfamiliar. The clay chimney was patchy with areas already dried out and cracking and other parts still darker with retained moisture. Smoke or steam crept about the structure, some finding its way through small cracks in the clay. The charges of crushed iron ore and charcoal were poured in with a metal scoop at the top of the chimney at frequent and regular intervals and each time flames shot up, causing heat distortions in the air, beyond the furnace. Fido called out something to Dolores, who then responded by dipping the metal scoop into a plastic bag, she then cast what looked like loose corn into the top of the furnace, immediately withdrawing away from the intense heat.

The last charges of iron ore and charcoal were added and a small thermometer, that had been buried into the wall of the furnace was checked regularly. I felt compelled to stay and watch, fascinated by this intensity that had been created out of a few basic raw materials.

Finally, looks were exchanged and Fido grabbed a long metal poker, and broke open the aperture at the base that had been blocked up with clay and sand. Immediately a blazing flow of molten liquid trickled forth, spreading out onto a concrete slab that had been positioned for that purpose. Fido poked about, encouraging more of this blinding residue to be released from the smelting process. The flow was short lived as it cooled rapidly, turning from brilliant orange to a dull grey, but with the shape of the flow preserved.

"That's the smelting slag," said Marlon, "now he's going for the money."

Fido, his face raging with delight, then wrestled a pair of giant iron forceps into the aperture at the base, wriggling and pushing his way through the intensely bright, molten accumulation.

"Ahhh," he said, with satisfaction, "gotcha."

He then withdrew the coagulated fiery bloom of freshly formed iron, the size of a large human brain, and slammed it down onto an old stumpy log, where it branded itself into the wood, flaming and steaming and Dolores and Harrison then rained sledgehammer blows down onto this fiery solid mass, with sparks flying in all directions.

It had been an intense and brutal birth and I had viewed the whole procedure like an uninvited guest, peering from behind the immediate family.

A forge had been prepared, in advance, in an old clay lined wheel barrow and the darkening mass of iron was quickly heated up again, with the hair drier now being directed to the base of the fire in the forge. Repeated heating and beatings of the infant iron on the anvil, quickly squared up and reduced the size of the lump and my ears were ringing with the intensity of these blows. I withdrew, whilst everyone's attention was on the process in hand and returned to my desk.

"Well, I'm off home," said the chap from the other end of the building, popping his head around my office door, "those artisan bakers are noisy blighters aren't they?"

"I'll get your loaf to you in the morning," I said.

"Excellent," he said, glancing out of my office window, "ah, here's the wife now."

I stayed on for another hour, feeling a pang of responsibility for the proceedings at the bottom of the yard but my cat needed feeding and so I left them to it, with an assurance that they would not burn the place down and would lock the gate on their way out. I also made a mental note to call in at the bakers in town in the morning, to buy a small loaf.

Later that evening there was a knock on my front door and it was Marlon, standing on the doorstep, holding his crash helmet.

"Hello Mr Wayland," said Marlon.

"Oh? Hello," I said, "I think I must have nodded off. Um.. would you like to come in?"

I had made a recent resolution to invite callers into the house and not leave them on the doorstep. This was after some reflection about Hywel, the first aider, who had kindly seen me home after the branch had fallen on my head and I had not invited him in.

"No," said Marlon, "that won't be necessary, but thanks anyway. I just wanted to give you something. Something that you asked Fido for, a while ago."

"I don't remember asking him for anything, I think there's been some sort of misunderstanding?"

"No misunderstanding," said Marlon, calmly as he held out a closed fist.

He nodded for me to open my hand to receive whatever it was that I had apparently asked for. As Marlon opened his hand, there was a gentle chink of metal and I felt something in my palm.

"A ring?" I said, inspecting my open hand, "in fact two rings. Are they made of iron, is that what that whole operation in the yard was about?"

"Try it," said Marlon, "the bigger one."

I slid the larger solid iron ring over the third finger of my right hand. It fitted perfectly and I turned the ring around and around.

"It's a perfect fit," I said, "how did that happen?"

"Clay?" said Marlon, "sheep shit?"

"I see, very...clever. But what about this one, who is that for?"

Marlon shook his head gently.

"It's for a much more slender finger?" I said.

Marlon nodded slowly. Leadbelly had just woken up and after

wandering sleepily out into the hall, he took one look at Marlon and bolted, clattering out of the cat flap in the back door.

"Goodnight then, Mr Wayland," said Marlon, turning to leave.

"Hang on, don't go," I said.

Marlon retreated down the path.

"But I'm really confused," I said, "..um..how do I find out who this other ring is for, it's obviously meant for someone?"

Marlon stopped and then returned to my door step, placing his crash helmet down carefully on the concrete path.

"There are unimaginable forces," he said, pointing down at the ground, at my feet.

"Under my doormat?"

Marlon smiled.

"Way, way below your doormat. Around the earth's solid iron core is an outer core of molten liquid iron. In this swirling mass there are currents, even a jet stream, these are extremes beyond our comprehension," he looked me in the eye, unsmiling, unblinking and then brought his hands together in front of him as if to cup an imaginary cricket ball, or the centre of the earth, "inside here is generated the earth's magnetism and polarity, but it's all in a state of flux."

Marlon's brow puckered to display his uncertainty as his hands continued to caress this uncertain sphere.

"At some point in time, maybe next month, next century, next millennium, next whatever, this polarity...is going to...shift," he said, suddenly twisting his cupped hands completely around, "and that will be interesting."

He then pulled his hands apart and I involuntarily twitched, as if I needed to catch this uncertain object that had been left to fall.

Marlon smiled and picked up his crash helmet.

"Goodnight Mr Wayland," he said, turning and walking back down the path.

I closed the front door slowly and shortly afterwards I heard a motorbike start up and then drive off. I located my reading glasses and sat back down in my armchair to study the two rings. They had both been formed in the same way, with a very narrow strip of iron being beaten into the round and the two ends meeting to leave barely a gap. I racked my brain to think about any conversation that I had previously had with Fido. When I had no option but to ask him to move back out of my tin shed, when he had been furiously fixing things, I think I ended up by saying that circumstances may change at some point in the future. It was a very laudable service that Fido was providing. I was probably just softening the blow but I had asked him to get back in touch sometime and give me a ring. Fido, I now realised, was someone who could not differentiate between literal meanings and implied meanings and had done exactly what I had asked for, he had given me a ring, in fact he had given me two rings.

"I'm really confused," I said to Nancy, after I had rung her to tell her all about the strange goings on, "and tired, I didn't sleep a wink last night."

"How extraordinary," said Nancy, "even by Harrison and the gang's standards, that is extraordinary, but I'm really intrigued about the second ring? Who is it intended for?"

"I have no idea," I said.

"Well you've got to find out. Somebody out there is waiting for that ring and they probably don't even realise it."

"But it's all based on a misunderstanding," I said.

"Nonsense Victor, don't be ridiculous," said Nancy, "there are forces at work."

"You're not kidding," I said, staring down at the threadbare carpet in my office and trying to imagine the centre of the earth.

Nancy stated that she was late for a meeting and had to go but insisted on regular updates about the mysterious second ring.

When I had first arrived at work, quite a bit earlier than usual, I had purposefully driven down to the bottom of the yard but any evidence of iron smelting or forging had been removed. It was only the ring on my finger and the smaller ring in my pocket that demonstrated that an ancient activity had been performed in the depot car park yesterday. This very same activity had transformed the world and enabled the modern world to exist, as we know it today. I thought about Marlon's words, spoken softly on my doorstep, about the possibility of a polemic shift at any time. I thought about the effect that this would have on a modern digital world, a world so complex and delicately poised. I then saw the chap from the other end of the building being dropped off in the yard, by his wife.

"Bugger," I said, out loud to myself, scurrying to locate my van keys, "I didn't buy that sodding loaf in town."

17
BOB STRIMMERMAN

"WHY DO YOU keep whistling that Helen Shapiro song?" I said, to the chap from the other end of the building, after I'd heard his fluted whistling coming from the kitchen for the umpteenth time.

"Walking Back to Happiness? Did you recognise it? My wife always says that I am a tuneless whistler, amongst other things. Yes, it's on the radio a lot with Mr X doing some walking weight loss campaign. He's going to walk all the paths in the county where there is a X in the name of the parish, apparently."

"He told me that he had something planned involving walking and I'd forgotten all about him doing that song," I said, "actually, I'm probably instrumental in him recording that song, in a roundabout kind of way."

"No, no, Victor, I think you'll find that it was solely the new director's idea, he's certainly been on the radio taking all the credit."

"Of course, silly me. He hasn't been in touch since the cricket match at Little Shits Wood. I think he was a bit miffed that it wasn't at Lords." I said.

"Miffed? He showed himself up to be a bad sport and his refusal to leave the crease after he had been given out by the umpire was very poor, very poor indeed."

He went off whistling and before setting out on my rounds in the van, I tuned into the local radio station.

Mr X singing "Walking Back to Happiness" came on almost immediately and it was fairly faithful rendition of the song albeit with a bit of a clunky key change towards the end. There was some talk about his progress and how many followers there were out on the ground and thousands more on social media.

"I thought I'd be walking on my own but there always someone to chat to," said Mr X, "and...we've met so many lovely dogs, haven't we Larry G? I'll be back on those bathroom scales live on the show on Saturday night so..tune in ..and.. I'm HAPPY...yeah. Walking back to happiness, woopah oh yeah yeah..."

It all sounded very positive and he was over in a large parish in Nancy's area, walking all the paths in Boxworth because there was a letter X in the parish name. After the next record there was a report about a man who wished to remain anonymous but was so fed up with overgrown public footpaths that he had bought a strimmer and set to work.

"Suddenly, from out of nowhere," said the mid-Atlantic tones of the radio presenter, "public rights of way have become the new rock and roll. There's Mr X singing Walking Back to Happiness as he's tramping the paths and now we've got an anonymous guy out cutting footpaths with a strimmer. He's been strimming his heart out, night and day, he's tangled up in green, god bless him and so.. we've decided to give him a rock and roll name, let's hear it for BAAAAAB STRRRRIMMERMAAAAN. Yes, Bob Strimmerman, so, we've caught up with Bob and I've got him on the line right now. Bob?"

"Hello?"

"Is that Bob Strimmerman?"

"No, I mean..er..I suppose so, yes."

"Tell us what you're doing out there Bob?"

"I'm strimming."

"And why are you strimming Bob?"

"Because all the footpaths are overgrown and I'm doing something about it,"

"Surely the council should be doing it, that's what we all pay our rates for isn't it?"

"I've tried to get them to do it but the man said not to bother him."

"Ok, so the guy responsible for clearing the paths, when you contacted him, said "don't bother me about it"?"

"Yes, well, actually it was at a darts match."

"I remember you," I said, sitting bolt upright in my seat, as I was driving through town, heading west.

"He just said, ring me up when I'm at work," said Bob Strimmerman.

"Hang on a minute," I said, "I was throwing my darts at the time and you were blatantly trying to put me off, Bob Strimmerman indeed, I'll strimmer you..."

We lost that darts match because I had been deliberately put off mid throw and I had intended to complain to the league about it, but it must have slipped my mind.

"So, there we have it, the man from the council just didn't care," said the radio presenter, "that was Bob Strimmerman, not his real name, he wants to remain anonymous so we've given him a rock and roll name. We'll be back to check up on Bob's progress later on and, of course, we'll be catching up with Mr X, but now, it's competition time, what did I have for dinner last night....?"

"I bet he wants to remain anonymous," I said, turning the radio off with a jab of my finger, "making accusations like that. I may have to break a rule of a lifetime and ring up that wretched radio station to put the record straight."

I reached across into the glove compartment and found a Bessie

Smith cd to put it on.

"I need a little sugar in my bowl," sang Bessie Smith.

Periodically during the day, I took out the slender second ring and turned it around and around between my thumb and forefinger. It was a simple and beautiful object. I thought about Liz Friendly and envisaged the bloody map, being passed between us and I recalled her gnarled, working hands. She would have had different looking hands if she had fulfilled her childhood dream to become an actress or a dancer, but this second ring was intended for somebody else, someone with slender fingers, elegant even. It is a very significant event to offer or accept a ring. Supposing I did not want to get married? This was all very hypothetical and I could dismiss it all if it were not for the two rings, one of which was definitely mine. Perhaps if I accidentally lost the second ring then that would be the end of the matter and Harrison and the gang would not bother to go to all that trouble again? However, by the presence of a second, much smaller ring, one decision had been made for me. Things had moved on and this was not just Dolores doing a bit of voluntary matchmaking. As Nancy had said, there are forces at work.

The next morning Harrison walked past my window and was let in by the smoker, on his way out.

"'As you any small nails for these?" said Harrison, entering my office.

"Good morning," I said, turning the iron ring around on my finger, making sure that my hands were in full view, "you've got some waymarks? Let me see? Is that Chinese writing?"

"Yeah, they is paid for by the Chinese," said Harrison, ignoring my ring turning display.

"Yes, that's great but they don't actually have to be written in Chinese, or Mandarin, do they?"

Harrison shrugged.

"It don't matter, you just follow the signs," he said.

"Well, I suppose that's true, but it's just a bit odd. There's loads of different characters, what does it all mean?"

"It means you don't have to pay for them and we is putting them up."

"I know, I should be grateful, please thank your sponsors from me."

"Has you got any nails boss?"

"Oh yes, no, I haven't," I said, locating my wallet, "..but here's five pounds."

Harrison frowned as he took the money.

"Fanks boss," he said, as he left.

"And please get me a receipt," I called out after him as an afterthought, raising my voice in the hope that I could still be heard, "not that we operate a petty cash system anymore and another thing, I haven't thanked you for the iron ring, or rather the iron rings."

Harrison had gone and I had the feeling that the Trust Harrison gang would all be a bit tight lipped about the two rings. From the outset, this was going to be a waiting game.

The distraction of the activities of Mr X and Bob Strimmerman, out there on the public rights of way network, meant that I was forced to listen to snippets of local radio, until I got incensed and turned it off again.

Nancy rang and said that she had heard about the anonymous man out clearing public footpaths, night and day.

"Why do all these good things keep happening in your area Victor?"

"Well, you're welcome to Bob Strimmerman, for a start," I said.

"But he's out there, night and day, strimming his..what nots off, by the sound of it."

"I'll strim his flippin' what nots off," I said.

"Don't be so ungrateful Victor."

"Our darts team got relegated because of him."

"What's darts got to do with anything?" said Nancy.

"And they've been giving the council a good kicking on the radio, as usual, we're a soft target aren't we? The radio presenter said that "the guy from the council just didn't care"."

"Well, ring them up and tell them that you do care."

"And another thing, it's detracting from Mr X's walking campaign, which is really positive and he seems to have got the nation behind him. They'll be people out there, actually getting up off their sofas and going for a walk. He's out in your area at the moment, isn't he?"

"Yes, it's amazing isn't it?" said Nancy, "but because he is walking every path in those parishes, there are some that just don't go anywhere, or there are bridges missing or they are obstructed and that then raises all sorts of other issues but it doesn't seem to be putting him off. So, any news on the second ring?"

"That's why you've rung isn't it?"

"Well, come on Victor, we can't stand the suspense," said Nancy.

"Don't worry," I said, "you and Gina will be the first to know, if there are any developments."

Later that morning the chap from the other end of the building popped his head around the door.

"I hear that you've got some help clearing your paths? Isn't it strange what some folk are prepared to do, he's out there strimming his nadgers off, night and day, doing your job.."

"I'll strim his wretched nadgers off," I said.

"Oh, dear Victor, you don't seem very pleased about it? I thought you thrived on volunteers, over in the rights of way department?"

"He won't be covered through our volunteer insurance as I

don't even know what his name is, or whether he is trained to use a strimmer, or where he is working, or..."

"Sorry, forget that I mentioned it, I've obviously struck a bit of a nerve," he said, retreating back to the other end of the building.

I had a missing footbridge to inspect and I set out in radio silence. I tried to empty my mind of all the circulating thoughts that were keeping me awake at night.

There is a point after the harvest when the narrow country lanes are lined with gold. This is the fresh golden straw, snatched from the enormous passing bale carts by the tight, thorny bankside hedges where it swirls about a bit before settling to gleam in the sun along each verge. Soon a heavy downpour will wash it all off down the lane to block the drains but today was a gleaming day. I parked up and followed a path over some uneven pasture land, down towards a stream in a wooded valley. I had been trying to locate my digital camera over the last couple of days with no success as I wanted to photograph the stepping stones that provided access across the stream. I had received a complaint, a while back, suggesting that a proper bridge was the answer, especially for the winter when the stream was much more active. I had no money for a bridge but promised to take a look and it was a good excuse to get out and walk in a remote and beautiful part of my area. There was a certain charm about the stepping stones, and the path was even referred to as "Stepping Stones", so there was more to it than just finding the money for a new bridge. I had got into trouble year's ago after installing some effective drainage in a byway called Watery Lane. Similarly I had been accused of levelling the "Humpy Bumpy Path" and perhaps a greater crime against local custom and distinctiveness was being instrumental in moving the Mill Path, well away from the mill.

In the heavily dappled shade, I sensed someone approaching as they negotiated the slope on the far bank, making their way down towards the stepping stones and the chattering brook. It is often very useful to ask people, whilst they are using the actual routes, what they think of any proposed changes.

"Ah, good," I said, "a member of public."

A lady emerged from the shadows and steadied herself in preparation to step across the stream. She had long amber hair and was wearing a white linen dress with black plimsols on her feet and no socks.

"We were thinking of erecting a footbridge here," I said.

"Are you talking to me?" said the lady.

"Sorry, yes I was."

"A footbridge? why?" said the lady, as the second stone wobbled

on her way across the placidly flowing brook. One reaching my side of the bank she stood to observe me with her hands behind her back.

"It's not always like this," I said, "it flows faster and deeper in the winter."

"I don't come this way in the winter," she said, "I like it in the summer. You don't often meet people on this path?"

"I just wanted to have a look down here, to access the situation with the stepping stones. You don't have a dog?" I said.

"No, why?"

"I just wondered.."

"Why would you wonder whether I have a dog or not, you've no idea who I am?"

"No, but, it's just that most people do walk dogs, they don't very often walk on their own, without a dog," I said, feeling a bit red faced, bordering on embarrassment.

"I prefer walking on my own," said the lady, "I just like walking and I don't need a reason or an excuse."

"Actually, I like walking on my own as well," I said, "and I haven't got a dog either."

"Well, that's nice, perhaps we should start an antisocial walking club, one's company but two's a crowd and no dogs?" said the lady, smiling, as she began to walk on.

"But you haven't answered my question about the bridge?" I said.

"Would it make more people use this path?" said the lady, pausing.

"Maybe, well yes, that would be the idea."

"Well, as a founder member of the antisocial walking club, then the answer is no, don't build a bridge."

"But you wouldn't have to wobble across those stones?"

"I can assure you that I didn't wobble."

"Not you," I said, hastily, "it was the stone that was wobbling."

I then apologised for not introducing myself at the outset and explained who I was.

"Well Victor, meet Victoria," she said, revealing her hand for the first time and offering it up to be shaken.

"Ok, hello Victoria," I said, shaking her hand.

"Victor and Victoria," she said, releasing my hand and walking on slowly, but pausing to look back at me, "so much in common that they nearly shared the same Christian name? But seriously, you had better get other people's views on the question of a new bridge. I think I'm probably just being selfish. It's a quiet path so you might have a long wait for somebody else to come along."

Victoria continued on her way, without any further backward glances, as she climbed up the path, away from the stream. I waited until she had disappeared from view before returning back towards the van.

That evening I took off my iron ring and placed it in a drawer along with the smaller iron ring. It was too much to think about, carrying around a ring that would determine my future and that was affecting my behaviour. Victoria at the stepping stones had struck me as an interesting person, probably a bit younger than me and yet once we had shaken hands, I knew that the slender ring would never fit her normal sized fingers. This was a ridiculous scenario and why was I making such presumptions about people anyway? It was as though the iron had now taken possession of me and then there was the prospect of the world turning upside down at some uncertain point in the future. All I wanted was a decent night's sleep and I would try to forget about the two rings.

The next day, curiosity got the better of me and I turned the radio on in the van when I was out on my rounds.

"..And he eats when he refuels," said a caller, giving an update on Bob Strimmerman's progress.

"So, he is refuelling himself and the strimmer at the same time?" said the radio presenter.

"Yes," said the caller.

"And sleep?" said the radio presenter, "surely he's got to sleep?"

"He says that he's not going to sleep properly until he gets to his mother's house in the village of Hammerbridge."

"Just like Motorhead then?" said the radio presenter, laughing at his own joke, "yes folks, that's no sleep 'til Hammerbridge for Bob Strimmerman? Rock and roll."

"Actually, he's an Abba fan."

"Is he now? Well you can tell Bob that we'll be playing an Abba song for him every hour, for as long as he keeps strimming."

"But he won't be able to hear it, with his ear defenders on."

"So, there we are, no sleep 'til Hammerbridge, but we're not going to play Motorhead, we're going to hear "Gimmie, Gimmie, Gimmie", a man after midnight, a man with a strimmer, a man with a mission, out there strimming his cojones off, can I say that..?"

"I'll strim his cojo..whatevers off," I said, putting on a Scrapper Blackwell compilation cd instead.

"Nobody knows you when you're down and out..," sang Scrapper Blackwell.

I inspected a couple more reported issues on the public rights of way network and at lunchtime, after eating my sandwiches, I must have nodded off for ten minutes but felt all the better for a power nap. Before I headed back, I made one more visit to a house where a lady was concerned about some tall ash trees that were growing on the verge of the public footpath that passed to the rear of her property. After establishing that she had larger than normal hands, I explained that the trees probably belonged to the neighbouring landowner and she should try contacting him, if she had any concerns.

"But they're on the footpath," she said.

"Ah yes, but we do not own the land over which public rights of way pass," I said, "they all cross other people's land, a footpath is a right rather than a thing, goodbye."

I left the lady looking rather mystified, staring up at the mature ash trees that overshadowed her house. On my way back to the depot, after some deliberation, I turned the radio on to see whether there were any updates on Mr X's progress.

"...so, my advice is just throw it in your bin, or better still, throw it in someone else's bin," said the radio presenter, "and now, we've got a caller on the line. It's Raymond, hello Raymond, I understand that you've been following the progress of our strimmer marathon man, BAAAAAAB STRRRRRIMERMAAAN?"

"Yeah," said Raymond the listener, "it ain't right is it, when Bob's bin aht there, strimming his orchestras orf, night n' day.."

"Orchestras?" said the radio presenter, "I don't..?"

"Yeah, Orchestras, it's cockney rhymin' slang, stalls or pits, you takes yer pick. So, he's aht there strimming his orchestras off, when the council bloke's in a layby, asleep in 'is van. I've jest seen 'im today, maahf open and dribblin' like a good 'un."

"Ok, thanks Raymond, so whilst Bob Strimmerman is out there, strimming his little socks off, the chap from the council, who should be doing it anyway, is asleep in a layby.."

"That's outrageous," I said, turning the radio off immediately, "I'll strimmer his wretched little socks off and the stalls, the pits and the entire bloody orchestra."

After another sleepless night, I had decided that enough was enough. When I arrived at work in the morning, I looked up the telephone number for the radio station and was just in the process of ringing them up when the chap from the other end of the building popped his head around the door.

"Well, that was a bit of a sad end to the strimmer marathon, wasn't it?" he said.

"Why, what happened?" I said, lowering the telephone back down on its cradle.

"Didn't you hear? Someone stole his strimmer after he had nodded off for a moment. That's rather poor isn't it? I know that you said there were issues with him working out there, but even so."

"Oh," I said, "so no more Bob Strimmerman?"

"Nope, he says that he's done his bit and hoped that it had made a difference to people. Mr X is still going strong though, he's back in your area, over in Sixinch, I believe? Aye, aye, here's the old Shining Path gang," he said, as the Trust Harrison van clattered into the yard.

As I watched the lads emerge from the side door of the van to stretch and yawn and scratch themselves, I reflected on Bob Strimmerman's attempt to make a difference. It had been a selfless act and yet I had been very churlish and ungrateful about the whole strimming marathon. That I bore such a grudge after being put off whilst throwing my darts by the anonymous strimming volunteer, perhaps I should have been more receptive at the time, or asked him after the match for the details of the overgrown paths? Even with Mr X, I had been put off by the fact that he had once had a catchphrase that included the misnomer, "we'll always be together like chalk and cheese". As a consequence, I had not been as helpful or as friendly as I might have been towards Mr X from the outset, which on hindsight is ludicrous. What reasonable person would care whether chalk and cheese are compatible or not? Mr X was now out there promoting the benefits of walking and making a real difference up and down the country with previously sedentary people beginning to walk to improve their health and fitness. People everywhere really were walking back to happiness.

A number of facets to my character had been revealed to me over the passing months, behaviour that may have scoured my path in life. Perhaps there are reasons why someone ends up living on their own? If so, can one change, can a person recognise these moments when they come along and make different decisions? Different decisions that cause different outcomes? Choosing the right path.

I went out to catch up with Dolores and Harrison as I had seen very little of them since the iron smelting and the making of the two rings.

I noticed Dolores glancing at my finger but she did not ask me why I was not wearing my ring. I enquired whether they had encountered the chap out there strimming the paths, night and day.

"Yeah, we heard something about it, didn't we?" said Dolores, vaguely, glancing across at Harrison, who shrugged.

"Apparently his strimmer got stolen, when he was taking a nap beside the path?" I said.

"Oh dear," said Dolores, "that's a shame. Didn't he get a strimmer donated to him?"

I glimpsed Knocker in the back of the van and his head popped back out of sight when he saw me, with only his grey beard jutting out in view.

There was the customary vagueness in response to all enquiries about the activities of Harrison and the gang. Dolores was more receptive but when it came down to it, there seemed to be a tacit agreement that I was only told anything on a need to know basis, even if my future seemed to be at the heart of an activity, such as the making of two iron rings. There was so much uncertainty that I had even managed to convince myself that Harrison had temporarily turned himself into Mr X's dog, Larry G. I had been there and witnessed some curious transformation that coincided with Harrison's unexplained disappearance. As a consequence a very small dog, that had previously only been carried everywhere, suddenly began dragging its owner all over the place on public rights of way and in doing so had Mr X now promoting an extraordinary national walking campaign. I looked across at Harrison as he sat in the passenger seat of the van and he appeared perfectly normal, for Harrison. Then of course there were the two iron rings and the threat of a polemic shift. I just wanted some clarity, some sort of resolution. I became aware that I was standing still in the yard, near the Trust Harrison van. Normally I would have conducted a short, often one-sided conversation and then returned to my desk but I was fixed to the spot. I could see Dolores glance across at me as she slammed shut the bonnet of the van. Harrison had stayed put in the passenger seat and the lads had returned to the back of the van and closed the door.

I could not move. I could not walk away, back to my office. Harrison got out and wandered over towards me.

"Is you ok boss?" he said, after studying my face for a while.

It now felt that not only could I not move but I could not speak either.

Harrison walked away to talk quietly with Dolores for a couple of minutes and then returned to haul open the sliding door of the van.

After being rooted to the spot, I felt myself moving towards the van. The lads made a seat available for me and I got in. Harrison slammed shut the door as Dolores started up the engine. In no time we were bouncing over the speed hump, on our way out of the yard.

18

THE SCREENING

After Dolores had dropped the lads off in town, I sat in the back of the Trust Harrison van on my own. We continued out of town and after ten minutes or so we turned off the road. I recognised the private track that led to where I had been shown the great tangle of scrap parkland fencing, a few months before. As we approached the small yard and outbuildings, I could see the Hunter Scavenger caravan parked up. The van stopped and Dolores switched off the engine. Harrison opened the side door to let me out whilst Dolores walked across and opened up the door and front hatch of the caravan. There was a plastic table and a few chairs set out on the piece of hardstanding between the caravan and an outbuilding.

"Sit down, Mr Wayland," said Dolores, as I emerged slowly from the back of the van, "would you like a cup of tea?"

"Yes please," I said, lowering myself into a chair, "I would love a cup of tea, thank you."

"Are you ok in the sun, or do you want a bit of shade?" said Dolores, filling the kettle from a plastic water container.

"A bit of shade might be a good idea, the sun's quite hot," I said.

"Let me open a sun umbrella," said Dolores, "there we go, can I ask you a favour Mr Wayland, may I borrow your mobile phone for a moment as I have to text somebody?"

"Of course," I said, handing my phone to Dolores. After a

couple of minutes she placed it back on the table.

Harrison had disappeared and Dolores went off to feed some chickens. I listened as the kettle on the gas in the caravan groaned and then began to click with the expanding metal. Dolores returned carrying a small wicker basket full of eggs as the kettle rushed towards boiling and silence was restored with the brewing of the tea. Dolores placed a mug of tea on the plastic table.

"Thank you," I said, "aren't you having one?"

"No, I might a bit later. Do you want a biscuit, nothing fancy but they are homemade?"

"Lovely, yes please," I said.

Dolores returned with a large biscuit on a small china plate.

"Thank you very much," I said.

I took a small sip of tea and then crunched on the oat biscuit, chewing with my eyes closed.

I became aware of some gentle music, a nylon strung guitar and a woman's voice. I opened my eyes and it was Dolores, sitting on the step of the caravan in the shade, picking out a tune and singing gently in Spanish. I closed my eyes again until the song had ended.

"That was beautiful," I said, "what was it?"

"Thank you," said Dolores, "that was an old Cuban bolero, Lagrimas Negras."

"I had no idea that you played guitar and sang so well?" I said.

Dolores began another song and Harrison reappeared with a large pot of paint, a roller, a wide paint brush and a painting tray. Wearing a floppy hat to protect him from the sun and what looked like a pair of ladies' sunglasses, he soon set to work painting white the old rendered wall, directly in front of the caravan. This glaring, fresh whiteness spread with each song Dolores played. Harrison worked his way along the wall, painting in blocks, in turn reaching up, crouching and standing, blending in the blocks to a solid whiteness.

I could have offered to assist Harrison but I felt no pressure to contribute anything. By Harrison's immersion in his activity, it was clear that he was intending to paint the entire wall on his own. I rested my eyes periodically and when I looked again Harrison had made some progress, as if it were time lapse photography. By the silences in between the songs, a comfortable easy silence, I knew that I was amongst friends. There was nothing to say in these moments, I was not on the outside looking in. Unanswered questions now seemed trivial and unimportant.

Dolores played Summertime, singing in English, a bluesy version of Summertime with lovely instrumentation. I had never felt this calm before. I sensed that Dolores would have played guitar and sang and Harrison would have painted the wall, if I had not been there. By bringing me here to share in their world, it had calmed me down. It must have been obvious to them that they could not leave me, standing motionless and speechless, in the yard.

Dolores put her guitar down and stepped into the caravan. In time I could hear what sounded like the chopping of vegetables. Harrison had painted without a break with three quarters of the wall now a solid whiteness.

I heard myself sigh.

"Thank you," I said, "thank you for bringing me here this afternoon."

Harrison did not reply or look around and Dolores continued to do whatever she was doing in the caravan.

"It's been lovely," I said, "but I'd better get back to feed my cat, Leadbelly will be wondering where I am."

"It's sorted," said Harrison, with his back to me.

"What's sorted?" I said.

"Your cat has been fed."

"My cat, who by?"

"My bruvver."

"But Leadbelly dashed off when Marlon came to the door, with the..." I said, pausing and not wanting to specifically refer to the two iron rings. I was trying to forget about the two iron rings.

"Yeah, but he'll come back, he's a cat," said Harrison.

I thought about this for a while.

"Ok," I said, "but that's very kind of your brother, to go to all that trouble."

"We'll have something to eat, in a bit," called out Dolores from the caravan, "would you like a glass of elderflower cordial Mr Wayland?"

"Yes please," I said.

Dolores brought out two tall and narrow glasses of elderflower cordial, placing one on the plastic table and she handed the other one to Harrison.

"Thank you," I said.

"Fanks," said Harrison.

It tasted of early summer and it was a beautiful delicate colour in the sunlight.

I sipped the cordial as Harrison concluded painting the wall. He stood back to check that there were no patches or gaps.

"Looks good to me," I said.

Harrison nodded and then collected up the painting gear and carried it all back around to the other side of the farm building. I could hear him running a tap, presumably to wash the brush and the tray and roller.

When he reappeared, without his floppy hat and sun glasses, he gestured for me to follow him. I stood up, stiffly and walked around to the front of the farm buildings. In a long shed a metalworking workshop had been set up with metal cutting tools, welding equipment and long benches.

"This is very well equipped," I said, "don't you get any problems with theft, I mean it's a fairly isolated spot out here?"

Harrison shook his head.

"Knocker is 'ere," he said.

"He stays here, in the building?"

"Mostly in the woods, back down the track," said Harrison.

Standing against one wall of the shed were a variety of different designs of kissing gate. None were conventional and they displayed a range of different colours.

"Where are they going to be used?"

"They is goin' on Mr X's land."

"On a public footpath?"

"Nah, it ain't a legal route, it's one of them uvver fings?"

"A permissive path?"

"Yeah."

"So, it's a link between the two footpaths than run either side of his property?"

"He's got them sheep wiv long necks, in some fields."

"Alpacas?"

"And a real big one to keep the foxes away."

"A llama?"

"Yeah, it don't like me."

"And what's that," I said, pointing to an enormous and heavy, flat metal plate with a figure cut out from the middle.

"That is Mr X, before he started walking. He don't look like that no more."

The rotund figure was standing with his legs wide apart and arms stretched out at the sides. The edges of the cut-out figure had all been rounded off to remove any sharp edges.

"I imagine that it would actually be stockproof?" I said, "and you've got to climb through it?"

Harrison nodded slowly.

There was one gate that was freestanding, away from the wall, which comprised a series of concentric hoops. I was able to move them around and it looked as though you needed to work out the right sequence of moving hoops to pass through it.

"That's interesting," I said, "some designs of kissing gates were called cow puzzles, as the cows could not work out how to get through them. This one looks like a people puzzle."

Harrison smiled slightly.

Leaning against the higher gable wall at the end of the shed was a huge kissing gate, conventional in design but it must have been twelve feet high.

"It keeps them animals in," said Harrison, "it's just big. There ain't no places where fingers or hands get squashed, they is all safe."

"It's amazing," I said, "it's like access sculpture?"

Harrison frowned and then shrugged.

"It's amazing that Mr X has embraced rights of way and access in such a wholehearted way," I said, "how on earth did he get in touch with you?"

"We went to see him and said what we could do and he said yeah, go for it, do something different."

"You've certainly done that," I said, "and he is welcoming people onto his land as well, which I wouldn't have anticipated after our first meeting?"

"We is putting them up next week. He is payin' for a big truck to shift it all over to his place."

"What can I say?" I said.

Harrison shrugged.

Back outside, the sun was still warm but the afternoon was leaning towards early evening as shadows began to lengthen. Tucked under the eaves of the single-story brick farm buildings were a number of mud nests and under each, an accumulation of bird guano on the concrete below. We looked up and the swirling and twittering house martins were feasting on a batch of unwitting flies, darting and twisting as they gathered these easy pickings. It was then express delivery, back to their respective nests to feed the unfledged young of perhaps a third brood who must themselves, in only a matter of weeks, gain enough strength and body weight to make that return trip to sub Saharan Africa.

"These fields is organic," said Harrison, "there's loads of flowers and bugs and fings. Most of the birds is doin' ok here."

By the time that we returned to the caravan, more tables and chairs had now appeared.

"Expecting company?" I said to Dolores, who smiled, "those are amazing metal gates and it's great that Mr X wants folk walking on his property."

"They're fun aren't they?" said Dolores, "Mr X has been really up for it, which is brilliant."

I sat back down in the shade and wondered who else was coming over, presumably to eat something, a bit later on. Just at that moment I heard a motorbike approaching. My stomach did an involuntary flip in response to this sound at the thought of Marlon and the world turning upside down. Marlon had no pillion rider and parked up the bike before taking off his helmet.

He smiled as he approached.

"Hello, Mr Wayland," said Marlon.

"Hello," I said, "I understand that you have fed my cat."

"Yes, I have fed your cat. Well, I say fed, it pushed off when I arrived. I put a plate of food through the cat flap. Hope that's ok?"

"That's fine, many thanks. Did you see any neighbours?"

Marlon shook his head.

Dolores offered Marlon a glass of elderflower cordial and asked me whether I would like a glass of cider.

"Yes please, that would be lovely, just a small one," I said.

Dolores handed me a half pint of cider that looked clear and golden in the sunlight and Marlon accepted the paler cordial. Marlon placed his helmet in the caravan and then wandered away towards the entrance to the outbuildings.

There was nothing for me to do but wait. Things were obviously going to follow their own course.

Harrison appeared with a black box and what looked like an old record carrying case. He put them down on the table and opened up the black box.

"There you go, dj Old and Easy," he said, placing a small tin next to the antique record player, "and here's them needle fings."

"A wind up record player?" I said, "I used to have one of these but it never worked properly and you've got some 78 rpm records and the proper needles? Where did you get all this from?"

Harrison disappeared again and I was left to it. After putting on my reading glasses, I sifted through the old shellac records in the box and chose the West End Blues by Louis Armstrong and the Hot Five. With a bit of fiddling about, I fixed a new needle into the clamp at the end of the playing arm and wound up the mechanism. After releasing the brake, the plate spun around furiously and I lowered the needle onto the record. The band started up and I was amazed at the vivid intensity of a sound that had been recorded in the late nineteen twenties.

"That's loud," I shouted out to Dolores, in the caravan.

She laughed and started dancing up and down in the galley of the caravan.

I was in my element. There were some fantastic records in the record carrying box. I had heard before that you needed to change the needle after each record and there were lots of spare needles in the little metal box. You also needed to wind it up each time so that the mechanism did not flag and slow down, half way through the record.

A couple more people arrived on the old tandem that I had seen Dolores and Harrison riding once before. It was Fido and the short chap called Boxer who had helped to fix things in the shed. They both came across and greeted Dolores before shaking hands with me and then wandered away towards the outbuildings. Shortly afterwards, the chap who had placed my Joe Venuti and Eddie Lang record in his mouth when I was about to play some records at the coppice open day, appeared on foot with a girl taller than he was.

We shook hands and I did not catch their names over the Harlem Nocturne, played by Johnny Otis, his drums and his orchestra, as it read on the label. In time, they all drifted back towards the caravan and the very appetising aromas from Dolores' cooking. The chap who ate my records, popped into the caravan to give Dolores a hand and I spoke briefly with Fido between records. I wanted to forget about the two iron rings but I felt that I should at least talk to Fido about what I considered to be a misunderstanding.

"I didn't mean for you to give me an actual ring," I said, "well, two rings."

Fido's head turned upside down as he smiled.

"Oh yes, we made rings. We made a knife, for the chef," said Fido, and he then gestured to Dolores to pass him the knife through the caravan hatch.

"I'm not using it, it's the chef's knife, it's got a blackthorn handle," said Dolores, carefully handing the long kitchen knife to Fido, "local iron, local wood, how about that?"

The knife was extraordinarily well balanced in the hand. The blade and the iron running through the handle were all one piece and the blackthorn had a lovely warm colour and a complex grain.

"So, it wasn't just the two rings that you made?" I said, rather relieved by this news but reluctant to relinquish the feel of the long chef's knife in my hand with its smooth and tactile blackthorn handle, "that's a very nice knife."

Fido retrieved the knife and taking a tomato from the caravan counter he sliced it, effortlessly in his hand.

"Oh yes," he said, "nice knife."

"So, where is the Hunter Scavenger chef, I don't think we've met?" I said to everyone and no one in particular.

No one answered and the knife was placed back in its special place in the caravan kitchen.

I put on The Flat Foot Floogie by Slim and Slam as a small car appeared and I realised that it was Gina driving with Nancy as a passenger. Just at that moment, Dolores announced that we should eat and so the tables and chairs were shuffled about so that there was one long table and a nice brightly colourful tablecloth was draped and smoothed over it.

I went across to meet Nancy and Gina and gave them both a kiss.

"Hello," I said, "what are you doing here?"

"We're not sure," said Nancy, "but we were invited so we thought we'd come. Dolores said that you would be here."

"I'm not sure why I am here, but it has been very pleasant," I said.

"We love a mystery," said Gina, "and that food smells good. We've brought a bottle of wine."

Dolores beckoned for everyone to come and eat and she came out to greet Nancy and Gina.

"Hi, it's great that you could both come. It's all vegetarian, unless you're vegan and then I'll just leave out the eggs? Would you like a cider, elderflower cordial, apple juice or spring water...or wine, thank you?" said Dolores, accepting the wine.

Gina and Nancy were very happy with vegetarian and once drinks were sorted, we all sat down.

"Johnny Swift sends his love, by the way, to both of you," said Dolores to Nancy and Gina, "we've had a postcard recently, from the West Indies."

"I was looking forward to meeting Johnny Swift," said Gina, "we thought he might be here, Nancy's told me all about him."

"He's jumped ship apparently," said Dolores, getting up and reaching into the caravan for the postcard, "here we are, he says; "I seem to have been mistaken for an ex Middlesex and England cricketer, by a bunch of ex-pats, anyway, they have dragged me off on a guided tour around the island. Just remember, volunteering is voluntary, so don't work too hard. Love to you all, also to Nancy and Gina, if you should cross paths, good luck to them both. Big kiss, Johnny S." So, there you go. Everyone should cross paths with Johnny Swift, at least once in their life."

"I can't wait," said Gina, as she gave Nancy a hug.

"That's very sweet of him," said Nancy.

"Very sweet," said Dolores, sliding the postcard back onto the counter of the caravan, "you do realise that he's going to turn up at your wedding whether you invite him or not? Anyway, let's eat."

The meal was described as huevos rancheros, a lovely rich vegetable, chilli and tomato base, with roasted paprika flavours and fresh eggs poached in the juices on top and served with whole grain brown rice. There was also a large mixed salad of various types of lettuce, rocket, cucumber, radish, herbs, water cress and roasted sunflower and pumpkin seeds. Suddenly all was quiet as our attention was focussed on the food.

Drink and conversation soon flowed and candles were lit as dusk crept into this secluded world. Two plump and rich red summer puddings followed with fresh cream and bowls were licked clean.

"This really is a piece of heaven isn't it?" said Gina, to me as the coffee appeared.

"It's extraordinary," I said, "this morning I was all over the place, anxious, worried, doubting everything and now..."

"And now.." said Dolores, echoing me, "..and now..let's get all this cleared, move the tables back.. but keep the chairs."

The tables were stacked away and then all the chairs were turned to face the freshly painted white wall. From inside the caravan, a small movie projector was placed on the hatch and pointed at the white wall. An extension lead was run out to the caravan from the farm buildings and in no time at all a bright rectangle of white light was being projected on to the freshly painted wall. We all seated ourselves and I moved slightly to make sure that my head was not in the way

"So that's why you painted that wall?" I said, in Harrison's ear.

Harrison nodded gently, without turning around.

"Are you sitting comfortably?" said Dolores.

After the flickering "Super 8 Productions" logo, the words, "A Stuntman's Holiday", appeared on the white wall as the music started. It was obviously intended as a silent movie but with a digital musical soundtrack, from a device on the counter.

"That's the Tiger Rag," I said, as the frantic solo piano started up, "by Art Tatum."

"Shhh," said a voice from the front.

A flickering and black and white silent Harrison appeared on the screen, disembarking from the carriage of a steam train, amidst swirls of smoke. He had an old rucksack on his back and brandishing a hazel stick he set off from the small station towards a range of hills. I thought that this must be somewhere in mid or north Wales. He was walking on his own but it was a sped up walking, even for Harrison, keeping time with the blur of Art Tatum's fingers. At a path junction he encounters a two-way signpost displaying the options "This way" on one finger and "Not that way" on the other. The hero scratches his head and with a shrug sets off in the direction that says "Not that way". Numerous scenarios were encountered where imminent danger threatened the relaxing stuntman, who was just trying to get away from it all; a charging bull, a large branch falling on the silent Harrison's simple picnic under a tree, after walking unwittingly into an army firing range the word "BANG!" appeared on the screen followed by a blackened faced, silent Harrison standing in a shell hole. His blank expression was well suited to the silent screen, touched with melancholia and pathos, emulating the greats of the silent era. A subtle and knowing gag followed as the silent Harrison passed a large wooden building with a high window at the gable end. This referenced the classic Buster Keaton scene where the wooden side of the building falls and by the narrowest of margins, real and certain death is cheated as the wooden wall crashes down and the open window frames the oblivious figure, sparing his life. In this scene, the silent Harrison glances up at the wooden wall and high window and then looks at the camera, shaking his head before he trips over a log and lands in a muddy puddle. A small ridge tent is erected and the silent Harrison, in his pyjamas, brushes his teeth before toddling off to enter the tent. No sooner had the tent door been fastened when, in the bright moonlight, a vehicle appears from nowhere and drives over the tent. The vehicle was the Trust Harrison van and Dolores spoke up, apologising for not having the budget to hire an old vehicle for the scene. After the vehicle has disappeared, leaving comic book tyre marks across the canvas, the tent flap burst open and the silent Harrison appeared, running around in circles, dazed and confused in his old fashioned, stripy pyjamas.

The final scene involved the silent Harrison walking past a broken sign post with a detached finger on the ground that read; "Danger, cliff edge, go no further!" As Art Tatum swirled across the piano keys, the silent Harrison continued ahead, whistling blankly, in ignorance of the certain peril that awaited him. A drone must have been employed to undertake an extraordinary perspective as the camera followed the silent Harrison to the edge of a deep quarry, the camera position continuing out into open space, looking back at the figure on the edge and then looking down to the dark water, way below. The audience groaned uneasily at this experience. The silent Harrison briskly retraced his steps, back towards the broken sign but then met an invisible wall, knocking him backwards. Not only was this barrier invisible but it was advancing nightmarishly towards the cliff edge. Attempts by the silent Harrison to halt its progress by pushing and straining at the face of the invisible wall, were fruitless. There was a lot of very convincing miming undertaken as the panicking figure ran frantically, back and forth, along the wall in both directions, but found no escape from impending doom. Space and time were rapidly running out for the silent hero and with only ten paces or so to the precipitous edge, desperate attempts are made, flinging himself and bouncing off the murderous wall. The piano music grew louder and faster as the silent Harrison was pushed onwards, on towards the edge of the cliff. He quickly took off his backpack and flung it out into open space and watched it plummet, eventually hitting the dark water, far below. The word "Splash" appeared on the screen. The silent Harrison frowned. A last second check on the progress of the invisible wall confirmed that there was only one course of action left, our endangered hero, in a matter of seconds, would have to jump. Exclamations of anxiety could be heard from the small audience, myself included, as the silent Harrison took up position, with the toes of his boots extending beyond the edge of the almighty drop.

"I recognise those boots," I said, unable to contain myself.

"Shhh," said the audience.

There were a number of camera positions in fast edits; from behind, above, below and hovering in open space, in front of the poised figure. The illusion of the invisible wall had been so convincing, I fancied that I could now see it about to push the silent Harrison from the cliff and then he dived. We gasped and held our breath. From behind we saw the figure dive out and disappear over the edge. A more distanced view showed the arc of the dive. From above you could see the symmetry and balance of the figure, receding towards the black water and from below the control of the diver, about to make impact with the water. Gasps for air from the viewers were coincident with the word "Splash" appearing on the screen. Art Tatum was fast approaching the end of the Tiger Rag as the ripples from the dive spread and then faded but with no sign of the silent Harrison in the black water. Suddenly, a splashing figure appeared on the surface, to great cheers from us all. Rather than swimming in a conventional way, the silent Harrison began to doggie paddle towards the edge of the pool. He hauled himself from the water, his clothes dripping. He scratched his head. The words "it's far safer being a stuntman", appeared on the screen as the silent Harrison scuttled and squelched away in the steel toe-capped safety boots that I had bought him when he had first started as a volunteer. The words "The End" appeared on the screen and we all clapped and cheered. We cheered the production and direction of the short film and the silent hero who had evidently been practising his diving at the swimming pool in town, rather than learning to swim. I had forgotten that the swimming pool in town had a competition standard diving pool annexed to it, that was now run by volunteers.

There were lots of questions directed at Dolores about how the film had come about and an insistence from everyone that we watched it all through again, straight away.

"It was a bit of an experiment, to be honest, I mean, come on, it needs a proper plot and a heroine, come to that," said Dolores, after the re-run.

"Well, you're the obvious choice for that role D, but I'd give it a go next time, if you want?" said the tall girl.

"Yes please, would you really? Thanks Patti, as long as you promise not to forget us, when you're a megastar," said Dolores, "I'm a happy bunny behind the camera but put me in front of one and I'm like a rabbit caught in the headlights, BAAM."

"I'll get my shovel," I said.

"Ha, ha," said Dolores, "actually, I think we've got your shovel."

"An awful lot of work has gone into those four or so minutes, I mean how long did it take you?" said Nancy.

"It took probably four weekends, altogether, to do the filming," said Dolores, "editing takes a long time and there was a lot of driving around beforehand, finding the right locations. Fido and Boxer were brilliant as crew and drone operators."

"And there's me thinking that you were learning to swim with all those visits to the swimming pool?" I said, to Harrison.

"Yeah, fanks for them lifts boss." said Harrison.

Gina wanted to know about the invisible wall.

"Where did that idea come from, it seems very resonant of the situation in the world today?"

"That was his idea," said Dolores, pointing across at Harrison, "he just started doing it when we were filming."

Gina assumed the affected voice of an arts critic, on a review show.

"To me, it was the advancing wall of intolerance, fascism and extremism, pushing all those in its path over the edge, forcing them to jump into a dark uncertainty.."

"I dunno.." said Dolores laughing, "but talking of dark uncertainty, we had to check what was under the water and how deep it was. There were one or two cars down there, but it was real deep."

"How high was that dive?" asked Nancy, "it was terrifying."

Harrison shrugged.

"I ain't done one like that before," he said, "it were high wiv them boots on."

"Right, who wants another drink?" said Dolores, "do you want to see some more short films, whilst we've got it all set up?"

We spent another hour or so watching more extraordinary films, some of which Dolores had made. We talked and drank and laughed until Gina announced quietly that she was giving me a lift home, as it was not really out of their way. I had given no thought to how I was getting home and I thanked her, if she was sure that it would be no trouble. We said goodnight to everyone and I had a list of things that I wanted to thank Dolores and Harrison for but when it came to it, an exchanged look and a simple goodbye said it all.

Outside my house, I thanked Gina for the lift and I gave them both a kiss goodbye. Leadbelly was nowhere to be seen but the plate of food that Marlon had placed inside the cat flap was empty.

I lay awake in bed, replaying the silent film in my head, smiling in the darkness.

19
DOWN

I HAD NOT seen my digital camera for a while but after a lengthy process of elimination, I searched in the pockets of my cricket bag in the loft and sure enough, there it was. When I arrived at work, I downloaded what was on the camera and found that the last picture taken was from the Past V Future cricket match near Little Shits Wood, on the edge of town. It was a group photo of both teams, seated and standing and I thought that the participants might like a record of this event. I sought out an earlier group e-mail that I had sent out, prior to the match and after attaching the photo, I circulated it to all concerned. Within five minutes I received a call from Dave Barlow in Comms.

"Victor, for christsakes, that photo.."

"The team photo, yes sorry it's taken me a while but I couldn't find my camera.."

"You've got to delete it, everyone needs to delete it now, have you seen it?"

"Of course I've seen it, I sent it."

"But have you looked at it properly?"

"Well, yes, but what do you mean, properly?

"Look at it again," said Dave Barlow, obviously quite agitated, "look at the banner."

I got the photograph up on my screen and squinted at the

banner.

"It says Past V Future, what's wrong with that?"

"Not that, it's the writing underneath."

"Oh, hang on, I'll have to zoom in on the screen, it's these reading glasses, the lenses are very scratched. It says..oh..I hadn't noticed that.. No more houses, piss off developers.. and leave our cricket pitch alone."

"Exactly," said Dave Barlow, "and it's displayed above the corporate head of council services, who is responsible for all planning matters. He is also responsible for ensuring that the government initiatives for new housing quotas are met and it is a site where there is a proposed new development comprising of much needed social housing, on our own land..and there he is telling everyone to piss off."

"I see," I said.

"So, Victor," said Dave Barlow, trying to remain calm, "you've got to e-mail everyone again and tell them all to delete it immediately, and make sure that they also delete it from the deleted folder as well. Do it now, we can't have this getting out into the public domain."

"No, quite, I see, I'll do it now," I said.

Dave Barlow rang off and I circulated another e-mail, as instructed. I then looked again at the photo. It was obviously the Little Shits that had pulled off this stunt as there was one at either end of the banner, holding it up. At the time I had not even realised that there was a banner. It would be a shame to lose a record of the event and I wondered whether I could doctor it and remove that part of the photo, but leave the rest. I thought that I might try doing this at home and so I sent the photo to my home e-mail and then deleted it, as best I could, from my work computer. I received fairly swift and compliant responses from all those within the organisation to whom I had circulated the e mail and photograph and thought that the end of the matter.

Late summer was still in denial at the prospect of autumn and things had settled down, in that I was no longer concerned about the two iron rings or the world turning upside down. The afternoon and evening in Dolores' and Harrison's company, with their friends, had been really beneficial. It had been a significant step towards not being an outsider and I now felt part of something. I was not quite sure what that something was but it felt friendly and a lot of positive things were happening. That being said, I had hardly seen the Trust Harrison gang since that evening and concluded that they must have been busy erecting huge sculptural kissing gates on a permissive path for Mr X, on his land. Mr X had now concluded his walking tour of all paths in the county, where there was an X in the parish name and had progressed to national trails and also a chat show planned for next spring that was going to be called Walking In Step. I had read in the paper that Mr X was going to chat to invited celebrity guest's, whilst walking on public rights of way, in various parts of the country. Rather than relaxing in a studio, promoting their latest film, album or book, the guests would have to keep up a brisk pace and battle with the elements and the vagaries of the public rights of way network. Talking and walking can be a challenge, if you are not used to it.

Liz Friendly had rung and left a message to inform me that I was a waste of space and that she was now selling up and it was all my fault. Harrison had already informed me that she had actually sold up some months before. I had also heard from a neighbouring farmer, when talking to him recently, that Liz Friendly's husband was not dead, as she had stated, but had run off with a vet two years ago. I did feel genuinely sorry for Liz Friendly but then I had been misled from the outset. If the sheep farm had been bought by developers and was now going to become housing, as had happened directly over the border in the neighbouring county, then I would certainly be involved again in the footpaths that crossed the farm. It may be an opportunity to tie up the paths so that they did meet at the county boundary, although I hated the thought of all those pastoral green fields disappearing under the footings of yet more houses.

I had almost forgotten about the incriminating photograph when, a couple of days later, Nancy rang me up on my mobile as I was leaving home for work.

"Have you heard?" said Nancy, with excitement in her voice.

"Heard what?" I said, "you know that I'm the last person to hear any.."

"That team photo of the cricket match is in the daily newspapers."

"But everyone was supposed to delete it," I said, with alarm.

"Well, somebody didn't, anyway, he's been suspended, the new director."

"He hasn't? Seriously?"

"Yes, seriously," said Nancy.

"Oh, god, I suppose they'll think it's all my fault? I know he was annoying but he's the director..."

"Get a paper Victor, a tabloid, it's all in there, I mean we're all in there, in the photo," said Nancy, "I've got to go, speak later, bye."

On my way to work I stopped at the local community shop and lingered at the newspaper stand for long enough to leaf through one tabloid. A couple of pages in and I read the headline; "Bellringer drops clanger, council planning chief tells developers to p*ss off". The team photo was rather small but they had encircled the seated director with an expanded image of the wording on the banner alongside. I could not find myself in the team photo at first, due to the rather poor definition and cheap printing but also due to the fact that I looked like an old man. Nancy, on the other hand, looked younger and happy. Harrison's expression was so bland that his features did not amount to more than a few dots, clustered together.

"Are you going to buy that paper?" said the bossy manageress.

"No, on second thoughts I don't think I will," I said, heading for the door, "good morning."

When I got to work, I crept into the office, thinking that I would just grab my camera and disappear into the depths of my area for a while. It might then all blow over, I thought, optimistically. There were a number of messages left on my answer machine, which I imagined would be from Dave Barlow in Comms. There were also a batch of e-mails from Comms that I could not bring myself to read and I turned the computer off again. I was just taking my camera out from the desk drawer when there was a tap on my office window. It was the smoker, on his well-trodden path to the front gate, with what looked like a postcard in his hand. I opened the window.

"He's gone off on his cruise today, away for three weeks, so I'm doing the post. This arrived this morning for you," he said, passing the post card in through the window, "sounds good."

"Thank you," I said, as I plucked the postcard from between his thumb and yellowed forefinger before closing the window.

It was from Hywel and by chance his jazz orchestra were playing in town in a few weeks and would I like to come as his guest and bring a friend. The picture on the front of the card was of Whitby in Yorkshire, where he was due to play a concert that evening. Hywel had included his mobile phone number at the bottom, so at least I could now make contact with him.

On the smoker's return journey to the front door, I reopened the window slightly.

"Have you heard about the new director," I said, "you did delete that cricket team photo didn't you?"

"Yeah, it's bad innit?" said the smoker, pausing to haul open the window and make himself comfortable by leaning on the window sill, broadcasting cigarette exhaust fumes into my office, "it weren't me, honest. Maybe he's upset someone and they're getting their own back?"

"Maybe, anyway, if you'll excuse me, I've got to go out now, thanks for delivering the postcard" I said, beginning to dislodge him by closing the window.

"I used to play sax," said the smoker, pointing at the postcard, as he moved back from the window.

"Did you?" I said, pausing with the window half open.

"Yeah, be-bop mainly."

"Be-bop? Charlie Parker?"

"Ah, Charlie Parker, now you're talking.."

"Look, I'm very keen to continue this conversation..but I've got to go out now," I said, as my office phone and mobile phone rang simultaneously.

"Sounds like someone's after you then," said the smoker cheerfully, heading back towards the front door.

I ignored the ringing phones and grabbed a recently received handwritten letter that highlighted a complaint somewhere and hastened out of the office. Wherever it was, I would drive there and hopefully there would be a poor mobile phone reception and it would be in the middle of nowhere. I needed to get lost.

I stopped in the first available layby to check the location of the obstruction referred to in the handwritten complaint. The letter referred to somewhere called "Down" that I could not initially recall in my area. There was a grid reference and after checking one or two maps I struggled behind the passenger seat to extract a rarely used map that included, on one edge, a very small corner of my area. I remembered now that there had been a boundary change some years before and a small hamlet in a neighbouring county had been annexed to a larger parish in our county, to which it had originally belonged, a century or so previously. It was certainly not on my radar and I could not remember having ever visited Down before. I worked out my route but there would also be some walking required, which was ideal.

On the way I kept thinking about the new director being suspended and who could have leaked the photo to the press? Jolyon Bellringer had certainly grasped the whole walking back to happiness campaign with both hands. It could have easily been something else as he had been desperate to make his mark but the introduction of Mr X into the mix, had made it all possible. I was prepared to overlook the new director's egocentricities in the knowledge that foot soldiers, like myself, would never claw their way to the top and, as I had mentioned to Nancy, it all rather came with the territory, he was the director after all. I wondered whether Mr X would now distance himself from his associations with the county, as Mr X's star was now on a new trajectory and the last thing he would want was some toxic banana skin to slip up on.

I reached for a handful of cds and chose a Memphis Minnie compilation and was soon listening to the Hoodoo Lady's Blues in an attempt to forget about everything else.

After stopping at a very minor crossroads I consulted the map again and took a left turn that soon began a long and winding descent down a narrow lane with a grass strip growing down the middle. I passed a broken village name sign with the word "Down" dangling vertically on its post. The telephone wires that ran alongside the road between lopsided poles were looping right down to touch the grass and an old metal public footpath sign leant at forty-five degrees to point at the ground. A cottage was little more than a ruin with its brick chimney toppled over and elder bushes sprouting up everywhere. Barbed wire field fences were slack and hanging between intermittent broken fence posts, whilst doomed elm trees in the fields and along the roadside verges were either propping themselves up or lying flat to display their roots, having succumbed to gravity.

I recalled a telephone call to my office some months ago when a caller had declared that everything was down but had not stated where he was referring to and that I should just "use my eyes". Driving this narrow road, that was barely more than a surfaced track, my eyes told me that this little hamlet had indeed suffered from neglect, in all respects. Before I knew it, I had passed through Down and I again stopped to consult the map. I established that I should continue on for a short distance and then I would have to park up and walk for a good mile, to get to the point specified in the letter. I pulled over into a disused field entrance but before I got out of the van, I ate a biscuit and re-read the postcard from Hywel. From the misfortune of getting hit on the head by a falling branch, good things were happening but I had no idea who I could take along as a guest to the concert. At one time I would have asked Nancy, even if she was not a big fan of jazz, but things had changed. The Smoker certainly seemed keen, as he used to play jazz saxophone, so if no-one else was interested then I might suggest it. Rather late in life, I had begun to realise that you cannot judge people by first impressions or even longer term impressions, as they will invariably surprise and confound you.

Reassuringly there was no phone signal so I decided to leave the phone in the van but I took the map, the letter of complaint and my camera and set off up the narrow lane.

After a few deep breaths and some gentle rolling of the shoulders, I began to relish the walk ahead. I told myself that I do not walk enough. I drive. I sit in front of a screen. I go for a short walk to look at a problem. I get in and out of the van and occasionally I do a bit of manual work. I made a silent resolution to walk more. If I cannot find an excuse for a good walk then it is not the best job in the world, or rather, it may be the best job in the world but it is the wrong person doing it. I checked the map again for my route and a little further on I found the bridleway that I needed to take. Surprisingly it was not too overgrown but it was steep and I resisted stopping to get my breath back until it levelled out at the top of the hill. The path then opened out and I walked along a grassy field edge. The field was in stubble and as yet unploughed, as fields used to be, long after harvest. In times gone by the gleaners, women and children, would scour the stubbles for ears of corn and over the winter it would provide a source of food for birds and small mammals. Often, these days, there is an indecent haste in ploughing after harvest but here nature was able to take its turn and if it were to remain as stubble throughout the winter then this moderately sized field would provide riches galore. As I was about to enter a wood I heard a large tractor on the far side of the field and stopped to watch as it dropped its mighty plough into the soil and then revved away up the field. I watched the lengthening dark line behind the plough, like thick brown crayon on blank mottled paper.

The wood was quiet and I could neither see nor hear any bird life, even in and around the fringes of the wood. Beyond the wood, the bridleway continued along the edge of a field that had just been mauled over by the same tractor and plough, with barely a strip left unploughed for the bridleway itself. My footpath branched off and left the bridleway at this point and continued south, along the outside of the wood, in a grass field. Access was through an old galvanised metal field gate that was down on its hinges and scrapped along the ground as I hauled it open and closed it again.

The crux of the complaint was a missing stile on a public footpath but I had not reached that point yet. I had a quick look at the map and before the site of the missing stile there was a dwelling and I had to pass through the garden, by the look of it. One never felt comfortable passing through someone's garden on a public right of way. As I approached the property, which looked like a bungalow, perched on the side of a hill with a grand view to the south, I employed my usual approach in such circumstances, which is to whistle and behave as though it is perfectly normal to walk through someone's garden.

The whistling provided a rather self-conscious, early warning to the resident, before I burst into view. After crossing a lawn, I had to duck under an empty washing line and the only route ahead appeared to be between one end of the bungalow and the perimeter hedge. I whistled louder. I passed before the kitchen window, looking determinedly ahead but in my straining peripheral vision I was conscious that there was someone sitting at the kitchen table. Through an open window I became aware of a man's voice but decided that it was the radio that I could hear and I was quickly gone from the garden. It occurred to me that the bungalow must have a separate private vehicular access that was not a public right of way, which I must have missed in my attempt at not being nosey. I had noticed a proliferation of bird feeders and also a couple of children's plastic toys dotted about the garden. I continued through another difficult field gate, into a grass field that looked as though it might have been left to provide a last hay crop before the autumn. The missing stile was beyond the bottom fence line of this field and I headed down into the corner where I found another old field gate and then met another footpath at a T junction of paths. At this point, on a field boundary, stood an impressive new wooden kissing gate, constructed of hand cleft oak with a substantial oak hanging post and timber surrounds. The hinges and catch were unusual in that they were not the standard galvanised metal but were forged from wrought iron and looked as though they had been made by a blacksmith. I checked the letter again and the map and this was definitely the position given by the grid reference but it seemed as though someone had already sorted out the problem. On one of the uprights was a new round waymark. I put my reading glasses back on and peered at it and it was one of the same Chinese waymarks that Harrison had showed me recently, that had been sponsored by the Chinese takeaway. I checked the date on the letter and it had been sent less than a week ago. The kissing gate looked quite new but you can tell when work has just been undertaken by the fresh sawdust and the trampling of the grass around the immediate area. I guessed that this gate had been erected perhaps a month or two before the letter had been written. This was not unusual in that the public did not always report problems immediately, after they encountered them and may have not been back to check, before contacting us. I studied the name and address on the handwritten letter and it looked like one of those examples that demonstrate how to fill in your name and address. The name given was "John Smith" and the address was "1, New Terrace, New Street, Newtown." There was obviously something going on here, given that the letter was effectively anonymous and sent a while after the problem had been sorted out. The presence of the Chinese waymark fairly indicated that this had been the handywork of the Trust Harrison gang, even in such a remote quarter as this. The fact that the robust kissing gate was very well made from hand cleft oak did intrigue me and the gang had obviously obtained a different source of timber to the few scrappy remnants that I had to offer. They had even gone to the trouble of making all the metal gate furniture. In fact, I now wondered whether the Trust Harrison gang actually needed me at all, any more. They were obviously no longer dependent on what materials I could provide and I never knew where they were working anyway. This structure signalled their independence, even the Chinese character waymark had been supplied by a take away restaurant. Had I been directed to this spot to highlight a significant break away moment in the evolution of public rights of way maintenance?

I took a photograph of the kissing gate from both sides and in doing so I noticed a small branded mark on one of the oak upright posts. It was a small figure of eight. As I looked more closely I could see that the eight was in fact two circles of slightly differing dimensions, placed adjoining each other and branded into the wood separately. Two rings together to form the figure eight. Two rings. Two iron rings?

Whilst I was here, I traced this footpath for a quarter of a mile or so in both directions and there were further Chinese waymarks and it must have formed part of a longer trail or circular walk. This bold new structure was pretty much on the county boundary with the waymarked path wandering off, across the border. It seemed as though the gang had now spread their wings and were extending their activities into the neighbouring county.

Returning to the new gate, its presence made me smile and it confirmed my view that here stood a landmark, signifying the end of something old and the beginnings of something new.

I began the mile or so walk back to my van. The footpath up towards the bungalow did not form part of the newly promoted route, which was probably a good thing for the residents, as there could be plenty of people wandering through their garden from now on. As I started my whistling approach towards the property, I could hear some music being played. It sounded like old jazz and as I got closer I stopped my whistling and tried to work out what it was, slowing down before I passed the kitchen window. The saxophone playing was unmistakably Coleman Hawkins and the tune was "Honeysuckle Rose". I had this on a cd and it was recorded in Paris in 1937 with Django Reinhardt on guitar and, rather unusually, Stefan Grappelli on piano. I continued on beyond the kitchen window and was about to glance in to see who could be listening to this fabulous old recording, when a lady came out of the back door, carrying a wicker basket of wet washing.

"Oh, hello," said the lady.

"Um, hello," I said, "I'm sorry but I'm just using the footpath."

"Ok," said the lady, "you came through earlier didn't you? I've just got to hang this washing out, I got waylaid by listening to a play on the radio and now I'm feeling guilty, please don't report me to the washer women's guild."

"I..I.. certainly won't do that. Is this playing on the radio?" I said, pointing vaguely towards the source of the music.

"This? No, it's a single actually, a forty five."

"You've got this on a single, Coleman Hawkins and Django Reinhardt?"

"You know it? Yes, my husband had loads of jazz records and forty fives."

"Has he sold them then?"

"No, he died last year, I've still got all the records."

"Oh, I'm sorry, I see, I didn't mean.."

"That's all right, he'd been ill for some time and had suffered enough by the end. I play the records a lot, I put this one on just to get me going sometimes, it's wonderful isn't it?"

"Yes, I really love it, I've got loads of jazz records as well and blues, in fact, I have played some fairly recently, as a sort of DJ, if that isn't too grand a description."

"So, what's your name, or alias, which I believe is the correct term? I think I've heard my daughter say that once?"

"Well, it seems to be "dj Old and Easy", although I didn't choose it myself. It was fun, I enjoyed it. Look, I'm holding you up from pegging out your washing. I'm the footpath man, by the way, I work for the council and I was just checking something down in the valley."

"Ok, I hardly ever see anyone using this path. A couple of months ago some people came down my track and asked whether they could unload some stuff, that was something to do with a footpath, down there in the valley. Nice bunch actually, at first I thought that I had been invaded by a bunch of revolutionaries, but it was fine. They explained that they used waste oil from a Chinese take away as fuel for their van as I couldn't understand my sudden craving for a bag of chips when they arrived. I gave them all a cold drink after they had finished doing whatever it was that they were doing, it was a really hot day. They stayed on for a bit just chatting, actually we talked about music quite a lot and I put on a few records while they were here."

"Yes, they work with me, well they're volunteers really but they just sort of get on with it."

"There was something on the radio, just before you came back up, on the news, about the council? Apparently, the boss has just been sacked for some sort of scandal, involving giving a celebrity permission to erect some Graceland gates at the entrance to his drive? I presume that these are copies of Elvis Presley's Graceland gates? Anyway, the director, I think he was the director, gave this celebrity the go ahead when it hadn't even passed through the formal planning process and now these very grand gates have got to come down."

"Oh?" I said, rather stunned by this news, "was his name Jolyon Bellringer?"

"Yes, that' it."

"Crikey, well that's a relief," I said, "no, I mean..that's a shame, actually he did some pretty good things regarding the promotion of walking, you could even say he put his job on the line because of it. The celebrity is a chap called Mr X?"

"That's him, I've sort of heard of him but he was on the radio saying that he hadn't realised that he had done anything wrong and that he'd always wanted Graceland Gates and now his dream had been shattered."

"Oh dear, I see, well thank you for letting me know, I can't really tell you why, well I could, but suffice to say, it is a bit of a weight off my mind."

"Look, I don't wish to be rude but I'd better hang these sheets out," said the lady, turning to walk up the garden, "I should have done it much earlier."

I followed her towards the washing line. It must have been an ep single playing, with two tracks on each side as the Coleman Hawkins All Star band now launched into Crazy Rhythm.

"I suppose my washing line is obstructing the footpath," said the lady, putting down her basket and untangling a white sheet.

"Well, I suppose it is, sort of, but never mind about that now," I said, "er..I've got a mate playing in a jazz orchestra, over in town, in a couple of week's time and I can take a friend, would you like to come, I mean.. I don't know whether you're..?"

"You must have some other friends who like jazz?"

"Well, no, not really, I don't," I said, "well, apart from the Trust Harrison gang but I've only got one spare ticket."

The lady paused, with a couple of wooden clothes pegs in her hand.

"I see, ok, right.... dj Old and Easy? I can't quite believe that I am being asked to go to a gig by a complete stranger who has just wandered into my garden..but.. um, I think I would like to come, yes, thank you...that would be great."

She cast the white sheet over the line before pinching open clothes pegs between her long and slender thumb and forefingers.

Lightning Source UK Ltd.
Milton Keynes UK
UKHW022110060919
349238UK00011B/874/P
9 781906 978754